A Compendium Of Lovers

FRANCIS STUART

A Compendium Of Lovers

FRANCIS STUART

Raven Arts Press/Dublin

A Compendium of Lovers
is first published in 1990 by
The Raven Arts Press
P.O. Box 1430
Finglas
Dublin 11
Ireland

ISBN 1 85186 077 0

Raven Arts Press receives financial support from The Arts
Council (An Chomhairle Ealaíon), Dublin , Ireland.

Cover design by Susanne Linde. Back cover portrait
of Francis Stuart by Edward Maguire, reproduced by
permission of the Hugh Lane Gallery of Modern Art,
Dublin. **A Compendium of Lovers** is designed by
Dermot Bolger & Aidan Murphy and printed in
Ireland by Colour Books Ltd., Baldoyle.

A Compendium Of Lovers

FRANCIS STUART

To my wife, Finola

1

One evening when driving into town with Maya who was taking me to dinner, she pointed to a rather dimly lit window on the second storey of a house in a busy side street. Maya loved to take short-cuts through dingy parts of the city that in fact took longer than the direct route.

- That's where Paul lives.

I waited. I was wondering about letting her take me out. Wealthy, and, although generous, I didn't want to become one of her 'beneficiaries', even if she might not look on them as that.

- An extraordinary character; wrote a book nobody could understand. Well, nothing unusual in that. Our city is full of these geniuses.

- Never heard of him, Maya.

- And now I believe he reads all day long; doesn't write a line. You should go and see him.

- Why?

- He's an admirer of yours, Joel.

The dinner with Maya, which should have been relaxed and enjoyable, turned into one of those unexpected minor dramas that occur out of the blue. Or not exactly out of the blue because, looking back, I see that I have provoked them by an impulse to assert myself, or at least to prove (to myself in the first place) that I'm not just 'anybody'. In this case not one of Maya's hangers-on.

As soon as the waiter came to take our orders, I asked her if she'd made up her mind and even suggested one of the more expensive dishes, as should a hospitable host in case the guest is hesitating because of the price. The same procedure with the drink. Disregarding the house carafe, I consulted Maya about which of several vintage wines she'd prefer.

Meanwhile, I put on a casual air, or rather entered into

one of the many parts that came naturally to me, while at the same time deducting the likely amount of the bill from a rough estimate of the total sum in notes I had in my pocket-book. (I have never got into credit cards.) It wasn't as if Maya would notice, but it was for the sake of my image of myself. Indeed it was likely that she wouldn't as much as recall who had paid by the time she was home.

Even these small dramas take unforeseen Dostoevskian twists; we'd hardly started the meal when a group of three young men and a girl presented themselves at the table and started to play Hungarian gypsy laments, or so they sounded to me.

Would Maya pick up her bag from under her chair or wherever she'd deposited it and hand them a crumpled note before my thin line of defence was seriously breached? But no, of course not, that wouldn't fit the pattern of the evening which, like it or not, was becoming clear.

- 2 -

A few days later I wrote to Paul Keller (admirers were rare in those days). The answer surprised me. At first I took it for a joke, supposing that this eccentric living alone and impecuniously (I was recalling Maya's passing comment) was resorting to a rather hackneyed kind of humour. He directed me, in a typed letter, signed Paulus Kellery and initialled by a secretary (another comic effect, as I thought) to take the lift at the end of the corridor to the fourth floor and so on....

However, the lay-out of the building was as described. The lift rose smoothly (what was I expecting?), stopped without any tremor and when the doors slid open there was a small illuminated '4'.

After that the association, if any, with an office block belonging to a prosperous consortium vanished. I knocked at the door I had been directed to, entered an office and was greeted by a middle-aged woman, introducing herself in a slightly foreign accent as Nicole Senlis, though of course I didn't catch the surname at the time.

- Come along, please, Mr. Samson.

Paul was sprawled on a couch whose day-time transformation from a bed wasn't very thorough. He got up, bowed, and we shook hands.

We sat down and, coming to the second stage in my appraisal, I saw that what the room really suggested to me was a chemical laboratory.

Having greeted each other with, at least on my side, considerable expectation (of what?), a hiatus, or silence, followed. I found it awkward but Paulus (that's how he had introduced himself) seemed to be elsewhere. Indeed the thought came to me: I've interrupted a difficult piece of research.

It wasn't turning out well.

Here I was, still hoping for something, but not very much, from this visit. What was I looking for, not just from coming here, but in general? In a word: A woman.

I had come to the point of not disregarding any hole and corner in my search. And I hadn't had as much as a passing vibration if I didn't count Maureen, a check-out girl at the local supermarket, who, handing me an extra lot of competition coupons with my change, had said: What about taking me out, darling, if you win first prize?

The only woman in sight was the elderly Madame, but she, I soon saw, was not without attraction.

What was it all about? Why the pictures of racehorses?

I met a couple of the staff, or fellow visitors, and I felt it was a show put on for my entertainment, though that isn't exactly my impression either. It's a lazy way of reporting complex feelings.

The room where he had received Maya - a twin-burner cooker with its tea-pot and greasy pan in a corner, and two remarkable paintings I didn't recognise on the peeling wallpaper - seemed to be Madame's bedroom and her showing it to me I took as a special favour.

The only reassurance - I know that sounds a funny term and I'm not suggesting I saw it as such - was meeting Dr. Cornelius Graft.

He told me about himself, that he was the consultant neurologist at St. Bride's (the hospital down the street). He told me that Paulus was an outstanding, though controversial, astronomer.

- He has a small devoted following, Maya among them, who visit the bed-sitter and venerate him as a sage.
- But isn't that what he is?
- Possibly. A clown and a prophet. He believes mankind is being subjected to genetic invasion by extra-terrestrial bacteria in the course of a fantastic evolutionary process.

Of course I was somewhat out of my depth, but my first thought was that I should stick up for Paulus. I was misunderstanding the doctor, however, because, as I began to realise, he was also 'sticking up' for him.

Then he started telling me about myself. He had read my novels, several of them - the only person I'd met that day who had - or at least had seen fit to mention them.

- And you are at the heart of them, Joel. No need to keep up the misters.

When he asked me to have lunch with him of course I wasn't going to decline and miss hearing more about myself from an intelligent and sympathetic reader, with the added attraction of being an expert in the mysterious science of psychology.

He had first to call at the hospital - this was the first I'd heard of St. Bride's which goes to show how basically healthy I was - and which was only a five minutes drive. There he suggested I accompany him while he checked on three or four of his patients - that was in any case my understanding of it although he only actually paused at one bed in a semi-private ward and that briefly.

It took me some time - as it always does for anything vital to me to sink in - to realise that he'd brought me to the hospital for quite another reason.

At the hotel restaurant - the same where Maya and I had dined recently - he was welcomed deferentially. On his suggestion, we drank whisky while studying the menu in which, with far more pressing matters in my head, I had little interest.

I let him choose and declined a second aperitif, as he called the whisky.

Evidently a dedicated - I wasn't going to employ the word

'heavy' - drinker. Or perhaps one of those who have discovered the restorative value of alcohol, as I thought I had done years ago. At a certain hour of the evening, which tends to edge forward if one isn't strong-willed, say around six, I resort sometimes to a glass or two of spirits to ease the pressures of the day which by then are intensifying my habitual sense of a vague apprehension.

- Look, Joel, meeting you like this out of the blue, was for me one of those shifts forward, or perhaps sideways, let's say obliquely, across a gap that, left to myself, I'd no hope of crossing.

- I don't know about that. I mean, I don't really follow you.

- Now, if you let me, we can talk about some of those extreme preoccupations in your novels that I too am concerned with.

- Like what?

I was somewhat cautious, the more so because I sensed so much was at stake.

- Your merging of the physical and the metaphysical.

- Well...

- Or of sex and religion.

- Ah...

I was on the alert.

Like certain chemicals, if mixed, they form an addictive drug or elixir that is more likely to destroy than help you in the struggle for survival. And I'm not just speaking in social or economic terms but at the psychological level.

- You must know what you're talking about, Doctor.

I wasn't sure that *I* did, and yet...

- Cornelius, please, unless you prefer the formalities. In your fiction your alter-egos manage to find the rather rare kind of woman they need. But they don't turn up with such regularity in real life.

We were into our second bottle of *Chateau Neuf du Pape* when the doctor, with whom I was also well into the Cornelius-Joel relation, remarked ('remarked' is correct; there was a touch of off-handedness in the tone which naturally alerted me):

- The first-person narrator in your novels would indeed be desolate, not to say desperate, without an intimate accord with a woman.

As far as I remember - it disconcerted me that I was very hazy about much of what I'd written, as if it had happened when half-asleep - they never are.

- What about the old campaigner himself?

Campaigner? Captain? Brigadier? What was this? Were there rumours, distant sounds of a battle?

- Do I seem bereft?

-You'd hardly have come on what for you was a daring step all alone if you had an available companion.

Was he referring to my visit to the laboratory?

- Maybe so...

- Come on: drink up, let out a couple of loops in your tether, and I'll show you some green, green pastures beyond your close-cropped circle.

- Ha!

I don't suppose I let out a syllable, not certainly this one which would have indicated a loosening of several loops in the imaginary rope.

- Hasn't it dawned on you yet why I took you to St. Bride's?

- Where?

Yes, I was slow all right, but out of tension and not slackness.

- To show you a place where there are a number of women whose vocation it is to care for people with various disabilities and afflictions. Some are utterly whole-hearted, many are attractive, they're all healthy, there's little danger of any of our contemporary plagues that Paulus believes are sent from the heavens. What you need you'd come across in such a place, even if in doing so you'd have to do some adapting on your own behalf.

What was that about a plague from heaven? Were not such recorded in the Old Testament? I have a tendency to linger on incidentals.

- With your nerve, Sergeant Major, not to speak of my co-operation, you can carry the day. Luckily for you, I haven't any scruples either.

There was now no pretence of adhering to the standards of good citizenship, or behaving as an upright member of society.

- I don't quite get it, Cornelius.

- An inside job. First you have an accident. But make sure before it happens that I'm the doctor summoned.

Anti- or at least a-social I might be, but I wasn't good at simulating a beneficiary under the public health board.

- Don't try anything like missing your footing jumping off a vehicle already in motion. Nothing public. Just a topple-over coming downstairs from your study of an evening and an unlucky landing on one of the frontal lobes, or, better, the rear top of the cranium. But that's for me to decide on when you manage to crawl to the phone in the hall before passing out.

I live in a garden-floor flat, no stairs, no study, no cat to let out or in   - but had he mentioned one, or wasn't I thinking of the beloved creature whose death had so affected Noona?

- 3 -

Everything, or almost, went off as planned. But then something unplanned and unforeseen   - by me that is, for I believe Cornelius suspected this might happen   - took over. It's hard to report what I made of it at the time, and I am not, if I can help, going to be more precise about ambiguous experiences by drawing on a grasp of them that only came later.

While I lay in my cot in the large ward, incommunicado (feigning unconsciousness), Cornelius, having diagnosed a hair-line fracture of the skull, and none of the other doctors or nurses presuming, or caring, to look under the bandages that cocooned my cranium, half-waiting for what I supposed corresponded to what Cornelius called a leap forward, or sideways, I took in the doctors, nurses, nuns, matron, visitors and fellow patients, above all the nurses, from behind an apparently comatose veil. And all this without any sense of pressure, hurry or fear of some sort of blunder, such as was usually at the back of my mind in the world outside.

Several of the medicos were young, pleased with themselves, lightweight. A few were serious and worried, which was presumably equally obvious to those in their care. One middle-aged surgeon stood out in this microcosmic world. However, surgeons don't, it seems, appear in the wards at all frequently and this one was obviously not a favourite with the matron whose authority was of the other, exterior, bureaucratic kind.

These observations were the result of my unique position of keeping in touch with what was going on from a point outside. To return to the central issue, or why I was where I was: the nurses. Did I imagine that when the heightened intuition which I'd been bestowed with revealed the one with whom I could escape loneliness, become absorbed in conversation with on summer evenings, in whose company share an aperitif at the magic hour of six, and at a still, indeterminate, even more magic hour, the inhibiting barrier would be raised, she would consent?

It was by all known means impossible to come to a conclusion about which of the Sisters had any of these attributes, let alone all. A mistake could be fatal. The writer, Joel Samson or Samson Joel as it read on the hospital register, while being treated for a mental disorder, had been persuaded by a woman half his age into an alliance which would bedevil his last years, while the girl, discarding nothing of her former ways, had the run of a comfortable home and money, and a tour of the shops on her days off (she had kept her job at the hospital).

In the end I had little or nothing to do with the miracle that I had put my faith in. But nor had the other person. As Cornelius observed, when I confided in him, there is a factor in nature, to which he gave a name or initial, that I at once forgot, ensuring that growth or evolution moves in small leaps or quanta.

I had of course noticed an Arab girl who in a slow, stately walk - but which because of her plumpness was sometimes close to a waddle - drifted through the ward taking, it struck me, random temperatures. She had irritated me by winding the band round my lower arm and attaching the tube to the gadget she held against the folds of the voluminous garment she wore in contrast to the trim rig of the other nurses, a few minutes after I had had the routine blood pressure testing.

She didn't open her full lips and I supposed she didn't speak English. By overhearing the gossip that passed from bed to bed, crossing my silent one at often a late hour of the night, I heard that she was the daughter of a wealthy sheik who had sent her here to become a qualified nurse so that she could return home to work in one of the oil state's less than efficient hospitals.

She seemed to do more than her share of night duty, perhaps an arrangement to get her out of the way. Or, as later seemed more probable, because it relieved some local nurses with whom, the married ones I suppose, it wasn't popular.

Anyhow, on this particular night there had been no hint of a quantum-like activity in my neurological stagnation. She drew, as usual, the curtains round my cot and in her leisurely fashion settled herself on the edge of the bed with her apparatus and what looked like a roll of fresh bandages. I was dismayed by the possibility - unlikely as it was - that she was going to dress the fictional wound at the back of my head. The event, the Epiphany, as I later thought of it, took on a fictional, dream-like dimension. We were in a tent in a desert under which lay the lakes of black, liquid gold. It was one of those hours in the ward of utter silence, with, for us, an expectant hush.

- I think you met my father, Mr. ...Samuel.
- On what occasion, Sister?

I was tense and startled at her opening those dark greyish lips in a face framed in a white turban, not unlike my own head wrap and pronouncing a precisely-articulated English of a kind nobody here, or in my circle of acquaintances, spoke.

- At Mr. Paulus's.

I was a little distrait at the time, Sister. I didn't catch the details of the personalities behind the new faces.

I was adopting a formal style that I must have thought suited this daunting pre-dawn encounter.

- You wouldn't have forgotten him.
- Ah, I had to be cautious. Did I recall an oriental countenance? Gathering my scattered wits and recalling what I'd heard in the ward, I exclaimed (I tried for an

exclamation rather than a more casual response to make up any loss of ground): Ah, the Sultan!

- Prince Ahmed.

She pronounced the name and prefix with a casualness that was notable - to me, anyhow. It reminded me of an incident in one of Dostoevsky's novels where late at night on the famed Nevsky Prospect in Petersburg (how familiar it was to me in those long hours of reading!) one of the great Russian's anti-heroes has to step aside as a woman in furs runs down the steps of a hotel. he bows slightly and raises his top hat: - Sergei Dolgorouky. She smiles a ravishing smile.

Prince Dolgorouky?

But he isn't a member of that famous family.

What on earth has this to do with the so far almost equally short conversation between myself and the night nurse? Nothing I could rationalise, but there was a connection, if only in reverse.

- You see, I'm bad at names, I didn't even catch yours.

She hadn't told me what it was, but now she pronounced such, to me, a strange one that I had to ask her to repeat it.

- Abdalla.

- Abdullagh?

- Not quite, but you'll learn it.

- Your father lives in our unhappy land, Sister?

Why had I thought fit to put in the romantic sounding clause?

- Oh no, he's on a short visit to see how the undertaking is progressing.

She scribbled something on the sheet where she'd noted the two sets of figures for my blood pressure and showed it to me: '15.2'.

This was hardly a blood pressure count. Was it some other assessment of my condition, possibly of my skull measurements?

- We're breeding Arab thoroughbreds of that height.

- Huh...

What she was telling me was that, despite the general assumption that any cross-breeding of Arab blood diminished the size of European race-horses, her father was proving the

contrary. I was not ignorant when it came to the tap roots of
the modern thoroughbred: the Brierley stallion and the
Darley Turk.

She fell silent, sitting at the side of the bed in the brightly-
lit tent. I had reached - *we* had reached - the still centre
where the previous words and whispers take on another
sense, to which the nervous system responds before the
mind. Perhaps blood is drawn from the head into the
instinctive centres, but I shouldn't speculate on matters of
which I'm as unknowledgeable as the next. I knew it was
now or never, that this was the initial leap, and, rising
slightly in the bed, I put a hand at the back of her head-dress
and pulled her face towards mine on the pillow.

The pressure I exerted, if not minimal, was easily
resistable. This was both out of fear of a rebuff and in accord
with the faith I was putting in Cornelius's explanation of
nature's mysteries.

She didn't respond. I daren't increase the pressure, and
was within sight of panic, shame and desperation. She rose
from the bed and stood beside it, about, as I thought, to
depart, her face averted while slowly, leisurely - though
that wasn't quite the word - moving one hand inside the folds
of her long cream-coloured -or at least distinctly off-white
compared to the nurses' uniforms - robe. I had no sense of
what was happening. She could be taking her time about
refastening an undergarment - a girdle, if she wore one
beneath all that material, that had come undone.

I felt my recently-registered pulse rate jump before I fully
took in the folds of her robe around her on the linoleum, out
of which she was stepping almost sedately.

Nothing could have been less furtive or conspiratorial than
her bearing as she drew back the bedclothes and climbed in
beside me. She was - that much I'd realised - still not fully
naked though I didn't explore her state of undress.

- 4 -

I never knew with Cornelius whether he was here at my bed
in his clinical role or as a visitor. Always accompanied by a

nurse - hospital routine, I suppose - who watched and learnt as, after the curtains were drawn around, he undid the bandages and with his surgeon's (pianist's) finger tapped out a tune (a message?) on my skull.

This time he brought a bottle of 48% volume, duty-free spirits and a small black flask of Bitters. When the Sister fetched glasses he concocted a golden liquid.

- A pink gin's just the thing to put you right at this hour, he chanted, as he might if reciting a poem. The words were to me evocative of a past era in closed circles of male society in the semi-tropics, probably at sundown on a hotel or club balcony.

Cornelius was offering the drink to the patients on each side of me, one an old fellow who hardly spoke and was perhaps senile, the other a lad who drained his glass in a couple of gulps without turning a feather.

As for me, the potent brew was arousing memories that had been hidden in a corner of my mind since early morning. An instinct to postpone reviving on a kind of mental video what had happened with the Arab girl after getting into my bed was reversed, and I withdrew my attention from Cornelius and the nurse for the very short space of time it takes for the interior scenario to be run through.

She lay still, and quite relaxed, as if nothing surprising or unexpected had taken place. Perhaps this was to put me at ease. The pause might be a breathing space. But hadn't I had years of breathing space, if it came to that?

Then   - the next leap   - I took her in my arms and clung to her. However, I haven't yet learnt to leave well alone, and I realised that this moment of tenderness would normally lead to a more uninhibited sexual union. But we weren't a normal couple. I unclasped an arm from around her and thrust it down through the coverings in which she still was clad, over her ample stomach and into a grove of pubic hair.

I was ready to risk all on the shock of this contact producing the nervous and muscular reaction that, for the first time in ages, would give me the magic power to enter - and what a secret, hidden aperture - her body. I couldn't be sure. But I never am at vital moments in quite different contexts. Without a hand to my own flesh, which might have spoilt everything, there was no sure telling.

Fumbling, as I knew from of old, was fatal, or would have been had not Abdallah revealed the first signs of her gifts: her insight into how to respond to somebody like me. She whispered a shameless sentence in my ear that completely reassured me.

The next couple of nights she didn't linger at my cot and I hesitated to detain her. Perhaps her night duties had become more onerous. There may have been a sharp increase of casualties for all I knew. But I couldn't dispel the other conclusion. I having failed her, despite her generous reaction, she had sought a lover elsewhere. And indeed had I not seen the hospital as a kind of dating agency with the possible partners on show rather than in a photo album?

Having wandered in trepidation so far up this desolate alley, I shall not break off to return to the latest point reached, that is: to Cornelius at my bed-side with the drinks.

On my way back from the lavatories   - there were only five for this whole wing, three of which were reserved for female patients - passing the entrance to the next-door men's ward I saw a lit tent pitched in the semi-darkness.

A sluggish imagination isn't one of my weaknesses and I instantly conjured up a vision. At first I didn't dare take in more than the small floor space by the cot. And of course there was the off-white wreath made up of folds of linen out of which she had stepped. I remonstrated with myself: How despicable to give way to a voyeurism that isn't even factual.

I was quite clear that, for my own sake, for Abdallah's, for that of us all (who were they?) I should continue back to my own ward, get into bed and dismiss my suspicions. When next we met all would be resolved. Had she been in bed with a man whose, say, broken leg had not reduced his virility there would be no temporising, prevarication. She was in no sense pledged to me.

I got as far as my bed but hadn't the courage to get into it and confront the hours till the lights were switched on and the early morning bustle commenced. As I stood there irresolute, I envisaged her astride a patient, he being the one who must not exert himself, her veiled head bent over a bearded face.

There was nothing for it but to admit utter, shameful defeat and return to what could only seal the disaster. For that's what I had made sure it was.

I found the spot where the two curtains overlapped and pulled them carefully half an inch apart. Abdallah, a surgical trolley beside her, was bent over a cot, cleaning with wads of what looked like soaked cotton wool a suppurating wound in the abdomen of an elderly casualty. She deposited the pink-stained material in a white receptacle in the bottom tray of the trolley.

Coda: Jealousy.

I was now, if briefly, in the degraded company of the illustriously jealous. That is to say I chose these as confreres, not indeed as any kind of self-mitigation but because they had left the most comprehensive reports. It was not so much the fictional persons in whom I sought some understanding of the condition but in their creators.

Shakespeare had evidently experienced first-degree jealousy to have made credible the passion that turned Othello into a monster. But of all those who have left records of this degrading anguish Proust's is to me the most agonising. What he suffers imaginatively over Albertine - a stand-in for Albert, his chauffeur - in the section of his great novel called in English 'The Sweet Cheat Gone' would, I think, be unbelievable fantasy to anyone not having been at least a small way down that vile alley.

Note: There is no jealousy in Joyce's 'Ulysses', although the little Irishman was tormented by it in regard to Nora. Bloom's lack of it is almost as incredible to those who have been a prey to it as is Proust's description to those who have not.

Incidentally, in Shakespeare's last great trilogy there are monsters - Caliban - but not this traditionally green one.

What of the company of the obscure men and women, perhaps especially the latter, whose beloved companions have betrayed them, though they may not let this word slip into the constantly re-drafted account they give themselves of the disaster in mostly vain attempts to understand it? Even to discover some possible failure in themselves, however minor, could make it marginally less desolate.

2

Dinner at the Village dining room downstairs at the Avenue Hotel; the place has two restaurants and a dining room, of which the latter was the most expensive.

It was the celebration of my discharge from the hospital, or so Cornelius had suggested, but for me there was a far more important reason to rejoice which can be surmised.

We had hardly ordered our meal, the items of which I haven't time to mention, when Maya entered in tow to Paulus. Although he may have been, at least in her estimation, one of her proteges, there was no doubt who was in charge of the outing at this point.

Maya sat down and waved to us; Paulus disappeared into the gents. So far so good; my *Lobster Bisque* with toasted bread would be here in a moment. We were already well into the bottle of Schnapps Cornelius had asked for before looking at the *Speise Karte,* as I translated 'Menu' to harmonise in my mind - at the moment all was harmonious - with the German spirits.

Paulus emerged from the lavatory bent double, dragging a leg, one hand on his hip and cupping the other under the nose of a thin dame draped in pearls seated opposite her husband at one of the tables, and exclaimed in a raven's croak: 'Spare a note, my lady, for an incapacitated Hussar'.

The woman seemed to take it in her stride - no doubt a frequent traveller to exotic lands - and did indeed put down her fork to take a couple of notes from her handbag. Maya was pretending not to notice, which gave her a lofty and rather ridiculous expression. I took a swig of Schnapps so that if I had to burst into laughter I could behave as if I was choking on the fiery spirit.

Paulus was making the rounds without any interference from the maitre d'hotel who I took it had either agreed to the little act - after all, he allowed the clientele to be pestered (I wasn't unbiased) by students in the guise of musicians.

After a few appeals to the diners, some of which were rejected, he ended up at our table at Cornelius's invitation.

I didn't suppose he'd recall my face, but he greeted me with

- Mr. Samson, sir, I should explain my behaviour.

- That isn't necessary. I fully...

He interrupted a sentence that I wasn't sure how I should end.

- I trust it doesn't embarrass you, Mr. Samson, to have a clown sit down at your table uninvited.

What was I to say? Nothing, a welcoming (false) smile and a headshake.

A bit of levity to lighten all the earnestness around. An oblique glance, a poet's perhaps or an astronomer's, reveals a farce: the solemnity on the face of a gentleman trying to figure out if the *Sauce Hollandaise* is a fit accompaniment to boiled carp. Why, the little show I put on is crude comedy in comparison.

Cornelius was drunk, as drunk as I ever saw him, a condition, that is, from which I've seen him revert to instant sobriety when necessary at the hospital.

A poet, a cosmic explorer, a colleague of Copernicus and Pushkin, he murmured, apparently to himself.

The latter was not a heavy drinker, though a sad and lonely man, Paulus remarked, a *non-sequitor* as far as I could see, but the conversation - lecture more like - despite Paulus's stricture on earnestness - was rather out of my ambit.

- Listen to this, Mr. Samson, Paulus went on, intentionally, it seemed, excluding Cornelius.

The poet dwells absorbed in vanities
And common worries and toils
Until Apollo calls him to holy sacrifice
His soul dreams in cold lassitude
And his days are perhaps the most wretched
Among the wretched sons of earth.

The first personal communication I'd received that evening. Probably I made of it something different to what was actually said, but isn't that mostly so with the important communications?

It was clear enough if I interpreted it without too much analysis (or the earnestness that perhaps Paulus had meant) of my present situation. Apollo/Abdallah would, if I trusted her, lead me from the company of the most wretched.

Paulus left, doubled up and limping, just after Maya and, as I later heard, catching up with her on the corner, and Cornelius started telling me about his 'foundation'. Again another picture, quite different from either the tatty bed-sitter or the extensive block on several floors.

I heard it was being transformed into a much more modest edifice. Cornelius described Paulus arriving in our city as a refugee (from where he didn't say).

And then something extraordinary happened, one of those miracles that come about when various quite disparate circumstances fuse in a flash of energy and a gap is leapt across, a solid wall is passed through.

One of the conditions in this case was Cornelius's drunkenness, which was not at the incoherent stage - if it ever was with him - but, by weakening certain rational restrictions, allowing intuition to emerge from being dormant or subconscious, he revealed to me the inside story of Paulus, the wild, destructive spirit among the tamest of the tame, the astro-physicist extraordinary as at home among the stars as the others were among their calculating machines.

How deeply Cornelius himself grasped the realities of Paulus's and his team's joint discoveries I am not sure. He told me of them in language that I could just about follow, whether a simplification for my sake or because for him too it was a field where he felt lost, I'm not sure. But it is, of course, roughly the language which I'm going to use in this part of the report.

Certain minute living cells - those of bacteria were the ones Paulus had for long been researching - emit their own signals on wave-lengths which he had been recording. He had arrived at what seemed a dead end in his experiments and although instinct - which the pure scientist relies on as much as the poet - told him he was skirting one of the more important aspects of reality, he was about to accept an invitation from colleagues in Australia to have a look at a new radio telescope in New South Wales.

Dispirited, he would have declined had Nicole Senlis not persuaded him to go.

He went, without Nicole, to Australia (I am paraphrasing Cornelius) and was soon recording through the radio telescope signals that corresponded almost exactly to the wavelengths of the organisms he had cultured in his laboratory.

These, of course, had been noted before but explained as radiation from mineral particles, as was well known. But, and here came Paulus's vital break-through, the radiation waves from his micro-organisms corresponded exactly to those recorded in space at a height above the earth at which it was impossible that they could have come from the planet.

There, for the moment, I'll leave the matter, because it is a strain to maintain for longer, and also because it is now more appropriate to follow the line leading to the relationship between Paulus and Nicole.

She was his guiding star (Cornelius's inspired expression). I now began to grasp the very strange picture. If Paulus had indeed hit on an utterly unexpected and revolutionary truth, exploding all the accepted evolutionary assumptions, then life had not its origins in the primal oceans of the planet, in amino acids and the fortuitous intervention of an electro shock by means of lightning. On the contrary, we came from the stars, and, in a very factual sense, are composed of star dust to varying degrees. Certain women's attraction, including Nicole's, came from the high proportion of these galactic particles in their make-up, according to Paul.

And now what, to me, was the final fitting together of all these new concepts in a final harmony: Nicole, as a very young girl, had been the mistress of the Lithuanian painter, Soutine, in Paris at the time of the last war. And his paintings, those I'd seen, were inspired by extra-terrestrial mysteries. Yes, even the plucked hen!

- 6 -

I shall make a fresh start: Day one, take one, one step

forward, two back, back to Nicole forty years ago when, at most just into the magic teens, she was picked up in an obscure Paris cafe by a failure of a Balt-Jewish painter, with perhaps no clear intention towards her, whose first name was Chaim.

He was nearly fifty, underfed, and Nicole, three portraits of whom he painted, cared as best she could for him before he died of tuberculosis and semi-starvation a year or two afterwards.

They were lovers because that's what he wanted, and to Nicole it was comforting though she could not really make it out.

(Almost all of this re-introductionary report I got, though considerably later than the lunch with Cornelius, and, at different times, from Nicole herself who liked nothing better than to talk, though not to everyone, about the past.)

From the very first day, he started to touch her. When he made her come she was so astonished and enthralled (had she never masturbated? No. And I believed her) that she thought he had some kind of necromancy about him.

She would have stayed with him for that alone, and perhaps in the early days that's all that concerned her. She became quite weakened and exhausted, and I saw her white face and large eyes with the stains under them in the first of the portraits he painted, which she has in her room.

Soon, though, he turned her more outwards, towards himself and his own body. She found it very curious and its changes in relation to her very funny. But also attractive to the point of obsession.

His painting and his sensuality, these were what fascinated her in a naive, childlike way: the studio smell, the texture and colour of what came out of the tubes, the viscous stuff that came out of him and clung to her belly. Of course in a vague way she knew what it was, *semence* (that's what she still called it) and it excited and reassured her, because, as she put it: - I never dreamed an uncouth urchin like me could have aroused a mature man, let alone a great painter.

The paintings: She couldn't make them out for a long time, but they fascinated her too. Such a storm in some of them, the trees, even the buildings, all leaning madly over in one direction. The still ones too. The plucked hens that he painted dangling from her hand looked to her as if they'd lost their feathers in the tornado. When he asked her why they made her laugh and she told him, he looked grave. She was sorry she'd come out with such silliness. But he wasn't really angry with her. He made love to her with the minimum delay and without undressing. it was only that night when they were in bed and she was in his arms - though a more precise description would put it the other way round - that he told her about the comets.

- Comets, Nicole?

- You see, he told me stories about comets from the stars that come rushing past the earth, bringing storms and whirlwinds and also tiny bits of life, smaller than a pin's head, from which we all had come, plants, animals and humans. All this thrilled me, and I believed every word. When I looked at his pictures, at my portrait, I looked like something blown in on one of the comets and the hen he dangled by its feet in one hand while he painted with the other, with all its feathers torn out by the hurricane.

Comets or no comets, and it was a theory I didn't reject there and then, and which, as I shall relate, I've come across recently proposed by the great astro-physicist Paul himself and also by the Indian astronomer Wickramsinghe.

To make a brief diversion: Meeting her helped confirm another of my convictions: that certain important events occur in pairs without one causing the other. By what might seem an extraordinary chance I met the one woman with whom I could share what had doomed me to solitude, first Abdallah, and then - after a lifetime during which I'd never caught a glimpse of anyone like her - another, Nicole, crossed my path.

Nicole's attractiveness was less hidden - there were not all the folds - than Abdallah's. Anyone with a grain of perception would be drawn to her, despite her age.

She had had all kinds of love affairs before meeting Paul. (I'm leaving out the 'us' from now on.) It was a relief to her, I think, to tell me about them in detail, for in doing so she was explaining them, and her own peculiar gifts, capabilities and failures, to herself. Another thing: she couldn't have confided like this in another woman and only in a man who was a fulfilled lover because a lot of it involved quite shameless intimacies, shameless, that is, I suppose, in those cases where love didn't enter into it. Shamelessness? Love? Listening to Nicole I too was learning more about myself, having to think clearly about what went on in the recesses of mind and body, unswayed by niceties, unabashed by shock.

When I came to consider these sessions with her I saw she couldn't have spoken so honestly to Paul without provoking him to jealousy, and in a particularly dangerous form: jealousy of the past.

- Doesn't he question you?

- Not much, there are thresholds he doesn't cross. He likes to hear of the very rare real loves in my life after Chaim. Especially about - (she mentioned a painter, far more successful than Soutine, with whom she'd lived several years, and, she said was still alive at a good old age, but whose work didn't now fetch anything like her first love's.)

Did she never wonder what effect some of her tales were having on me? Was she sometimes attempting to provoke me? On balance (by which I mean I'm not absolutely certain) I don't believe so. She was a too caring, not to say loving in the unegoistic sense, person. My having Abdallah made her happy, though the two women had very little in common.

Most of these conversations - and that's what they were, not just monologues - took place in the room whose lit window Maya had pointed out to me that fateful evening. So, in a sense, I was back at the spot from where I had started.

It had always belonged to Nicole, the bed-sitter that is, having taken it on her arrival from France to our city. She had lived alone in it, though not without lovers and, I surmised, even casual pick-ups.

I soon realised that I'd come to a point where I'd have to make a vital decision, something I don't like doing. I could withdraw from the company of Paul, Nicole and their world - though I hadn't really grasped it - and let Abdallah take over and fill my days and nights. That was all that I wanted. A short time ago it would have seemed to have excluded any other world. But what I was learning was that the more you have - this applies to the greater gifts as well as the lesser -

the more you're given.

In the end I don't suppose I made a conscious choice. Where I've failed in this report is in not presenting it from the start as one composed by a writer of imaginative, though very sober and serious, fiction. What was the point of stressing my sense of solitude, even alienation, my sensual fantasies that were hard to fulfill in actuality, if it didn't all lead up to, or devolve from, my being, beyond conscious choice, what is called an artist?

Brief diversion or interlude to ease any build-up of over-earnestness: Not long ago at a party, asked my profession, I replied 'writer', which was misheard by my slightly intoxicated hostess as 'rider'. For the rest of our prolonged talk, not having immediately corrected her, I had to keep up the misunderstanding, which meant embellishing it with all kinds of exciting and, to her, surprising experiences of an amateur equestrian who had competed in events at Deauville and Rome, not to mention - I manoeuvred her questions so that it seemed far from boasting, but was dragged out of me - having won the famous Czechoslovak Grand National on a grey gelding called *Sumptuous* who was now in peaceful retirement at my farm.

At the time Paul, in collaboration with an Indian astronomer, had published a treatise setting out his then (even now) unpopular proposition.

- This Asian told me my genes were sparks in a cloud of diffused star light. (Nicole.)

- In the forests of the night, I added.

Another extraordinary 'chance': because it had a picture of Soutine's - of a comet I think - on the cover, she had read Paul's book, 'The Truth about the Origin of Life' (an intentionally provocative title) of which she'd made out almost nothing except, disappointingly, that living organisms reached the earth as bacteria and viruses.

She had asked if she might interview him for a French magazine whose editor she knew - had been his mistress - telling Paul about Soutine, of whom he apparently hadn't heard, and about what he had told her of the cosmic storms that so often got into his pictures.

- 7 -

When I was discharged it was because Cornelius had persuaded them to grant Sister Abdallah leave of absence to look after me until I had recovered.

So I was living with a woman again after a long time of solitude. That is a miracle, not of course usually seen as such because of its frequency, or commonplaceness. I was conscious of it, having almost despaired of ever again achieving it.

To divert a moment - my head was so full of subsidiary ideas sprouting from this fertile centre stem: - We are all fragments of reflected reality, in the same molecular form as the cosmic structure. I had long had the illusion of being at the centre of reality which had been turning solitude into a very constricted state. Now I recognised companions, fellow-beings, whose cells contained the same basic quest for consciousness as mine, a consciousness that could merge to varying degrees with mine.

In the case of a woman to a few extra, but how sensational, degrees.

Such semi-scientific, pseudo-psychological meditations had to be discarded, or wither away, in the more immediate sensations of daily living if I was at long last to escape from over-consciousness into whatever state - I'd almost forgotten - lay beyond and all around it.

It happened of its own, as it must. Abdallah was at the kitchen table and I came up behind her. I saw, without taking it in, that she was preparing a favourite dish, *couscous*, and, without fore-thought, stooped and pulled up the skirt she had exchanged for the voluminous nurses' garb.

At first - though first to last went more quickly than standard temporality - she went on with what she was doing and afterwards I realised that this is what enabled me to carry it off, being under no pressure. Then, as this too was just the right response at the right moment, I felt the backward jerk of her buttocks. Was there a pause, a cessation of movement for a fraction of a second that may, for all I know, on another time-scale last as long as it takes for a petal to open, a leaf to fall, the moon to rise? Then - it was she again whose bottom made the necessary adjustment - I was inside her.

Now I was fully conscious again, and so was she, if she'd ever been anything else from the first move. We were both flooded with the consciousness of the other's sensation as well as our own - it's more than a guess in regard to her: we were exchanging communication at a mercurial rate - though when she came she added her voice to the other vibrations to leave me in no possible doubt.

A few moments before my own orgasm, had another woman been substituted I'd have gone on unabashed and unabated. I mention this because it later worried me, until I realised Abdallah would still have been there in some less stormy, undefined corner of my being.

Though the Paul set-up wasn't nearly so extensive as, in my daze, I'd supposed, it was costly enough. Where did the money come from?

- Oh, that was never the trouble. The sale of pictures of Soutine's, Nicole still has two, brought in the necessary capital and the stud fees of my father's stallion, Al Kareb, supply the running costs.

When it came to the hard facts, she had a clear grasp and was as adroit in explaining them as she was sensually.

And this particularly so when the act of love-making seemed to have cleared our heads. Apropos of which, Nicole had told me that the at-one-time famous painter she had lived with after Soutine invariably turned his back and went to sleep after they had copulated.

What had made her stay with him? I may come back to that, but at this point there are events from Abby's past that are of more concern to me.

There is the trip with her father, Paulus, Nicole, an Asian astro-physicist, two stable lads and two stallions belonging to Prince Ahmed. The way she related the journey, not making its purpose at all clear at first, made it appear bizarre, to say the least. But by now I knew enough about her to let her proceed in her own fashion, slowly, gravely, with the same marked decorum that I'd noticed as she walked down the ward.

I say 'decorum' because she was telling me this, sitting partly undressed after I'd seen her in one of her most indecorous postures while we had made love.

The journey was to Canada, to the most northerly part of Nova Scotia, on the coast opposite Prince Edward Island where, in March, she had seen pack-ice for the first time.

It had evidently made a deep impression on Abby, as it well might have on a daughter of the desert, and she was going on about it in her deliberate way.

- Please, Abby, don't leave the story up in the air. it's hard enough to follow anyhow, without diversions.

- I'm sorry. I was leading up to it. Where were we, though?

- In the far north of Nova Scotia with your father, Paulus, Nicole, an Indian astronomer, some horses, and two stable lads.

- One of them was a lass, as they're called.

- Don't let's get into racing terminology.

- OK. I was only.... You see, a colleague of Paul's discovered the comet, Zadopek, called after him, and had predicted the exact course it was on nine and a half years earlier when its tail - I'm putting it as best I can - brushed past that part of Canada; Prince Edward Island and the sea around it.

I was listening attentively, not so much to the scientific data - if that's what it was - but for what I sensed were important moments in Abby's past.

- Wait a minute. Why didn't the comet's discoverer himself go with you?

- He had died since, so Paulus said.

She didn't seem convinced that Paulus was telling the truth, perhaps they'd drifted apart, almost ten years is a long time, but there wasn't any point in going into that.

- Another thing: What effects had the first appearance of the - what's the name - Zadopek comet had on this island?

- Which island? Oh, you mean the Prince Edward one, and the Sound between it and Nova Scotia.

- Yes, that's the strange part, or one of the peculiarities in the story.

- A couple living there at the time had put down in their diary some changes in their hens - they had a poultry farm - and also in the garden. The old lady - we were shown coloured photos of her - also some in black and white - had noted in a small brown copy-book where I think she kept the accounts as well as egg-laying records, that these - I mean the egg production - had increased for no reason - they knew nothing about any comet at the time - for several weeks. There were also notes about unusually splendid roses, and some other species of flower that I've forgotten, in the garden. This was in French, which I don't altogether understand, and was translated for me by Nicole.

- Nicole, what did she make of it? With all her reminiscences, this was something she hadn't told me of.

- She said this person she'd lived with in Paris as a kid had known all about it, and made illustrations or something.

Abby had either not attended closely to what Nicole had said or else Nicole hadn't seen fit to confide in her.

I would ask Nicole to tell me her version of the Canadian expedition in due course. This would not in any sense imply that I doubted anything that Abby was relating.

Paul and the Indian questioned several other islanders but I don't think that they got any valuable information.

Hardly surprising. Imagine a knock on the farmhouse door. Two strangers - tourists? - 'No, thanks, we can't stay for tea. We were wondering if, a little over nine years ago, you noticed anything unusual in your live-stock or crops?'

But all this was merely introductory. They were there for the great event, if not exactly led by a star to this rather desolate spot, at any rate guided by a prophecy.

Zadopek, or Zadopeksi: he'd been a Pole and for convenience his name had been shortened when the comet was named, had not been able to predict its return more precisely than within a period of forty-eight hours. through laziness, a defect he shared with most Poles, so Paul had told them. Which sounded like one of his jokes. After a journey of hundreds of millions of miles into outer space and back to pinpoint its arrival within two days was surely an extraordinary feat!

It never came?

I had to end the suspense, and know the worst. Though, of course, I suppose in my heart (what had the heart to do with it?) I already had more than what is called an inkling.

3

The intrepid expedition stayed at the hotel which, according to the maps brought by the Indian and marked by Zadopekski was in the direct former trail of the luminary's tail.

The above is, as is evident, my own comment, though of course based on Abby's information.

When we resumed the discussion, for it was by no means a monologue, I reminded her that according to Paulus - and here he was the chief authority - what was transmitted from the comet were bacteria and viruses.

I saw that Abby was out of her depth in this area, as I myself was, but said that this did not worry her father whatsoever.

Why should it, indeed, I thought, if life on earth had thus arisen? If these bacteria, not all brought by comets because the original probes had revealed that living organisms were widely scattered in particles throughout the cosmic star-dust. As far as I have been able to make some sense of the theory - first postulated by three up-to-then highly thought of scientists, two Asians and Paul - these bacteria, whose side effects could produce epidemics such as influenza, had evolved from a simple molecular unit to ever more complex structures. Finally the most complex structure known to us, the human brain, evolved and, with it, consciousness. No good asking Abby how this tied in with causing an influenza epidemic. This was one of the questions, not one that had priority, for Nicole who seemed quite at home with Paul's controversial theories.

To get it out of the way of more sensational events, I'll say here and now that, putting it over simply, neutral researchers of outbreaks of influenza were still baffled by the fact that at least some strains of the disease - the Asian kind, for instance, if I'm not getting mixed up - are not transmitted from person to person. It may strike a whole community in, say, a small town and bypass the citizens of a metropolis not very far distant.

- We spent a couple of weeks at the hotel to be on the safe side.
- What about the animals?
- Oh, the horses. They were in the yard, exercised by their handlers.
- They could remain in their stables? They didn't have to be all the time in the open?
- Oh no. It would have been far too cold. Both the stallions and we were exposed to whatever was going to pass along the predicted route inside the walls and under the roof.

That made sense, given the first premise. I recalled reading that millions of neutrinos passed continually through our bodies.

- There were some funny goings-on.
- You mean in the hotel?
- Between Paul and Nicole.
- Oh.
- Paul returned from one of his night expeditions to find a hotel waiter in her room.
- How do you know?
- Oh, it was all over the hotel.
- Gossip.
- Don't you like gossip, Joel? Don't you want to hear it?
- Of course I do. I want to hear everything. What sort of night expeditions did Paul make then?
- He and Mukerjie took their instruments somewhere along the coast to monitor the comet's approach.
- Could you see it?
- I never had a glimpse of it.
- Did anyone?
- Oh, I suppose so. I think they tracked it by radiation and not visually.
- And then the day... the moment of truth arrived. Tell me about that.
- I didn't know which it was. It may have lasted several days, or perhaps only an hour or a few minutes.
- What happened?

- Paul said there was a Russian submarine under the ice.
- How did he know it was Russian? I mean, why did he think there was a submarine at all?
- I imagine he was in touch with it through his radio and Nicole speaks some Russian.
- Was she with them?
- She went once or twice. I'm not sure.
- It doesn't matter. What actually happened, that's what it all boils down to, doesn't it? Or don't you know, darling?
- Oh, I know very well.
- Go on, then.
- For one thing the stallions went wild.
- In what way?
- Heavens, Joel, in what way do you think? When I was brought to have a look at them in the loose boxes their penises were a horizontal yard long and when they reared up they stuck out like ram-rods with the purple tips gleaming under the electric bulbs.

When she got going about the horses Abby was more informative than about the visitor from space.

- How did that affect you?
- What a stupid question. How do you think?
- Go on, sweetheart.
- Daddy had to enquire among the local farmers about where there were mares in heat. It turned out there was a half-bred filly quite close whose owner was willing to have her covered. I'm not sure what my father told him about why the two stallions were there at all. But he showed the old fellow their pedigree from the thoroughbred breeders' compendium where their stud fee is advertised at something like twelve thousand dollars. So, you see, word soon spread and there were several locals wanting to bring mares to have them mated with these champions from Europe.

- Yes?

I didn't have to put any more questions. Abby was off on her own and described the scene in the barn where the mating took place.

Without adding, or detracting, any detail, I'll put it in my own words, those, that is, of a dedicated writer of true fiction. The first to be 'serviced' was the black filly who was backed up towards the chestnut stallion by her owner. The stallion was held by a handler on each side of his head gripping the bridle with both hands, a stable lad and a lass pulled almost off their feet, while the filly, being propelled backward, took short, delicate steps, setting her hind legs hesitantly on the straw and drawing them up quickly as if it was on fire, and what was being manoeuvred into position was the big dark buttocks, a sort of ark borne ceremoniously towards an altar where some sacred but bestial ceremony was to be performed.

The filly's big rump was thrust backwards, reminding Abby of how a woman standing with skirt hitched over arse, leans forward with her forearms on a table or the railing of a balcony, and thrusts backward and upward towards her partner.

Then the stable girl with a leg-up from Abbey's father got on the stallion's back - it turned out she was the only person who could handle him - a moment before he in turn mounted the filly and what everyone had been waiting for: the savage thrust of the long penis between the buttocks, that had now some pale specks not yet of sperm but sweat against their blackness, and into the filly, deep and deeper to the very neck of the womb, was accomplished. This, for Abby, was the epiphany, rather than the comet.

- What about the girl?

- What girl? Oh, the jockey? She had ridden races in France. I don't remember, I was too intent on the animals. Slid off I suppose.

After that, not surprisingly, Abby and I made love quickly and easily (I'd almost forgotten what a problem it had been for me before).

Here I'm going to interpolate a quotation from a tape of an interview that Nicole had with Paul for a French magazine. I think this was the first time she had met him.

NS: Of course nobody except a trained scientist understands the language in which you write about your discoveries.

PK: It's one of the secret languages as are all those that communicate anything worthwhile: the poet's, the imaginative novelist's, that of lovers, the language of the

Holy Books. All the rest is jargon. Political jargon, commercial jargon, that of the law, the Church. Nothing related or revealed, only the passing on of lies, prevarications, blasphemies and so on.

NS: When you published your first book, *Star Dust and Bacteria,* you received a lot of sneers and abuse.

PK: Yes, yes. Which confirmed my belief that I had discovered a missing piece of the great pattern.

NS: It was even suggested that you had perpetrated a hoax, that you were seeing whether you couldn't convince at least some respected colleague of what you would later expose as a huge farce.

The tape, evidently left on, ends in murmurs, whispers and finally, in Nicole's moans.

- 9 -

Now, although it comes as an interpolation between the two parts of what Abby told me, I'm going to give a resume of Nicole's report. Not in the form of question and answer, but a sober, edited version of the main events.

She hadn't been sure what it was all about. Paul called it a top-secret mission, but he could have been joking.

She dwelt on what to me were inessentials just as my dove had done, though different ones. She couldn't get over the unexpectedly luxurious hotel, but, as I suggested, the whole hard winter in those parts is compensated for by those who can afford it. Yes, but who are they? Prospectors? Mining engineers? Let's get back to the matter in hand. Or at least to a matter not totally unconnected, such as, if it meant so much to her, the hotel.

There were lushly carpeted open spaces (building space wasn't at a premium) and a sunken winter garden traversed by a real gravel path leading to a teak-wood counter that was the reception desk, then to their room, Paul's and hers, luxuriously appointed, with thick fleecy towels on a heated chromium rail in the bathroom.

She had never quite grown out of being a poor little waif,

often hungry, a lost urchin until she met Soutine, and then still most of these things, except lost.

They'd had a lot of fun, which she enjoyed describing, and even in retrospect it seemed to excite her. I wasn't sure if she was referring to long ago with Soutine or to the present and Paul.

Besides their luggage Paul had with him a black, heavy case which he never let out of his hand. They were no sooner in their room than he opened it, put on the earphones and started twisting knobs.

She said she didn't know what it was, some sort of sophisticated walkie-talkie with which he was calling up Deva Brata Mukerjie, whose room was down the corridor.

This struck me as unlikely. Did it really not occur to Nicole that it was a key part of the radio-tracking device to locate the comet? But I wasn't going to make any suggestion that might influence her report. The vital observations - if she made any - must come unbiased from her.

- Most men take it so seriously.
- Take what, Nicole?
- Why, sex, of course.

We seemed to be off again at a tangent. There was nothing for it but to follow her in these diversions and hope to circle back within sight of what was really going on.

- Not Paul, surely.
- That's, among all the other things, what we've in common. He's into all sorts of improvisations, not only setting a comic tone, but other tones too, like pretending he's in prison and I'm visiting him with bars between.

Paul shut the apparatus and told her he was going down to deposit it in the hotel safe for the night. She said nothing, though she told me she was surprised, because it would be perfectly safe in their room. After all, they weren't on some adventure barely this side of the law where it might be a shrewd move to act openly, even brazenly, and put the tell-tale tools into a safe deposit.

When Paul didn't reappear she lay down and dozed off in exhaustion, having switched off the main lights. She was awoken by a knock at the door and dazedly padded to open it. A trim-looking, middle-aged waiter stood with a tray balanced on one hand. The corridor lights, except for a pilot lamp, were out so she supposed it must be late. There was a dish with a silver cover, a bottle of wine, glasses and what looked like a sweet. Surely Paul hadn't ordered this. No good suggesting the waiter had come to the wrong room. Let him deposit the tray on one of the tables and depart.

- Does madame require anything else?

Evidently a foreigner, or perhaps a French Canadian.

- What time is it?

She asked out of nervous tension.

- Late, my lady. Was madame asleep?

Nicole didn't answer. She stood waiting. For the man to depart? For him to touch her?

This at any rate is her account of one of those moments subject to different emphases and interpretations.

What I think is that Paul, for it was of course he, resolved the ambiguities with a bout of love-making which was so noisy that the couple in the adjoining room must have overheard. Excited, they began coupling, according to Nicole who claimed she heard cries through the wall. She then imagined a chain reaction from room to room until it stops at an unoccupied one or where there's a solitary guest.

One night, perhaps the very next, Paul took her with him in the car to the mysterious destination that she supposed was the epi-centre of the whole venture. Turning off the main road that the snow plough had cleared, they drove down a track traced by red-striped markers on either side past shuttered frame dwellings, some no more than shacks, the summer homes of families from as far away as Halifax, Paul had told her.

He stopped the car and rolled down the windows on what she supposed was the seaward side, although in a misty moonlight there was nothing but a stretch of greyish, slightly undulating surface that reminded her of the view from a plane flying just above the clouds.

Paul handed her the binoculars.

Nicole gazed through them, uncertain what he was waiting for her to see.

There was what looked like a whitish wall, where the horizon should have been.

- The tundra! she exclaimed in desperation. She was both in love with and in awe of Paul and anxious not to fail him.

- Pack ice, he told her.

Now we were back at a point where the two reports met. But ice piled high, block over block, like the scene at an accident if two white trains had crashed into each other, hadn't impressed her as it had my little Arabian from the golden desert.

Paul rolled up the windows and switched on the car heating again before getting to work on the radio transmitter, as she called it.

When, after what seemed a long time, he was still twisting knobs and pressing buttons, bent forwards with the earphones clamped across his head, she undid her brassiere and slipped her breasts out of her blouse, the twin orbs dimly illuminating the interior of the car as the moonlight did the icy seascape.

These are *her words*. As a 'realist', I should have put it differently.

She was 'ready to relax him' when the strain of trying to interpret the whines and wails got too much for him. But what she wasn't ready for was his putting the receivers over her ears, with a layer of her hair in between, and telling her to talk in what Russian she could manage to the person at the other end.

She had picked up a smattering from Soutine - this turn of events had so taken her by surprise that she wasn't a very coherent reporter at this point.

Yes, she could hardly believe it, she was talking to a member of the crew of a Soviet nuclear submarine under the ice in Northumberland Strait. She told him they were also monitoring the return of the comet. Not an easy message to get across.

- Predicted by a Russian, or, rather, Lithuanian, she added proudly, though inaccurately.

- What was his name? But, first of all, what about yours?

- She told him, and then that of the great painter.

- Never heard of him, Comrade Nikolaya.

Their conversation was broken off by Paul putting questions to her to ask the commander of the vessel.

At this juncture she became reserved, just as I noticed she did at certain crucial points in her sexual reminiscences when, having done her best to provoke my curiosity - and succeeded - she would put on an air of embarrassment.

- You must understand, Joel darling, that we've come to the confidential part. What I heard and translated to Paul was classified information.

What wasn't classified and what I had to hear about was the goings-on in the car when the conversation, probably more halting than Nicole had recalled, was ended by the crew man who informed her that the commander - with whom she didn't speak - was switching onto the Moscow, or was it Mermansk?, wavelength.

Nicole either wasn't in on the stallion scene or preferred to dwell on her own and Paul's. Anyhow, whether it struck her or not, whatever it was, bacteria or star-dust (or are they one and the same?), that was borne on the tail of the comet, had a marked aphrodisiac effect on man and beast.

However, there was something more to it than that as I concluded when I gave my undivided thought to it - undivided between Abby and Nicole that is. A heightened imagination being one of my chief assets, I wasn't slow to fantasise about the comet's star-dust heightening the attractiveness of women exposed to it. Not only women perhaps, hadn't the black filly displayed an unusual sexual sophistication for an animal, not just by being in heat, but by her mixture of delicacy - in the manner of placing her hooves - and shamelessness in presenting her buttocks to the stallion?

- 10 -

Now Abby: she and the Indian returned to Europe by a night flight from Halifax on an Air Canada Lockheed that was almost empty. Of the others, Paul and Nikolaya visited a college of Paul's at a New England university, while Abby's father flew to the USA on business, no doubt connected with horse-racing rather than cometary matters.

Abby planned to compose a diary of the events she had witnessed during the flight and, although the Indian had suggested they sit together, she had declined. She could be quite determined, even ruthless, when she wanted.

She couldn't however keep her mind on recording her recent experiences. She was, I think, preoccupied with the immediate future, her father having insisted on her training as a nurse rather than assisting with his racing stables.

When the tall air hostess who with casual charm seemed to be running the plane by herself got talking to Abby after bringing her the miniature bottle of Canadian rye whiskey that she'd asked for, she told of her own small disaster (why, *own?* Was Abby left with a sense of disaster from the expedition?) the previous night. At a party at her boyfriend's she had drunk too much and behaved, as she put it, outrageously. There'd been a row, worse than their usual ones, and it looked to her like the end of the relationship.

Later, when the few passengers were asleep under the woolly pink blankets that she had earlier distributed, or dozing with earphones plugged into the radio transmitters in the arm rests, she brought a couple more bottles of whiskey and, pulling down the seat next to Abby, settled herself beside her.

They exchanged names, hers was Melly, and it soon looked as if she was going to confide some more intimacies to Abby, who didn't catch everything she was being told, partly because of the drone of the engines - more lulling or sleep-inducing than a fitting background to such converse - it's not all Madeira and tea cake where I come from, Melly announced.

She might have said: Sweet biscuits and china tea, but *qu' importe?* Abby was not very wide awake and neither completely absorbed by Melly's conversation. Natural enough, given what she had herself been through.

Melly went off to help a woman get a case down from the rack above her, and then spoke into the inter-com attached to the cross-fuselage that divided the big barn of a compartment they were in from a similar one forward. Conversing with the pilot, or co-pilot?

Abby poured one of the whiskeys into her glass and took a

sip or two to help keep her attentive, as she put it. It probably had the opposite effect because, some time later, when they were flying into the European dawn, she wasn't sure what Melly was recounting about a jade necklace. What it sounded like was: - Sometimes when I'm feeling like I do now, I put it inside and keep it there for the whole flight.

- Sounds fabulous, Abby managed to respond.

- Not fabulous like the real thing, better than nothing.

The hostess conjured up - not that it needed much conjuring with, presumably, the normal supply of complimentary drinks on board and the plane three-quarters empty - another couple of miniature bottles, both of which she poured into the one glass, remarking that although not permitted to drink on duty, she needed tonight a restorative. She also said it was in the way of a little celebration at meeting someone out of the blue.

Abby was about to ask: Who? But stopped herself in time. With one arm round her Melly held the glass to Abby's lips, and then kissed her on the mouth.

A pause, in which, I imagine, though Abby didn't explain it like that, the tall air hostess was sensing the lie of the land, or whatever the appropriate expression is. Then Melly's hand was up her skirt and burrowing around the top of her tights without hurry but persistently, while Abby was rather, but not altogether, taken aback.

- Did you facilitate her?

- Did I what?

- Accommodate.

- What lovely words.

- Open your legs, then.

- I did nothing, which was just what she wanted.

- Go on, Abby.

- That's about all.

- It couldn't have stopped there.

- No, of course not. I mean it took its natural course.

- Well, put it into words.

- She caressed me till I came.

Then had come the anti-climax of hanging round Heathrow until she got a trolley and then pushed it along the endless subways to another terminus - she was en route for

Paris, where she was staying with a relative until her father picked her up on his way back from America. Not that at this point I am going into her different movements - I mean geographic ones, ha! ha! - subsequent to the Canadian trip and before coming to St. Bride's hospital.

4

Where are we? If anyone is asking I'm not surprised.

First, where we are not, though had I followed a broader approach, that would have included, besides the two women's accounts, more of Paulus and his background than I do - Budapest, 1956.

As a mathematics student, perhaps with a leaning towards physics - or it could have been the other way round - after initial exhilaration and then heartbreak, he escaped as the Soviet tanks moved in. (I suppose it would have astonished him had it been predicted that he would, through a translator, be talking in a kind of comradeship to one of the crew of a Russian submarine on a secret mission all those years later.)

He had told Nicole that he and a group of fellow students, several girls among them, had laid a wreath on the statue of Stalin, that some citizens - many of them also students - had later pulled from its pedestal. I suppose even then he was aware of the grotesque, the incongruous, in the human condition. And this set him off in quest of a non-human, extra-terrestrial solution, at least a solution that would fit his particular temperament. In one sense it was farce, in another farce made the sense.

So much for what is rather heavy going, though that is my fault, for heaviness is not a characteristic of Paul, the clown-prophet.

- Well, boy, what do you know.

Not Abby addressing me in bed of an early morning, but Paulus at our apartment soon after his return from the United States.

What he had to tell us made another leap, forward or sideways, who can tell, in the saga.

He had come on - his expression, but I think introduced by the colleague I mentioned in New England - an old man who years before had written a treatise on the South African white ant.

Unexpected news? I'm not going to register bewilderment, not even surprise, any more. Just try to take it as it comes.

The typescript of the essay on these peculiar termites had been read by a quite famous French, or Belgian, dramatist and he had later incorporated it into a book of his own. I had better not name him in case of libel, though I don't suppose he could still be in the land of the hale and hearty.

The relevant point or connection, however, between him and Paul's work on the movement of life-laden cosmic star-dust begins nine or so years back when he'd been in the district of Nova Scotia, where the Zadopek comet's 'tail' had 'brushed' on its first recorded appearance. This he had mentioned to Paul's biologist friend quite casually after he'd known him for some time and discussed with him the behaviour of the African termites.

What he hadn't discussed, or known anything about, was his interest in the common or garden earthworm. He had only found out about it when he had visited him and the old fellow had brought him to the attic and shown him an ancient wooden (oak or perhaps mahogany) wine cask filled with a mixture of earth, manure and compost.

- That's where I keep them.
- You do?

Paul hadn't wanted to ask what. The old man was, it seems, one of those hyper-sensitive types, verging on the neurotic, constantly fearful of giving offence, and easily taking it himself.

Surely it wasn't a colony of the white ants, or, if it was, he had made insect history by successfully transporting it to such a habitat.

- The annelids.
- What?
- That's what he calls them.

Paul had brought him back with him, accompanied, I think, by the Prince, but it was all I could do to assimilate the more essential part.

Paul was evidently impressed by the old man and his unlikely obsession.

We had quite a bit of trouble getting his huge bin of worms packed in a crate cleared as consecrated soil being transported to Europe for use in the foundation of a temple that some visionary sect were building.

Not only did Paul indulge in, but he attracted the farcical. Mr. Margraves - I hadn't yet heard his first name - had been installed in a ground floor apartment in a suburb in our city. Access to a garden, it appeared, was essential.

- Well, let's hear it, Paul.

We'd come close enough by now for me to know that he hadn't called in for the sake of a mystification act or an elaborate piece of buffoonery.

- The earth to a depth that we haven't yet been able to be precise about is radiated either by the coma or the so-called tail.

- Did you say coma?

We were back at the heart of the mystery or reality, as he would have preferred to call it, where every new term or name, even if only a couple of letters were altered, might be vital.

- Did I? Anyhow, the gaseous halo or cloud that surrounds most comets. At the time of the earlier return of Zadopek, Margraves, who after his let-down over the African termites had - a sign of the real gift - turned to what was at hand: the common or garden earth worm.

I'm going to get through this part of the report as quickly and objectively as I can. It doesn't appeal to me greatly, nor does it concern Abby or Nicole, my two principle witnesses and informants, at least not directly.

I went to see Margraves with Paul. There was a smell of manure and rotting compost as soon as we entered his apartment. He entertained us in an over-furnished living room where every plush cover, curtain, piece of upholstery had absorbed the stench. Canadian rye was served (shades of my beloved Dove!) and cheese biscuits - who was paying for all this, but never mind - and there was no trace of senility or lapses of awareness. As I - wrong as usual - had expected.

The old man treated me deferentially. So much so that I think Paul had described me as having a far more important role in the 'whole business' than in fact I had. Referring to it as this 'whole business' is a kind of drawing back, of distancing myself at this point, which I was soon sorry for because of my fondness for and belief in, or wish to believe in, Paul.

We were conducted through the kitchen where I had only a glimpse of the bin - it could have been an old beer keg or water butt - but we didn't pause to look into it. Instead we went through into a small, secluded garden.

This I found strange. Am I particularly slow in adjusting? And when Margraves started to show off his vegetables, I was really startled. Not that I couldn't hold my own, as they say, in chatter about broccoli and cauliflower, coming up with runner beans, onion setts and the difficulty of propagating parsley in alkaline, or is it acid, soils.

Then the tone changed. A kind of hush descended - whatever I lack, it's not responsiveness to change in the psychic atmosphere - as when a gossipy conversation stops as the participants enter the church for Sunday mass.

Following the old fellow's lead, Paul and I stood looking down at a small plot of uncultivated earth, partly covered by a few common weeds. Was Margraves about to pray? That being unlikely, though I wouldn't have laid very long odds against it, I supposed he was going to tell us, that is me, something about his involvement with both the earlier and recent appearance of Zadopek.

Nothing happened. Or rather I missed altogether the happening, until Paul called my attention to it.

Several, four or five, earthworms had surfaced or were in the process of doing so.

Native to the soil, and not imported like those inside, the old man said, raising his head and regarding me to see, I supposed, how I would take it.

Several conventional vulgarisms such as: 'Well I never', 'You don't say' or 'You could have fooled me' suggested themselves, and were dismissed, as possible responses.

Before I could formulate a serious one we had moved on to a row of magnificent blooms along the hedge beyond which was a street. Then, in contrast but complete harmony, Margraves commented: - These lilies are good for nothing but loveliness that is also derived from out there. He gestured towards the sky - Not that this Sandwort - I looked round for another species of flower but there wasn't any - isn't just as wonderful, though with a wonder that doesn't so easily illuminate the consciousness.

The only worthwhile view of reality is holistic, involving the totality of consciousness. And at long last, partly thanks to you (to me? No, of course he was addressing Paul) this philosophy is slowly replacing the pseudo-science that has dominated most of the century that asserted that only the fundamental particles are real.

Back at the 'institute', as I'd heard Cornelius call it, with Paul and Nicole, I found out more about the old man whose unexpected outburst or confiteor in the garden I've recorded in brief.

Nicole told me that he had picked up a street girl and brought her to the garden flat but that when she had seen and smelt the beer keg, which she'd described to her street friends as a coffin, she'd fled before he could lay hands on her.

Nicole unfolded her plan. It was to visit an exclusive call-girl agency she knew - what and whom didn't she know or had known? - taking me with her and choose, under the Grande Dame's guidance, after appraising her of the facts, one of the women who would come and share Margraves' flat for as long as was required.

- Required for what, Nikolaya?

I had, as always, lagged somewhat in the dusty rear.

She rightly ignored me and went on telling us about this Mme Lissik d'Harcourt who it turned out was related, by no means distantly, to somebody who'd been the Russian poet Mayakovsky's one great love, for whom one of his pet names had been Lissik.

All this was in the strictest confidence, as indeed was all Nicole's gossip, but at the same time I was well aware that she and Paul both confided in me as the eventual chronicler of the events, both private and historic, in which they had been and were involved.

When we arrived at what Nicole had called an 'agence' but was evidently a high-class brothel at around noon the place was in a state of what struck me as hushed, or restrained, excitement. The girls, there were older women among them and one even elderly whom I took to be the proprietor, but as usual was wrong, were all getting ready to go out. They were fashionably, but soberly, attired, mostly in black, some with dark scarves over their newly brushed and burnished hair.

Nicole, who appeared to know several of them, came to tell me as I waited in the elegantly furnished 'parlour' that Madam d'Harcourt, the Russian directress of the - I'd almost written 'institute' - house had died a day or two before and they were about to attend the funeral.

- Touching, isn't it? They want to look their best for her sake. It's more important to them than when practising their calling.

'Calling'. We were learning flexibility in our use of words!

It *was* a strangely moving scene, at least to me. In the several rooms to which Nicole conducted me, they were putting the finishing touches to their costumes - the word came of itself and not inappropriately because there was, among other connotations, the suggestion of a sombre carnival. On the unmade-up, or perhaps very subtly made-up, faces of some of the mourners were tears. Nicole introduced me to two or three of them, in particular a woman of around forty whom she told me later was one of several society ladies or upper-income housewives who spent their leisure time at the house both for the company and the sexual satisfaction. Although Madame d'Harcourt charged the same for these as for her permanent inmates, they left the full amount with her for the upkeep of the establishment. Finally, I was taken to a small, cell-like room on the top floor where Madame Lissik, as they were now calling her in subdued voices, was laid out on a narrow bed. The old woman really did look, as in the hackneyed phrase, as if asleep. Frail and obviously light as a feather, she was dressed in a pale, not quite white (though perhaps it once had been) dress: her wedding gown, a girl called Rebecca whispered to me between, with several others at the bedside, reciting the rosary.

A little later we all assembled in a downstairs reception room, passing through the hall where I saw the coffin that, at our entry, I'd failed to register.

As well as the twenty or so women, there were a couple of men in the room, three including myself, a gardener and the lawyer who - the dark girl was now my informant - looked after their legal affairs which, it seemed, required a fully employed counsellor.

Funerals! How they impel me over emotional and psychic thresholds into areas that, I imagine, form a kind of no-man's-land between life and death. That is, as far as an ordinary mortal like myself can follow the departed on their long, lonely journey. (Though why 'long'? I am only speculating.) I'm speaking of the funerals of those whom I was bound to in the bonds of deep affection, in which rare cases - two or three perhaps in a lifetime, if one doesn't include the animals - there is neither the time nor repose for such meditations. The panic and grief obliterates everything but the almost-despair after the initial numbness wears off.

When it came to getting the coffin into the hearse that had by now drawn up at the front drive of the house, I was invited - and it was a considerable honour - to share in its carrying. Being tall, as was the gardener, who bore it on the other side, we found it hard without a marked stoop that made negotiating the front steps difficult, to shoulder a proportionate weight - most of which came from the coffin - to that which the women were bearing.

We drove - I and two of the girls - in Nicole's Fiat to a large, bleak (as I suppose city cemeteries always are) graveyard where in a light rain a monk appeared, and with one of the women holding an umbrella over him, read some passages that I recognised as from the Gospel of St. John.

What were my thoughts? I don't ask for the sake of self-indulgence but to try to ascertain whether communications of a certain kind, not exchanged in everyday experience, were to be overheard.

One very vivid recollection illumined the damp, near-twilight. Several years ago I'd been driving along a side road through a desolate, disused bogland, and had come on a youth on a stationary bicycle, propped on the grass verge by one foot, a black and white dog hugged to his chest. At first I thought the creature was dead, but I caught as I passed the black gleam of its eye gazing back at the boy. Each was all either had as they hesitated on the verge of a hostile vastness, fearing what was in store and not daring to turn back.

Am I imagining more to the not very extraordinary scene than is justified? No. It was not so much imagining as wondering. And the wondering was at something so familiar to me, so deeply present in my own consciousness, that, though this was many years ago, at certain hours - this was one of them - I remember those two mortal beings in a manner that makes a mockery of the tepidity of the word 'remember'.

- 12 -

After the funeral rites, Nicole brought me back to the small room at the top of the house where Lissik had been laid out. Yes, I was now calling, or thinking, of her by her pet name as one often does of the dead which one wouldn't dream of doing when alive.

She said she wanted to consult me about which of the women would be a suitable companion for Margraves. But in fact she was telling me more about the old man and his earlier researches into the 'soul', as he called it, of the white ant.

About this Nicole had heard from Paul and I was hearing it at third repeat. What Margraves had originally found out about these African termites was, I believe, very strange, so was what I now heard from Nicole but clouded over by the interpretations or adaptations it had passed through.

Here, then, are mine. I am leaving out a lot of what seem incidental but are no doubt crucial to the final theory or discovery. This I only grasp intermittently and must keep my attention beamed in its direction.

What it comes to is this: the queen ant spends her life in isolation, in a small cell in the ant colony, fed on nectar by a specialised group of her subject termites, neuter in gender. Another, much larger section, form an army whose main task is to defend the colony by repairing damage to the various ant hills that form it. These can be quite remote from each other, measured of course on the termite scale.

When one of these outlying structures is damaged, a fairly frequent event, a squadron of this militia proceeds across the intervening ground on what can be a perilous excursion. At first Margraves supposed there was a guide, but this raised, as they say, more problems than it solved. To cut a long and exciting story short, he discovered that this expeditionary force was under the command of the queen. Without leaving her cell or despatching any messengers, she had (a) become aware of the depredation, (b) had ordered the workers to repair it and (c) directed them to the spot with complete accuracy.

How had Margraves come to this astonishing conclusion? Very simply: by taking the queen from her cell and removing her to a considerable distance - man-measured - from her kingdom. After which the whole defensive system - and some others that I haven't really grasped - broke down.

So far, so intriguing. But why was it of such importance to Paul? If it hadn't been Nicole wouldn't have been so involved. Whatever the means of communication between the queen and her loyal ants - it was one-way. It struck Paul, according to Nicole, that it might be of the order (whatever that means) of the code by which a cosmic intelligence guides the minute - much tinier than an ant - living, bacteriological particles, among other destinations, to this planet.

There it is! I've done my best and, if I was asked, would say that I don't think I did too badly.

Now we were back, Nicole and I, to what I had supposed was the reason for her bringing me up to the room of mourning: the selection of a companion for the pioneer in the study of thought - or emotion - waves. Apropos of which there was, even earlier, the Russian biologist who took two newly-born leverets from the doe, transported them to a far-away district of the Soviet Union where he killed them and at the precise moment of their death, the mother hare back in the Moscow laboratory showed every indication of extreme anguish.

This latter obnoxious experiment, however, is lacking in all the significant aspects of Margraves'.

We had hardly arrived at what I'd taken to be the original object of our closeting ourselves in the upper room - how these biblical terms keep slipping in - when the dark girl whose name was Rebecca came to call us down for the funeral repast.

This was laid on a long table in a room that I hadn't yet been in, whose polished wood reflected the scintillation of a large chandelier. There were around twenty places. The hostesses were standing behind their chairs when Nicole and I came in and were allotted our seats, one on each side of the old lady at one end of the table. The only other two men beside myself were at the other end, placed each side of a woman of forty or so dressed in what I took to be the latest fashion in sombre femininity.

I had Rebecca next to me on the side that extended down the length of the table. What we ate and drank would take considerable concentration, and another consultation with Nicole to recall, and is largely incidental to the continuance of the tale, or furtherance of the plot.

Taking on myself responsibility for this, I told Rebecca what we had in mind for Margraves, at the same time supplying a brief sketch of the old fellow and his preoccupations, what is called a 'profile' in the media. I suggested that she might recommend one of the women, rather than a girl, who would be interested. I felt I was going about it as if I was in charge of personnel at a small but prestigious firm and was looking for somebody to fill a position of the highest responsibility. Which, looked at in one way, I was.

- Do you know, Rebecca, I said - I was in much the same position not so long ago myself. I needed a companion, perceptive and compassionate, or, from another aspect, pale, warm and clean.

- But you didn't come here.

- No. I'm a poet, or so I hope and imagine.

- Yes, I understand.

- How perceptive she was! One of the attributes I'd stipulated.

- I went to a hospital.

- And took home a nurse?

- That's right.
- I wouldn't mind giving it a try.
- Thank you, Rebecca.

I felt I'd achieved a small personal triumph in a delicate matter. I began to explain to her how cautiously we must proceed - here I was relaying Nicole's plans, which I considered on the over-sensitive side. I told her she would be introduced to the old man at lunch or dinner and, provided the omens were favourable, would ask to see his bin of annelids.

We were coming to the end of the meal and I had got this far when the small bombshell went off. I'm reporting figuratively of course, and the actual explosion was a limited one, taking place only within my nervous system.

The old lady beside me at the top of the table announced that the distinguished writer, Joel Samson, would now address the company.

'Ever ready' has been my motto. Or to put it less commonplacely, I regard myself, or one aspect of my not-uncomplex character, as a patient pack animal, submissive to what burden, habitual or unexpected, is laid on it. But also, like Balaam's pack-ass, one who on occasion could prophesy with accuracy and aplomb.

Sisters, distinguished laymen: at the end of this collation (laughter and applause) I am both honoured and abashed at the expectation you place in me. As an imaginative and possibly an original novelist, I shall try to express what you feel in your hearts about her who was a dear friend, a mother, a confidante and a comforter to you in an existence whose pleasures, distresses and anxieties I don't pretend to more than guess at.

I went on in this vein for several minutes while collecting my faculties for the assault, so to speak, on the peak.

It would be mistaken to suppose I was altogether out of my element. Indeed, when I recalled a recent international writers' congress which I had attended as a representative of the host nation I took heart from the learned, comparatively-speaking, and distinguished beings who were hanging - my impression - on my words.

At the congress I recall with a shudder a proletarian social commentator (his own description) of some renown with what's called a working class accent of which he was proud and a black wig of which, from his nervous fingering of it, he was evidently not.

Suddenly I could put that, and other literary occasions, behind me and was inspired by the spirit of history (a term that I coined on the spot and whose emanation shone). I told them about the dead woman's ancestor, Lili Brik, who was the Russian poet, Mayakovsky's, mistress though married to Osip Brik. I even recounted how when she rushed home in a panic to tell her husband that she and the poet had become lovers, he said: 'How is it possible to refuse Mayakovsky?' and then added: 'But we must never part from each other'. Is this nobility? Who knows? My audience was listening intently and, no doubt, interpreting all this in their own ways.

There was an extraordinary intensity in Mayakovsky, as if the molecules were packed tighter in his structure than is humanly possible, a comment that perhaps reveals my ignorance, scientifically that is, though the girls would not have so considered it. An intensity I imagine as particularly Russian, though I have known some fellow-nationals who burn, or rather smoulder, with this inner fire. I'm not thinking of Paul whose origins were somewhat obscure.

Lissik, which is what he ended by calling her, was to the Russian poet much what Nicole had been to the Lithuanian painter, Chaim Soutine. That, anyway, was my interpretation of these two events, separated, though not by that great a distance in time and space.

Nicole was very appreciative at the comparison I made, and, touchingly, the audience applauded.

- 13 -

I am leaving the funeral celebrations rather abruptly. I have an instinct to press on towards new, and what at the time to me were unexpected, developments. This doesn't mean that there won't be space for any important incidents during the obsequies to be noted. One, for instance, before proceeding any further: the old woman, Martha I believe she is called, showed Nicole a creased piece of paper on which some words in yellowed ink were written in Russian. Nikolaya showed it to me - in a frame under glass - and proudly translated it as 'Why don't you write to me, you wretched witch, Volodya'.

This was a note of Mayakovsky's to Lili Brik from around 1925 which I had already read in an English translation of his correspondence and could have supplied the more colloquial and correct version in which the appellation was not 'wretched' but 'meaney'.

Howsobeit - a word interlopated here which, for those interested in such matters as literary technique, and who perhaps attend creative writing courses, serves to create space between or before more relevant phrases start jostling for room - howsobeit, I hurried back to our apartment to tell Abby about the events of the morning and early afternoon. And to be consoled by her.

How and for what? A good question, as they say on, and off, the chat shows. For the loss, even if not mine, and the finality of death. The consolation lay in an early evening period of intimate caressing. Without any detailed commentary which I don't intend introducing - not because, as by now must be evident, I believe in drawing veils over, or curtains around, the indecorous, erotic or crudely sexual, but rather because there stretches in front of me a clear path or vista of narrative which I want to traverse without being lured down luscious or shady cul-de-sacs.

A few days later, Rebecca came to stay and it became evident that all was being planned, by Paul and Nicole, in what struck us as an extraordinarily devious not to say' absurdly sensitive fashion. Sensitive, that is, in regard to old Margraves and his presumed reticences. When I remarked to Nicole that these hadn't prevented him from shuffling out onto the street in his slippers and picking up the first available female he saw, who, it seemed, had seen him coming and stepped out into his path or orbit, she said: That was near-despair, fear of being cast into the outer darkness of human incompatability.

We were taken aback by this outburst from the usually

level-headed Nicole. Did she and Paul, or she alone, know more about the old recluse than we did? Did she, or had she once had, some closer relationship than was apparent? We both shook our heads, or shrugged our shoulders, and left it at that. It was a considerable time, a time I shall arrive at, all being well, in due course, until this small puzzle was solved.

A luncheon was arranged for Wednesday, the 24th. I put down the date, perhaps the first one I have noted, because it was accompanied by so many injunctions and so-called guidelines by Nicole - with Paul at her back - that it was, as they say, engraved, if not on our hearts, in our nervous systems.

Without arousing the least suspicion (suspicion of what? But we didn't ask) it was suggested in the most casual fashion that the old man give a small lunch party by way of house warming. When he agreed, or at least raised no objection, the date was decided on and the invitations sent to, besides Paul and Nicole, Abby, myself, Rebecca whom he was told was an old friend of Abby's from her hospital days and a Colonel Hanburg, an amateur expert on insects and fungi (a strange combination, I thought, but it didn't concern me).

This last addition to the party turned out a mistake, as when Margraves should have been hitting it off, if not actually getting off, with Rebecca the colonel kept butting in about the dance of the common gnat. He had also brought an illustrated compendium of exotic butterflies which he had collected in, I think, Borneo, brought home and had colour-photographed. This turned out an unnecessary distraction to the rest of us at the table. A personal, possibly irrelevant confession: under its open cover spread between us - we were seated together - I slipped a hand up Abby's thigh under the rather tight skirt she was wearing, a marked contrast to the voluminous robes in my early comments.

This helped me to preserve an inner equilibrium, if not complete relaxation. There had been disturbing intimations of an attempt by Nicole to tell Rebecca how to behave. And only for Abby's tact, and, more than that, authentic wish to heal any hurt that the girl may have suffered, she would, so Abby said, have gone back to the 'Firmament', as, for the first time, I heard the house was called.

Rebecca, it turned out, when at the mother-house in Geneva, had been one of the women most sought after and hankered for by some of the best-known public figures in Europe, and two or three from Asia. The others had been the society women, a couple of them, who were part-time voluntary members of the community. Come to that, all were voluntary, but what I intend to convey is that the former were in no way financially pressured.

Nicole told Rebecca that it was not the sort of party where one could let a breast slip out of a blouse. That she had taken as an affront, while Abby had assured her that this was almost certainly a message from Paul, one of his notorious jokes which, as she surely had heard, had alienated him from quite a few highly-placed citizens. Incidentally, so I had heard, one of those was Maya who at the moment had erased his name from her list. I didn't ask, her list of what? Proteges possibly, or guests, or even lovers.

All behaved with sober decorum, except for Abby and myself, whose slightly indecorous exchanges were soberly carried out and undetectable. So much so - I'm referring to the general mood - that this supposedly convivial house warming had none whatsoever of the delight, tinged with sadness, of the funeral meal of a few days before.

At what seemed to me the last moment, something happened that saved it ending in failure. I don't quite know what, but Margraves was asking Abby and Rebecca - I wasn't included - whether they'd like to go and have a look at his annelids. Abby glanced at me for a sign and I gave her a squeeze of the thigh on which my hand still rested which she took, quite rightly, as telling her to accept. They followed the old fellow out of the room, and a sigh of relief went up - as I imagined - from three of us at the table. Colonel What's-his-name seemed disappointed, was probably offended at being overlooked. After the door was opened into the upstairs room or attic where the load of well-manured earth and worms were kept, an unpleasant odour was wafted into the dining room.

When after ten minutes or so Rebecca returned alone, Paul and Nicole's hearts may have fallen, I don't know, but I

waited. I had a great confidence in Abby. Had she not been
capable of performing a miracle with me, and without for a
moment experiencing the slightest anxiety or familiar pang
of jealousy, I was fairly sure she was furthering the object of
the whole operation. And, sure enough, though this is to
anticipate, Margraves had detained her just as she was
leaving with Rebecca, and when alone with her asked her to
tell him about her dark, and - his own words - ravishing
young friend.

What Abby told him I didn't ask her in any detail. She
would know what to say and what to leave out.

Abby and I were taken up with our own affairs and
Rebecca was left to enjoy a short vacation which she did,
having many friends and acquaintances and a car in which
to visit them.

Money was one of our problems, not exactly pressing but
at the back of our minds, of mine anyhow. Abby went back to
the hospital for two or three nights a week and I entered into
negotiations with a book dealer about the sale of some
manuscripts. And then, out of the blue, Abby had a phone
call from her father in the capital of one of the Gulf states to
ask about our wedding arrangements because he was going
to give her - us - a three-year-old colt called Abby's Gift (it
had evidently been intended for her all along) that was with
one of our leading trainers, not the famous doyen of trainers
here or across the water, but a younger man with whom the
prince had a number of animals.

Which forces me into some precision about dates, the
month, if not the year. It was, in fact, early April - did I
mention the daffodils in Margraves' garden? - and this colt,
who had never run, was due to contest the first of the two-
year-old classics in a few weeks.

This banished our financial worries, or would as soon as
we got married. If it is asked - and I see my task as not
leaving the more obvious questions unanswered - why we
hadn't married already it was because Abby, influenced by
her father, didn't like the idea of a Christian ceremony, while
I thought twice about a Moslem one. And a civil ceremony
didn't appeal to either of us.

Rebecca started telling Abby about the developments in

her relationship with Margraves. And of course Abby related it to me, filling in her own imagined incidents that the very seductive dark girl was leaving out. These were to do with the provocation that nobody knew better how to assert, according to Abby - didn't I agree? - both subtle and when the signals from the old fellow were encouraging, crude.

I hadn't to ask before Abby went into it in more detail. She too knew all about provocation - hadn't her subtle skills been what had, against all likelihood and predictions (my own), got me going again?

- The bin of worms that he was constantly pottering with didn't do much for them getting together. It turned out there were I don't know how many species of earthworm beside the annelids that his main crop belonged to. The more categories he mentioned, the more hopeless the situation became in Rebecca's estimation. Until, that is, she invented a category of her own, of which there was only one member in the immediate vicinity, calling it the white worm and indicating by a gesture, possibly even a brief touch, its location.

- The old fellow was at first shocked, or probably only stunned, then amazed and, after a minute or so, delighted. How did he respond?

- Oh, Rebecca put on her modest act - its part of her repertory - and didn't want to tell me. I bet she knew how to drive him crazy and did.

- How, darling? Tell me what you think.

- No. But I'll show you.

5

On one of the evenings I was alone, Abby being at the hospital and Rebecca out at friends, I happened to pick up a tissue from which came the whiff of a perfume I hadn't smelt in years. It was one used by Abby - she went in for a few cosmetics - and must have been then discarded on to the floor - no, she was not well house-trained.

It evoked from years ago the early days with Noona. To describe a scent is a task beyond the ordinary range of communication and would require a cypher language of its own. This was not a particularly sensual or exotic one though it evoked femininity - I'm already making heavy going of it! It opened my senses to the world of women but not to that of sex, which came later, though never fully with Noona at all. The effect was, of course, erotic, I see that now but in an indirect or round-about way. The only way, as I now know, I can take. It transported me into the company of women, of one woman, without making any suggestions, let alone demands or drawing conclusions. I could take her or leave her, or, let's say, I could certainly leave her without any hint of failure or inadequacy from her. The scent assured me in its own relaxed way that where it had transported me was far from hotel bedrooms or dim-lit studios with inviting floor space, but somewhere where I could take my ease. And, naturally, in such a state of relaxed nerves and semi-dormant senses, anything could happen - to me, that is, not to everyone, or indeed most men, who, I imagine, go about it in a more direct manner.

What, as you've probably guessed, I'm getting to is that this perfume was worn by Abdallah, only a drop perhaps behind her ears or between her breasts, when she got into my hospital cot.

And now back to the white worm. According to Rebecca it has burrowed its way through history, leaving a silvery-grey trail of slime most of which quickly dried on flesh, sheets, carpets or was casually wiped away, but a very small proportion of which was ejected into the precious vessel destined for it from the beginning of the world, or, at least, from the beginning of multi-cellular organisms. This last sentence is not part of what Rebecca told Abby when relating her seduction - though that may not be the word - of Margraves, but my own embellishment.

- I wouldn't care to be burrowed into by a white worm, Abby had told Rebecca. - If I thought of it like that I wouldn't get turned on.

- What did she say to that? I asked.

- She said nothing. Girls like her are used to not being much taken with it, let alone carried away. Some of the women in our harems read travel books or listen to music on earphones while being fucked. And that's often what the men with us, and if they were honest, a lot of other men too, want. They don't want women to show too much enjoyment or share their excitement. They far prefer those who hardly seem quite sure what it's all about.

Another thing the one girl confided in the other, the dark pigeon to my still darker dove, was that the posture most favoured by many of her clients from their partner was that of the racing cyclist or jockey; buttocks higher than head.

This, though, was far from being the case with old Margraves when she had, very tentatively, tried him out.

In case I'm giving the impression that Abby and I spent most of our time gossiping, with her doing most of the relating, that is far from so. We talked intently of various matters, apart from those relating to Paul and his discoveries, such as horse-racing, the situation in Europe and the USA, which her father had brought her up to view with disfavour: as materialist, consumerist, godless, depraved, demoralised. We read poetry together, Keats, Blake and W. H. Auden (her favourite) and some post-modern as well as the great fiction writers of the past such as Dostoevsky and Kafka, and she read my own, starting at the top - I mean those two or three I thought worthwhile - and working her way down.

Now we were on the drive to the trainer's who had the colt

her father had given - or promised her as a wedding present - I was not quite clear about this, in his care. Abby was wearing jodhpurs, which she'd brought with her when she came to this country, though, as a nurse, the prospect of using them - apart from dressing up in them - seemed slight.

Her being so physically inaccessible reminded me of how she had appeared at St. Bride's, hidden away in her ample robes. Now it was a kind of armour below the waist.

Believe it or not (I'm joking, because if this report isn't accepted as the truth as far as I am able to perceive it, it's not worth reading) her attire intrigued but didn't provoke me, not at least on the outward journey. And we did actually discuss the world situation for a few minutes after listening to some of the constantly negative news on the car radio.

Abby was far from ill-informed which, I confess, surprised me at first. Had I really supposed that all Arab women shared a harem mentality, or sentimentality, occupied in pleasing their lord and master in all sorts of ways and so-called perversions, lazy, fond of sweetmeats, massage, warm, shallow pools and chatter? This - Abby's distinction - may have been due to her upbringing. Her father, Prince Ahmed, though conducting himself on his visits to Europe with grace and affability, looked with some contempt, derision too, on the kind of civilisation that had taken over in the West.

- Have you ever studied history, Joel?

- I wouldn't say 'studied'.

- It's one long tale of subjugation and exploitation, the misuse of power: social - the poor by the rich - religious and ideological - there have been more massacres in the name of God, the spiritual, the ideal, than in any other cause. Sexual - the subjugation of women by men. National - of colonial peoples and weaker nations. Racial: - of Arabs by Jews and indeed Christians, of Jews by Nordic hordes, of black by non-blacks... I could go on and on.

- Well, don't, darling.

It wasn't that I'm callous, but, as is generally accepted, reports of pain piled on pain don't increase the impact. Pain hides behind pain, there's only so much visible, and feelable, at a time. Not that I wasn't proud of my Dove in her guise as a social historian. But it was time - according to my interior clock - to discuss the purpose of the expedition, about which I wasn't completely clear.

Yes, we were going to have a look at, and perhaps Abby hoped to have a ride on, the colt her father had promised her as a wedding present: Abby's Gift. (Altered, I'd heard from Paul, but I'm not sure if he was serious, from Abby Gadaffy which might have been offensive to some racegoers.) But she had spoken of another purpose: to look at, and, especially, hear about a mare and foal in an adjoining yard. I wasn't certain whether this was also a gift to her, or us, not from her father but... No use getting ahead of schedule. I'll come to these matters in a moment.

Meanwhile I was pointing out the pastoral beauties of our land which Abby was seeing for the first time, and I don't think taking in because of what to her were more vital matters. What things? The horses, but, as it turned out, not just, not primarily, the colt from her father, but the mare and foal in another yard. But she had also us to think about, as she did, I believe, constantly, both emotionally, in the heart, neurologically in her erogenous zones, psychically about whether to marry me in a Christian ceremony and forsake the great visionary, prophetic, and historic Moslem world.

- 15 -

She was either a little disappointed in Abby's Gift, a smallish grey two-year-old colt by Sharif Dancer who had never run, or else was distracted by the thought of our next visit. Her father's trainer, called Macmasters, was at first hesitant about letting her ride the horse, but the stable jockey who happened to be there gave her a leg-up without referring to his boss - as a winner of a classic race in England for the stable I don't suppose he felt he had to - and, on another animal, with two stable boys on a third and fourth, they walked their mounts to the training ground, I following in the car, and after a couple of canters, galloped them over what I estimated was four furlongs. Abby could ride, there was no doubt about that. She held her own with the other three and even, towards the end, pushed her mount out with hands and heels to finish well up with the jockey and one of the lads, the fourth horse having been tailed off.

Then we were off to what I now sensed was the important visit, yet it seemed I was, as so often, wrong. I parked the car down a side road or leafy lane, then Abby asked the way to the dwelling of Mrs Eileen Cabbitt Bruce - a mouthful that of course I didn't register, but later came to roll off my tongue without thinking. We passed through a small but lovingly cared for vegetable garden - these are things I can spot off-hand - and the door of a small one-storey house was opened by a short, stout woman in pink. When Abby said we were expected, the caretaker-cook replied: You're very welcome, and showed us through a miniature conservatory - everything struck me as minute just as on my first visit to Paul the place had seemed quite vast - full of exotic plants and I thought I caught a glimpse of a tiny pond through some fronds but it could have been a reflection of the sparkle from a sun-lit pane.

Then we were in the salon as I at once thought of it: a quite small room with a window onto another small vegetable plot - not the same one from another angle as I'd first supposed - a door open into a corner of kitchen, a fire burning in the hearth and, enthroned, though not on a raised but in a deep arm-chair, a large woman with wide apart, luminous grey eyes, that reminded me of the dolphin whose glance as it surfaced focused on me one day on a visit to a foreign zoological garden.

My instinct was to take in all that I could and to make notes about it later - which I did on the way home when Abby was driving. Why? Hard to say without benefit of hindsight, which I try not to draw on. A presentiment that if this was the important visit I should try to get it straight from the start as I had so failed to do in the case of Paul.

However, this grading of our visits into degrees of importance is misleading. It was not Eileen, whom Abby hadn't met, that she had come to see, but, as I've mentioned, a mare and foal in a yard belonging to Eileen and just visible through the window and no doubt from the chair in which, as I soon learned, she sat in from when, with Bridie's and the gardener's help, she rose at one until quite late at night, after her last hot whisky sweetened with sugar or honey.

This we were offered. Abby declined gracefully, managing to suggest, without actually going into it that as a Muslim she abstained from alcohol or, alternatively, that she was on a long and arduous drive. She was served instead with tea.

As I drank the hot, sweetened spirits - a potion I hadn't tasted for years and had come to imagine, quite mistakenly, that I disliked, I was impelled, or pushed, into one of those leaps sideways, that Cornelius, perhaps quoting Paul, had said were the manner in which knowledge, and various other important attributes, were bestowed.

Without analysis or mental effort - as by now will be evident, I'm not a clear thinker - I was convinced that the genes of this woman had continuous retrospective links with an earthly or rather aquatic Genesis. Here was a confutation of Paul's theory that life came from extra-terrestrial sources. Not a laboratory or experimental refutation but, as truth can only be revealed, that is in its wholeness, and not in parts.

Eileen was a marine creature with salt in her veins, she even emanated a faintly saline odour and as for her eyes, at which I kept glancing, they shone dimly with an underwater glow and lacked any reflection of star-light.

As I learned later she attracted a circle of people, not quite disciples or acolytes, even less social run-arounds, mostly from the horse racing and breeding families in the vicinity. I take it they talked with her about matters unconnected with riding and training thoroughbreds, about what otherwise hardly got attended to in their rather preoccupied existences. She had been a concert and opera singer, had met and perhaps sung with Gigli, had known John McCormack and Dame Nellie Melba - or am I going too far back? - in any case she belonged to a gracious, dramatic, largely-lost era, where what couldn't be said was sung and 'when they wanted a song bird in heaven, God took Caruso away'.

Dare I say of what I was reminded? At the risk of being thought to over-indulge in fantasy, I thought of the queen of the African white ants as discovered and described by old Margraves when a youth, which unpublished treatise had fallen into the hands of the famous Belgian, etc, etc. I shall not further hold up this narrative with what may seem incidentals.

From Dame Eileen's - I'm awarding her an appropriate distinction - it was a short way to the small stud farm.

Instead of a running commentary on the next couple of hours or so I'm going to try to evoke both images and tone as when composing fiction. With the proviso that what I relate are the facts as I registered them.

The small breeding establishment belonged to a monastery and was run by some of the monks with the help of trainee young men - there were no girls. There was also a department, if that's the word, where genetic breeding was taught and studied.

Abby had to wait in the car while I entered the monastery to seek a monk whose name she gave me.

I told the youthful figure in a brown habit with hood resting on the back of his neck that my wife had come about the mare and foal that had recently been imported from Canada. I said 'about' and not 'to look at' which would to my mind have started off what I considered a rather delicate negotiation - not that I was at all clear about it - on the wrong foot.

The monk came with me back to the car: a longish walk through cloisters, an interior square, called, perhaps, a garth, the yard itself and a long barn. We were silent. It occurred to me that this might well be a time of day when conversation was proscribed by the rule of the Order. Or it could be, summoned out of his solitude, the little lay brother felt it was up to me to make an affable remark. But it was impossible. I rehearsed several, such as: - A nice place you have here! and - I do hope we're not intruding, Father. (He was too young for a 'Father', probably a novice. 'Brother' sounded too familiar because of its slang American connotations.)

Here I'll end the commentary and do my best to present what Brother Dunwoody, as his name turned out to be, had heard about these two animals.

The story had circulated around the northern coast of Nova Scotia opposite Prince Edward Island, and for some distance inland, and later to Europe and to the monastic stud. It was told by a couple from Halifax who, for reasons of their own, were holed up in one of the holiday shacks that Nicole had noted, as follows:

There had been comings and goings in high-powered cars along that part of the coast, always at dead of night and in intermittent snow storms.

On the fourth or fifth night the couple had heard an explosion from seawards and in the morning through their binoculars (were they ever interrogated about what they were doing there?) they saw that the thick ice had been broken leaving an expanse of clear water of about two hundred yards long and fifty wide. At first they supposed a bomb from an aircraft had been dropped, but then concluded that a bomb or even aerial torpedo would have produced a more-or-less circular crater in the ice.

- 16 -

Composing myself, becoming poised for what's coming next, I'll start a fresh page, a new section.

The night after the explosion, another freezingly snowy one, the disreputable couple - however, it's not up to me to pass any judgement - became aware of activity out there below the surface of the water, which had inexplicably not re-frozen. The man, who claimed he was a chemist, suggested to his companion that massive amounts of certain chemicals, which he named to her, were being pumped into the sea-water from some depth.

A likely story!

They had been keeping awake by drinking Bourbon and intermittent love-making, though this they didn't say and it's my surmising.

- Well, what's yours, girl?

- A gin and bitter lemon for a change. (Ha! ha! My attempt to introduce a lighter touch into what could get somewhat dense.)

The waters in the ice-free pool were troubled. They bubbled and foamed and seemed to be forming a tidal wave while from beneath there surfaced what the two vigilantes thought at first was a huge whale. Something monstrous and ghostly, gleaming faintly in the freezing mist - it had stopped snowing as if the curtains were being drawn back by some mysterious power - the 'mysterious power' is a verbatim quote from the monk to me.

The submarine surfaced and gradually came to rest in what could have been a dock and the couple had time to examine it through their binoculars - one pair which they used turn about while the other made notes. From the markings on the turret or superstructure they concluded it was a Soviet nuclear vessel.

What they had missed by focussing all their attention seawards was the arrival of what looked like a police van and a private car at the shore line. From the rear of the van, which turned out to be a horse-box, a ramp was lowered and two horses were led out. This was taking place within a few yards of the shack so that the two hidden observers could watch every move and detail, as well as hear the voices of the handlers and the neighing of the stallions. Meanwhile, on their hi-fi stereo, which they had brought with them to while away what they foresaw could be occasional interludes in their orgy-for-two, they were receiving signals in Russian, which neither understood.

The horses were wearing what in the notes were described as rubber galoshes over their hooves and a stable lad - or it might have been a girl - gripping the bridles at each side and wearing snow boots, were led out onto the ice, preceded by a figure on what looked like skis.

The rest of the proceedings were less observable, partly because whatever device in the vessel was used to bring the horses on board and accommodate them below was on the far or seaward side of the submarine.

A considerable time elapsed when nothing was happening as far as the man and woman holed-up in the shack were concerned. However, they didn't relax their vigilance and noted that when finally the handlers returned across the ice there were only three of the original five.

This was related to myself and Abby by the novice in the car parked outside the monastic cloister, though I take it we could have driven into the yard where there was already one female in the shape of the mare we'd come to see, and, presumably, others.

Brother Dunwoody was in the back with me and Abby turned to him from the front seat.

Not for the first time in this complicated saga I didn't know what to think. This young couple - I pictured them in their early twenties - had certainly not invented the whole story. Yet, I'd understood that the Prince's two stallions had been shipped back by plane to Europe. Understood or misunderstood? I needed to consult Abby before I got much further involved. I was afraid that she might now think it time to carry out what, after all, was the primary purpose of the trip and ask to see the mare and foal, which would have meant another hour perhaps in the close company of the monk.

Before, though it turned out that she'd had no such intention, she could open her mouth, I asked the monk if he, or the monastery - I knew that like most Orders the members shared all in common - were in possession of a copy of the notes from Canada.

- The Abbot.

- Could you obtain his permission, Father?

The monk seemed reluctant. Had he more to tell us, or was it that as a novice he wasn't used to approaching his superior with a request not directly concerning the monastic life?

There was a pause.

- We're just come from Lady Eileen Cabbit-Bruce, I said.

I was giving everyone titles not strictly belonging to them. But the information had the result that I'd hoped.

- Ah... The Abbot often visits her; she's our landlady so to speak.

- She spoke of him with affection and asked us to give him her warmest greetings.

Untrue, of course. She hadn't mentioned him, but it had the foreseen effect. The monk rose from the deeply reclined back seat of the car - more comfortable perhaps than his cell stool - and went off towards the monastery.

- I thought the stallions were flown back to Europe.

- Oh no, darling, there wasn't any question of that.

There surely had been a question of it, and more than a question, but, it seemed, only in my mind. I'd taken it for granted; they'd been brought from Europe to be the objects of an experiment - I was putting it reservedly - and what more logical than that they'd been flown back?

- So their only thoroughbred offspring in Europe is this foal we're here to see.

- Right, and I wish instead of sending off that youth for notes that he probably won't get and are of no importance, you'd asked him to take us there. And, even more urgent, I'm dying to have a pee and I don't suppose there's a 'ladies' within a mile.

- Don't be genteel, that's not like you. There's nobody in sight except me.

- OK.

Using the car as a screen - though from what? - she pulled down the jodhpurs, which didn't go that smoothly, and, squatting in the age-old, ever-new posture, released, with a sigh of relief, a long jet. Fitting back into the riding breeches took even longer than their lowering and while they were still half or, let's say, three-quarters way up, the novice was back on the scene. I hadn't noted his approach because I was watching Abby and by the time I saw him it was too late to do anything but laugh.

He was shaken, or maybe just excited, but terrified too, not, I imagine, by Abby but for fear of delighting, if only for a moment, in a possibly mortal or at least one of the addictive sins, as he'd been taught in the Novitiate. What did I know about the Novitiate? Little or nothing, a situation which has never stopped me allowing my imagination a brief flight.

Back onto remote control, that is to say an exposition of the next events in my own tonal manner.

Postulant Dunwoody conducted us through a yard of loose-boxes to a paddock in which were several mares and foals.

There you are, sir, he said to me. By now he dared not as much as look at Abby.

- Well, boy, which is Lucinda?

This was the first time I'd heard the mare's name, or the young monk either.

- Excuse me, he said, still addressing me: - I've no idea.

Abby was leaning with one arm on the wood fencing, while the fingers of one hand were inside the waist of her breeches. It looked to me as if, in her last few seconds' hurry, she got her knickers wrongly adjusted, unlikely as that might seem with such a simple garment. She was taking in the scene, deciding, for all I knew, which was Lucinda and her unnamed colt foal, a couple of which were staggering about on their too-long legs.

Abby wasn't in any hurry. Not that there was any reason to be, but it seemed to me that having seen - or failed to see - what we had come for, there was a next step, even a pressing one, to be taken. Not, of course, that I was sure what it was.

- Who does this animal belong to? I asked her.
- Which animal?
- The one in question.

I was getting impatient.
- To my father.

She called him 'father', I noticed, when matters of his horses, or, indeed, racing camels, were concerned, as well as when telling me of his social-historic philosophy. Otherwise he was 'Daddy' or what I took to be an Arabic term which, having never seen written, I cannot reproduce.

On the drive back to the city we had a lot to talk about, which wasn't unusual. The mare, or mares, though, were hardly mentioned. The main topics were Eileen Cabbit-Bruce, the perennial problem, in Paul's closed circle, of where life originated, the queen of the white ants, how Rebecca and her old man, whom she'd invited to lunch at our flat, were spending the day.

- How do you suppose, I asked.
- Calling up worms? But if she doesn't manage to 'call up' his white worm, then it's beyond all human wave-lengths. She even got X going (Abby mentioned a quite famous statesman) on his visit to a congress in Geneva.
- Where did it all start, Abby?
- I was thinking about Eileen.
- Adam and Eve.
- I don't mean how sex started. I was thinking of life.

It's much the same. Adam came from a celestial creator and Eve from Adam. The man from the stars, the woman from the earthly breeding-pen.

- Yes, well...

That raised, as they say, as many questions as...

- It doesn't much matter, does it, Joel. What we make of it, I mean of being alive, thinking, feeling and in obedience to the code.

- What code?

She was always introducing diversions, keeping quite ordinary subjects - not that this one was that - on the simmer.

- Ah, how stimulating she was! At home I'd only to lay a hand on her to feel the current. Or if she wasn't beside me and I wanted her, no matter why - to find a mislaid object, to ask a question, to make love to, or just to caress, I had only to call 'Abby!' to experience a pang of delight, perhaps related to the joy of a thrush that calls to its mate on the neighbouring tree.

- Oh, you mean the genetic code!

Not that she had. But an idea - I'll go all out and say 'an illumination' - had struck me and I was trying to translate it into speech.

6

- You see, Abby, we think it of the greatest importance.
- Think what?
- The origin of life, and so on.

I'd been catching a hardly perceptible murmur, a whisper of distant waves in the night of the subconscious that was now flooding my mind. Paul and his comets, the Prince and his race horses and camels, all very well and extending what might have otherwise been a somewhat limited life *a deux*.

This report I'm doing for Paul has been taking up too much of my time and thoughts. I paused. How would Abby take it?

Well, go on.

It might be just beyond me to disclose to her the bright-burning object (tiger?) after all this beating about in the jungle that had been revealed to me.

I'm a poet, not a journalist. And, anyhow, if Paul and his Asian colleagues prove they are right, as they probably will, so what? It's not the origin of life that matters that much to me but the conjunction of pain and love, an illumination that will send a beam into the future before it is finally extinguished. It was around that that I composed my fictions, and the rest was at best an often stimulating interlude.

We were sitting on the bed and Abby was getting out of her jodhpurs. She took me in her arms and for a moment or two I thought that the intense mental and nervous crisis of my confession was going to be relaxed in our usual way, and later discussed calmly. But this time it didn't work. I wasn't responding. This, in the state I was in, disturbed, confused, came as an unexpected blow from an unexpected quarter.

- It'll be fine again soon, I promise you, Joel. And the sooner the less you let it upset you.
- I believe you, my tender dove, my wise dove, my grey-

blue dove.

She rose and brought Rebecca's note from the hall and read it out.

Grateful, very, for loan of apartment. Your garden worms uncooperative. Because you spray your lawn with insecticide. My honey Daddy's - he's an authority on bees too - suggestion. But the white worm functioned perfectly - Abby glanced up at me to be sure I didn't let this faze (a good word, not in popular dictionaries) me. - Paulus phoned, I told him you were out.

The soul of discretion.

- They have to be where she comes from, Abby remarked.

She went to make us an evening meal, we hadn't eaten since morning. I came to myself, restored by my faith in Abby, itself a sign of the importance of my mission or vocation. I could now turn back to recent events without feeling I was neglecting the vital issue.

I reviewed the incidents at the stud farm attached to the monastery. A, Abby hadn't bothered to take the notes that the novice had fetched and was too embarrassed to hand to her. B, she couldn't have been sure which of the mares was the Canadian one, Lucinda, nor which foal was the only one in Europe sired by the 'irradiated' stallion. C, while still under the effects of exposure to the comet's tail or coma. D. Did the effect, if any - I was somewhat sceptical despite a considerable amount of positive evidence - wear off? E. Had Prince Ahmed sold (presented?) them to the Soviet Ministry for Sport (or some such bureaucratic department) because of his dislike of the West?

The aperitifs - bloody marys - were ready before I'd time to formulate the consideration under 'F'.

When Abby joined me from the kitchen she was wearing a narrow, striped skirt that came to just below her knees and a blouse with a view of the start of the deep, darkish vale between her large breasts.

This reassured me. I took it as a sign that she didn't attach much importance to my recent physical failure and was ready for a quick recovery, hastened by her get-up.

No need to report what, how soon, and where it happened. What matters is that we were as we'd been before while sharing what might have been too new or revolutionary a concept for Abby to assimilate after all the energy she'd put into Paul's and then her father's projects. Oblivious and unselfconscious love-making: this was the former, the rarer kind, seldom achieved in a brothel (I noticed in one of the rooms at the 'Firmament' a mirror on the ceiling).

We were still coming to ourselves, drained of desire and released from tension, when the phone rang. It was Paul.

There was a gathering of scientists, he didn't specify from which branches, being held in our city, an inter-European affair, to which he invited us.

Illustrated with equations, of which we'd make nothing.

- And slides. Did it ever occur to you that if the stars in our galaxy were orchestrated by a master conductor as roughly the same number of neurons in our brains are by us, a condition might arise not far short of godlike?

- Oh, many's the time!

I was, I thought, being funny, but Paulus (I'll call him that when he's tiresome), for all his clowning, was, I'd noticed, slow in seeing a joke, especially when it was at his expense.

Although the asembly of international scientists didn't take place for a couple of weeks and meanwhile matters of more importance happened in what I consider my smaller but I believe finally more eventful world - the events in theirs take place at so many light-years remove - I shall tie it up as neatly as I can before getting back to the personal theme.

For me the interest lay not so much in the talks read out by the speakers, most of which I didn't follow, though I don't say I wasn't at times diverted, but during the intermissions. By talking with some of the delegates I wanted to get an idea of what Paul's international reputation really was. Abby, too, in her own indirect fashion, received some sidelights from a couple of Arab astro-physicists (belonging to a tradition far older than the European one).

I had several talks with an Austrian Jew, a Nobel Prize laureate incidentally, who, when introduced to me, shook my hand with real warmth - I can distinguish between the kind that comes from the heart and that from the frontal lobes. Joel Samson! How is it you appear, I'm speaking as a serious reader of your work in German translation, never to have got your due, though I realise that may be a silly question. What writers from the past, now classics in their field, were household names when they were your age?

I am quoting this verbatim not primarily for reasons of self-promotion but because it (A) adds validity to my recent resolve and (B) seemed to indicate that this eminent scientist, whose name I won't disclose, would have something worthwhile to say about Paul.

Was there, I asked myself, some meanness, or slyness, a back-door mentality, in eliciting an opinion on Paul? I'm still not sure, though the counter-arguments were strong: Would I have resented a friend, say Paul himself, enquiring of an acquaintance who was a literary critic, what he thought would be the ultimate fate of the better works of Joel Samson? I'm not sure. I would, I suppose, given Paul's professed belief in them, have preferred he didn't call in a second opinion.

Be that as it may, having myself done something of the sort, I may as well give a summing-up of the verdict:
Paul was original, with a daring imagination, qualities very rare in pure scientists. And, in my interlocutor's opinion, very valuable if kept within bounds, by which I think he meant as long as there were not many of such innovators in proportion to the patient, hard-slogging, no-nonsense researchers who were dedicated to mostly lonely and unrewarded - publicly - vigil - keeping.

What he struck me as evading was whether or not Paul's cometary theory of the origin of life on the planet was taken seriously at the highest levels.

- It's significant, Mr. Samson.
- Could it be true?

I realised this was not what I needed to ask. It had little relevance to what I *did* wish to elucidate: my, and Abby's, close friend's reputation among his peers. And, possibly because of my inexperience as an interrogator, I wasn't, as they say, much wiser than I'd been.

Back to the immediate and vital, as I understand these terms. There were two developments, both absorbing, one surprising. The first concerns myself and Abby, the other,

Rebecca and Margraves.

- 18 -

A theory of synchronicity was developed by Carl Jung that postulated the possibility of the proximity of two similar events in time without their having a cause-effect relation. How, or if, he explained it, I don't know, but having personally experienced this phenomenon, it seems to me that if one is not cause of the other, both have a common one.

After this somewhat awkward and probably irrelevant lead-in, I became aware of new events taking shape in our small world within the not very large one of this report, from Abby as usual.

She related a conversation she'd had with Rebecca that was, to me, astonishing and exciting. And which produced a lightness of heart that the discoveries of the Paulus team failed to do (not that that was their objective).

Rebecca had confided in her - what it came to was an intimate and moving confession - that she loved Margraves.

- You mean, you're sorry for him.

- Yes, Abby, I pity him, but isn't that a large part of real love and affection?

I recalled Yeats' statement: 'A pity beyond all telling is hid in the heart of love', one of the very few lines of his that suggest he knew much about this mostly painful passion.

- Go on. This is Abby addressing the dark girl, lest there be any confusion.

Moving from the verbatim, and into my own words, Rebecca saw at last a purpose in her existence. Not that she hadn't found life entertaining and even, occasionally (the funeral?) moving, but it was mostly very lonely. The other girls at the 'Firmament' did not dispel this sense, nor were they themselves aware of it.

When Margraves went round the corner and brought back a street girl he wasn't sexually impelled, though sex entered into it. It was the despair of loneliness. So he had told her the day we had lent them our flat. Funny, I said to Abby, that she didn't mention any of this in the note of thanks she left us.

- For one thing it hadn't sunk in, it takes time, you know. And also the letter was to both of us and, to begin with, she could only confide something so unfamiliar and about which she was still insecure to another woman.

- The old fellow? What's his reaction?

- A miracle, that's how he sees it. After a long life that started with high hopes followed by one set-back after another until he was left with only his worms to show for all the work and deprivation, to have this sweet - that's what she said he called her - young woman say she loved him and wanted to be everything to him more than made up for all.

- And for her, Abby went on, to have been given out of all likelihood someone to whom to devote the coming years of her life that had looked like being progressively wasted and petering out in - at best - a respectable retirement of quiet - or perhaps alcoholic - desperation.

That, then, is one of the two similar events that took place in close proximity. The other was - is - a ripening, a maturing beyond the blossoming season - in ours.

As for me, this meant a shedding of some of the weight of selfhood.

How hard it is to present, not to mention comment on, these subtle, secret deepenings and enhancings of an already rare relationship. Yes, they take place secretly, and unnoticed, in a sense, as the grass grows. But, unlike the grass, seemingly accidentally.

It raised again the question of our marriage, and that we were both conscious of a need for a ceremony, traditional and solemn, as binding as is humanly possible, or rather bestowing a grace that binds closer than the humanly possible.

Traditional, that was the problem. My need and longing were for a Christian wedding, while Abby, although not a practising Muslim, had come, through her father, to distrust what she saw as the baleful influence of the Christian churches.

- Forget the churches, Abby, and let me tell you about the Gospels.

A strange suggestion? What about the blind leading the

blind? No, in all modesty, that is not quite the situation. I had reason, just now, to mention my novels and their being esteemed in unexpected, if restricted, quarters. The best of them, the more serious, which of course doesn't exclude comic, are myths, parables, prophecies that owe a lot to the Gospels. I know they are poor little tales in comparison, but that doesn't mean that if I put, as I did, my heart into it, I couldn't preach the 'message' of the New Testament persuasively. That is: to someone so basically simple and open-minded and open-hearted.

If the Gospels are in a secret or esoteric language, as the cosmos appears to its explorers in mathematical equations, then I could translate it and make an intoxicating story. That was not the difficulty. The problem was to at least make the suggestion that they might be also true not to seem to slip into fantasy. Of course I needed on my part to be at the height of what powers I have, or are bestowed on me. I needed, above all, what's often glibly called faith. Faith, that's to say, as indeed I've perhaps said too repetitiously, in an individual destiny that makes ultimate sense of even the most ruinous disorders.

I told Abby how, as a raw youth, I thought I sometimes caught a glimpse at dusk, or very early on a still morning, of a treasure that all else should be bartered for. Then slowly and clumsily I began to grasp that if there was such a treasure it was quite a common one and certainly not buried but, if not exactly on offer at street corners, still part of the texture of everyday living.

- OK, Joel, but let's get to whatever you're getting at.

- Oh, I was a long time getting to it in actuality, I was down all sorts of side-ways and some dreadful bye-ways and I don't want to falsify the past by wrapping it all up in a few brief sentences.

- No, darling.

- For a time, quite a long time, up to and for the first years of my marriage to Noona, I thought it was women. At first romantically, even poetically, but gradually more precisely and crudely, it turned into the cunt.

- You're not going to tell me how you were saved, converted from the sins of youth and middle age, like Tolstoi, into a follower of the Redeemer, isn't that what you call him?

A serious set-back. I was so far only repelling her. Indeed, the part of me listening to what I was saying was also repelled.

- I wasn't saved or converted. As you know very well, Abby, I'm an ageing man still obsessed - among other things - with the cunt, though not all that potent, and, in fact, would be impotent but for the miracle of finding you.

And then I was off at a tangent, carried away in the direction the conversation, or what I had just been saying, was taking.

- Oh, the mystery of it! The feel of it, like groping the grimly wooden beam of a barn in the dark and coming on a small, freshly-woven nest with eggs still warm.

- What are you on about now?

- Don't pretend you don't know! Listen, darling. All the sweetness and tenderness, magically, metaphysically, purged of the anguish, is hidden there in this grail of flesh that is also a very lowly receptacle situated between two drain-pipes. Think of the polarity, the deep, deep counter-currents in which we drown or are carried off.

Abby was silent. I was shivering slightly, a reaction to sensual stimulation that I used to experience as a youth and not since. I recall shivering - as if after a cold shower, and distinct from trembling - so much that I was awkward in undressing or helping the woman to.

- This doesn't stop the other obsession? Abby asked.

- Could it be that they're really the same?

- I thought the Gospels, unlike the Koran, were strong on asceticism, virginity, purity and all that.

- What about the women, Mary Magdalen and other Marys? Jesus in his heart of hearts liked their company more than that of his disciples, with the possible exception of John, but his public mission could, at that time and place, only be entrusted to men.

-You seem to know a lot about him.

-He came to associate with sinners, to 'call' them in the official phrase, and promised to keep this up throughout a future whose duration he doesn't seem to have clearly foreseen. He wasn't protected from harsh contingency, like the rest of us I suppose he could make mistakes though probably never really bad, let alone disastrous, ones.

- What else do you know about him?

- It's what he knew about me, and you, his dove, and all the other, unborn but not to him absent. Not, anyhow, after the resurrection when the dimension, so to speak, that he'd discarded to become human was restored. Whatever it was, it acted on the conventional time-scale, annulled it, so that during those few weeks he could associate, still human - more or less - with those of us who responded, though that was still to be established in what to us is the future.

I was, of course, getting out of my depth and Abby, who didn't miss the faintest signals, perceived it. I had to regain the attention of her deep nervous and sensory centres.

- What do you suppose occupied Jesus when he was alone during that short transitory period?

I didn't wait for an answer, not expecting one. But Abby, left momentarily in the air, with no foothold, through my clumsiness, exclaimed: How the hell should I know!
I put an arm round her, as I should have earlier, and went on.

- For instance, when he was kindling a fire at the shore of Lake Galillee, it was you and I - I'm not excluding all the others, just singling us out because I can't think in millions - who were there with him. A somewhat one-sided association? But no, because here I am telling you about it, and here you are listening and, however much of a shock it comes as, or with however many rational reservations, your heart is warmed, I can feel it.

- You're a fantastic story-teller, Joel. You've a fascinating imagination, at least it fascinates *me*.

- What is thought vividly enough takes form outside the imagining instrument, the brain, and becomes in a sense that I don't say I grasp, a small part of the truth.

- Give me an instance.

- I had to think about that, but it wasn't all that difficult.

Some years ago, when I was reading the autobiography of St. Thérèse of Lisieux, (popularly known as 'The Little Flower', though only in English), and meditating on the final chapters - the earlier ones are mawkish - I imagined having been born forty or fifty years earlier - she died a few years before my conception - and in Normandy instead of Australia, and having met her at a time before she was completely obsessed with becoming a Carmelite nun, she might have taken up with me. I realise this will strike most of her supplicants as unthinkable and possibly blasphemous. But I have thought and imagined it, not blasphemously because my life-long devotion to her altogether precludes that.

About our life together until her early death I'm not going to talk. That would be impossible. But in an astonishing passage towards the end of her book she takes as her own words of Christ uttered at the Last Supper about, among other mysteries, his coming and in-dwelling with his loved ones.

As a postscript to the story of my loving relationship with Thérèse Martin, I would not have dared approach her had she not written in *The Story of a Soul:* - 'Had I not been an enclosed nun I might well have become a street girl'.

- 19 -

I am not neglecting Paul, he is still part of my theme, if the minor one. Wasn't it he who inspired it, or anyhow selected me - not that he had a wide choice - as his, or its, chronicler. And, of course, Nicole who - this is no more than an intuition - drew his attention to me in this regard.

Have I given the impression that Nicole wouldn't have rejected any advances I might have made? Probably, but at this point I shall be more explicit, as I have been in the matter of the other two intimate relationships, Rebecca and Margraves, Abby and me.

Nicole wasn't young; if she had been thirteen, a guess, with Soutine in 1942, what does that make her now? You can work it out for yourself.

She doesn't make any apparent effort to look younger. That may have been due to a very percipient loyalty to the memory of the Lithuanian painter. it would have seemed to

her that to be taken as more youthful than she was would have separated her from Soutine, if only - but perhaps not only - in memory. She had a remarkable faithfulness to him.
To Paul she wasn't faithful. As I've recorded, she told me in some detail of other men, mostly rather brief but very sensual relationships.

Sixty or more, she appeared. Did I ever consider trying her out? That sounds a crude way of putting it, but I didn't love her nor she me. Perhaps I thought I did; that was before, though not so long before, I went to hospital and met Abdallah.

Making love to her would pose for me some kind of connection with Soutine, tenuous, but again substantial, in my estimation.   She and Paul understood each other better, I think, than anyone else did. And that's saying something for a marriage - they were man and wife. It doesn't mean, though, that the set up is a good one. While on the topic, I'd better admit that one reason I kept clear of Nicole sexually was my fear of not functioning properly. And for that sort of failure I felt she'd have no patience. Her standards had been set by Soutine.

But she hadn't given up on me. Like the susceptible women I've come across she had an instinct for the degree of virility in a potential lover, something far from easy to distinguish. Men are likely to be very far out if they try to assess another male's potency, often taken in by a crude masculinity.

Before I get to our next visit to Paul and Nicole I'm going to look back briefly on my first marriage, that to Noona. The other day I came on some old diaries, as well as more recent ones, of hers that she had left behind - this was unlike her - at her departure. This is the extract that, how shall I put it, brought her back out of the limbo to which it seemed I had consigned her by that universal and evil tendency to give the immediate present too much priority. For those who live passionately, and, in so far as they're capable of responsiveness, for those who don't, we are involved in what's happening now as completely and in so closed a circuit as if nothing of the sort had ever happened before.

"While I am dividing and replanting the blue violas and

look up at the lawn, there's something even lovelier than the grass and flowers that should be there and isn't any more. And if I think of what was there, at least on and off, keeping me company last summer and the summer before, I know that it was precious to me as nothing can be now."

No, we didn't have a child that died. Does it constitute an anti-climax to explain that the missing object was a black cat called, perhaps banally, Foxy? Not for me, it doesn't. It may even increase both my sense of my own failure in regard to Noona and bring her back into the company of those couples who had been so present to me of late.

I had started out to document - is that the word? - what at the time I thought of as the sensational discoveries of a somewhat eccentric scientist and champion them - not that my support would carry much weight - against the scepticism of most of his peers. And now I had come to the point of seeing them as secondary to quite different events, both historic and contemporary, factual and fictional. This was the love stories of men and women, those I knew and witnessed, those in which I was, or had been, involved, those I'd heard of or read about and those, as in Thérèse Martin's case, I'd imagined.

What I'd originally set out, and promised, to do was, compared to novel-writing, a smooth and pleasant task. But what I now envisaged might be either beyond me or requiring the acquisition -bestowal -of new and more original gifts than I now possessed.

Before I attempt it I know that I have to turn off my thoughts, at least from that direction, lapse into a state of what seems mental and emotional torpor, a general idling that comes quite naturally to me. And then, after a time, it may come about that the first quantum of energy I require will have been rather mysteriously supplied. I say first 'quantum' or installment because that is how the most vital of our needs - or should I speak only for myself - are given.

Meanwhile I'll record our visit to Paul and Nicole. It wasn't just a social or friendly call, but had, as usual, a purpose, if not several. One was to get Nicole to translate some cuttings from the sports page of a Russian news sheet which Prince Ahmed had sent Abby and which related to the importation of the stallions.

I had a very private and subjective reason for wishing to visit Nicole and Paul and that was because I saw in them a fascinating example of a couple whose relationship was relevant to my growing obsession. As it was, I had too little direct knowledge of other couples, though the main source of understanding would come from my and Abby's daily experience.

Ripeness is all (Shakespeare). As far as I know he didn't add: Love is the sun that ripens. It is in loving relationships that the human consciousness matures and develops, through loving rather than being loved, because that is where the pain is engendered - and without pain there is not much intensity, and intensity of experience is the measure of ripeness, the means of our evolution towards more loving complexity or complex love relations.

The above needed getting off my mind and heart, I hope in one fairly coherent piece, before I return to what concerns me more and what I'm better at: specific situations, tangible incidents.

Starting with the humblest and one of the nearest, Margraves had by now lost faith in his annelids, had even admitted to Rebecca that perhaps after all the Belgian writer had not stolen the result of his researches into the life-style of the African white ants but had himself studied them. By the time he and the dark Rebecca had formed their unlikely union he had recognised his failure and taken it as a blessing that in some way bound them closer. Here I am speculating, but I think because it brought them to the same status. Otherwise, as well as age, there'd have been this discrepancy between an ageing savant and an ex-inmate of a brothel.

In this case the necessity of failure can be rationalised. In many others not. To leap from the most obscure to a historic, at least in the annals of hagiography, St. Thérèse was during her short life an insignificant nun in an obscure convent in Normandy, for all her sense of a grand posthumous destiny. And shortly before her death overheard a couple of her sister nuns wondering what on earth there would be to say about her in the obituary that would appear in the Order's newsletter.

Mayakovsky, once the darling of the Russian revolution, whose poems were in the hearts and on the lips of the newly liberated generation, and whose love for Lissik I shall relate from inside (how so? You weren't privy to it?), lived to find himself isolated, out of touch, more or less forgotten.

And then there is Emily Bronte, with whom I recorded, in the third person, my own fictional relationship, in a novel called *A Hole in the Head.* By far the finest, most original and daring of the three gifted sisters, her *Wuthering Heights* failed miserably to evoke any response before her painful death still in her twenties on a horse-hair sofa - she had dragged herself out of bed and dressed that morning.

After these diversions, we - Abby and I, as well as the faithful reader - come to Paul. He too, after teetering on a tight-rope along which he hoped to reach the far bank of fame, or at least estimation, he must by now have given up and was only postponing the catastrophe.

At the risk of bringing any favourably-disposed members of my small but far-flung audience to the breaking point of their patience, another relationship, very significant for my purpose, is that of the murderer, Rashkolnikov and the street girl, Sonia - I'd almost written Rebecca - in Dostoevsky's *Crime and Punishment.*

Before going into that famous story, I'll return to the obscure one of Rebecca and Margraves.

Abby started to tell Paul and Nicole what to her, and to me, was the most exciting piece of news that had come our way for quite a time; the loving compassion, the merging of currents that had been submerged in both because if allowed to surface they'd have disrupted their respective lives. I'm presenting my own suggestions; certain songs demand the words that make them memorable, some words attract the crowning tune.

It was soon evident that our hosts didn't want to hear anything of the sort. A world, or a small corner of it, redeemed by loving relationships was the last thing that fitted Paul's view of reality. Disruption, disharmony, influenza epidemics, perhaps AIDS, a whirlpool that just about kept its centrifugal form, for he didn't quite go as far as to agree that 'the centre cannot hold, things fall apart'.

Nicole had become conditioned to much of this at an early age. Soutine had had his whirlpools, if of another kind. I'm not asserting that he wasn't wildly attracted to her, the portraits - the two that I've seen - romantically testify to that. But it had left her without belief in another kind of relationship, more tender, caring and companionable.

To change the subject, Abby took the clippings from the Soviet equivalent of the English 'Sporting Life'.

I don't think Nicole found them easy to translate, maybe because of some specialised terms, but most likely because her knowledge of Russian was sketchy. She didn't render them word by word or even sentence by sentence but gave us the gist, as she called it, of what was written.

I could have come out with what it amounted to myself by not very astonishing divination, and would in all likelihood have included more detail. But there it was.

I commented just now that Paul had a very personal sense of humour. When I, or anyone else, made a remark that I thought was funny he seldom laughed. Yet his clowning was sometimes hilarious. A contradiction? He was full of polarities, as Cornelius called them. Paul is your New Man, the prototype not of Nietzsche's Superman, but more a fallen angel, the anti-hero of them all, which he instinctively feels, and which is the probable cause of his passionate assertion about where we come from.

- Why would an angel, fallen or stable, go in for farce?

- That's self-evident, I'd have thought. The set-up here on the planet would strike him as so absurd and yet so seriously taken that occasionally he'd have to express his reaction. And, I suppose, his use of the local language would be less flexible than yours. Did it strike you what an awkward style Paul's treatises are written in?

I quote the doctor who knew Paul better than anyone except Nicole, not because I think his submission is correct - allowing for the fantasy, incidentally he wasn't sober at the time - but because it does throw a light, if a narrow beam, on Paul's psyche.

I had hardly recalled the words of Cornelius and decided to include them in this memoir along with a note of caution as to their worth, when Paul launched into a monologue, the trend of which - by the time I'd caught up - seemed to be that what we, mankind, I think, was suffering from was being totally cut off from the cosmos.

- It's an enormous conspiracy, though most of those involved aren't aware of that. The brains behind it, and that is what they are, mindless brains, a new strain in the species that has been evolving for only a few centuries - but inside the skull mutations take place at an astonishing rate - having lost all means of contact not only with the cosmos but with the natural world itself, in complete seclusion, the new monk in his cell furnished with computers, electronics of all kinds with hot lines to the world's money markets, but, like the monk, with the barest personal necessities, cot, water jug, slop pail.

Nicole put down her knife and fork, whether to give all her attention to Paul or in a gesture of impatience.

- Once they set up their kingdom on earth - 'their kingdom come' - and they are putting the last touches to it, the wonder, the splendour, as well as the fears and ambiguities, will be banished.

7

Having noted Nicole's fork, I may as well fill in the
gastronomic picture. It was a spoon and fork lunch, nothing
that required cutting. Salmon with what I think was Heinz
mayonnaise, warm garlic bread - a craze in our town for the
second time round - wrapped in napkins. Fresh raspberries
from the garden - whose garden? Margraves'? - and red and
white wine of which I availed myself to counter a sense of
dropping behind, of not keeping up with our host.

I won't put myself out of turn here if I mention some
personal matters touching on my general health. After all,
before a witness to a vital event, or a commentator on an
important experience, is to be fully trusted, he or she should
at least not be vulnerable to intermittent physical disorders.
I'll put my sense of my condition first as I present it to
myself: in visual images, though more briefly. Some years
ago, during the early years with Noona, I saw myself as a
strong, young tree - not an oak or chestnut, I didn't aspire
that high - but, say, as a maple or sycamore, straight and
sturdy, under whose leaves we were encamped for a time
while we took stock and planned the rest of our pilgrimage.
Romantic? Certainly. And so it still is, even if the word must
be extended and restructured from within to embrace new
meanings.

Here, I'd like to say that language itself evolves with the
intensifying of the experiences and the increased complexity
of the events it has to reflect.

To return to myself as the young sycamore. Disaster
struck, I needn't symbolise it, and the tree was cut down. For
a time, say, two seasons, there was the bare stump, rising a
few feet from the ground, with its concentric rings, that could
have been used as a table at barbecues or picnics. And then,
at the third spring, shoots began to grow from it and by now

there is a far greater bower of leaves from a number of stems than there was from the earlier trunk.

- They may think they are putting the finishing touches to their materialistic earthly empire, Paul. But meanwhile there is the beginning of a change of mind in a lot of people who had gone along with them a long way. And there's going to be a violent backlash, if not actually an independent revolution.

- Joel, old lad, you've never been slow with audacious predictions.

- No, and even if these were half guesses I am not going to give way to the professional weathercocks who think they know the direction of the winds and breezes.

I'm not placing Paul among these. No matter what he'd said I'd have disagreed. I was sorry we'd come. The food wasn't to my taste, and as for Nicole - who could have saved the day - she was, like the food, being a mixture of the attractive and appetising (the salmon), spoilt by a cheap sauce. Not the Mary Magdalen, as I sometimes thought of her, nor Marilyn Monroe, to descend a few degrees, but just a woman who had had too many men doing everything they wanted to, or with, her, because she enjoyed it too.

I intimated to Abby that I'd like us to leave as soon as we could. What I needed was to tie up all the men-women relationships that I knew enough about, directly or indirectly. Not exactly to form a theory, as Einstein had with his 'General Theory of Relativity' (while still in his twenties, though that's neither here nor there) but in order to see how it fitted or affected the overall picture. The picture, that is, of the 'all', the cosmos, that, apparition-like, manifests itself to itself, so to speak, inside the consciousness.

Having gone so far into the deep, I may as well take another step and assert that the person to whom this event has happened will never again be dismayed by mathematical equations involving billions of light years or galaxies.

As soon as we were home, even before, in the car, I could feel that Abby was upset.

- Oh, how my breasts ache!

She had large, darkish breasts, have I mentioned this before, not luminaries but, on the contrary, absorbing light and always in shadow. I could just about cup one in my hand, kneading it tenderly and, with both hands full of sombre bounty, I took the red bud at the centre of a dark-grey corona into my mouth.

- Paul got all that about the world falling into the hands of the barbarians from my father. But Daddy doesn't believe they'll have the final victory. No, don't stop, Joel. Can't you listen while you comfort me?

I hadn't withdrawn hands or tongue but only ceased the slight movements which, for all her concern in what she was telling me, she sensed at once.

- That Nicole's a bitch.
- Don't let her impinge.
- I'm frightened.
- Of what, Dove?
- Of it all turning out to have been a dream.
- I'll show you if it is!

I closed my mouth tightly and even brought my teeth closer together.

- I didn't mean you and me. But what about all the other couples who turned this nasty place into a haven, not a shelter because they shared a lot of pain, but where the nastiness couldn't enter, so that when you put them all together, through the ages, the world is refashioned.

This time I had to stop what I was doing, partly through surprise (though I should by now have known how she stored up and could repeat - more movingly - what I told her) and because I had to answer.

- It's a general theory, a dream, a myth, a revelation, as are the Gospels, Einstein's conclusions, and, more privately, Dostoevsky's, Leonardo's, Soutine's.
- Oh, leave Soutine out of it!

Abby was petulant, excited, darkly lustrous. I'd no doubt how the mixture of dialogue and touchings was going to end. But again I was wrong.

- Let's tidy up, she suggested.
- Tidy what up?

She wasn't presumably referring to all the loose strands, expecting me to make connections between myth and legend, apparition and hallucination.

- Ourselves.

She wasn't undressed; it was a matter of adjusting her clothing, as the saying is. What should I do? Pull her back into more total disarray? Is that what she was after? No, she might at times be petulant, but never coy.

We were sitting sober-seeming to all outward appearance in the living room that opened into the small plot of garden.

- Let's talk about something else, Abby said.

- Such as?

- Anything as long as it's, you know, not conducive.

Yes, I knew, even if I wasn't sure what the point was.

A few minutes ago I'd expected her to come up with some surprise in the way of love-making. Despite her comparative youth she had had more sexual experience than I. Not that, like Rebecca, and to a lesser extent, Nicole, she had had a lot of men, but with those she had had there had surely been a wide range of methods of coming to, or postponing, orgasm.

- Politics? Money? Golf? Horses and racing? Professional boxing?

- Yes, you've got it, Joel.

So I had, somewhat tardily. What she was planning was for us to begin all over again from the furthest point from our goal. Not to slide or slip into sex from emotional or nervous reactions as just now on our return from Paul's.

Does it work, such deliberation, I wondered. Yes; at any rate it did this time, and marvellously. Abby had brought me with her a long way since our first embrace in the hospital bed, not gradually, but on certain memorable occasions. She showed me in practice deviations to shock not just the squeamish but the sexually unawakened, devised by I don't know whom in what ferment of the senses.

- 21 -

If, as is generally assumed, the imagination is an old-fashioned faculty, largely obsolescent because of electronics, but to be given due respect for tradition's sake, any proposition based on its supremacy will be rejected by a huge middle segment of public opinion. A section starting at the level of primary education right up to the fringe of those with a gift for and training in the pure or speculative sciences and arts.

This is another way of putting the 'great conspiracy theory' expounded the other day by Paul, in opposition to both of which I am going to devote myself to proposing a totally contrary interpretation of the phenomena.

The premise is that the human mind, because its structure is an extension of the cosmic pattern, can, given the right conditions, add to or extend reality.

Having, with a couple of bold steps, crossed a formidable frontier, I shall not hang around putting finishing touches to the theory which doesn't stand any tinkering at, and can never be 'finished' or 'finalised' in the packaged and sealed sense.

No, let's get straight into one of these imagined experiences that, I'll repeat at the risk of alienating some of my audience, are as much part of reality as those events that happen before they are imagined.

Lord, may the tears of your handmaid, like those or your earlier one, Mary Magdalen, drop onto your feet, and in the mysterious reversal of roles that you initiated, let the washing clean be of her.

What's this, some girl asking to share the shower? Words that could have been whispered by Rebecca, by Sonia in *Crime and Punishment,* by many unknown women who in their love for another being - a man, because it is the history of lovers, not of saints I'm recording - prepared themselves, not just physically, with garments, make-up, hygiene and the rest, but with this touching spiritual humility which, in many cases, was abused and shamefully exploited. Maybe, but what I'm proposing is to compile an authentic record of vital but largely ignored or unknown historic events that, more than any others, give us, individually and as human beings, the promise - the old, but forgotten or derided one - of our longings not being in vain.

The prayer I have just quoted, or rather composed, could not, of course, have been uttered by St. Thérèse de Lisieux whose virginity was both clinical and spiritual. Not that she wasn't equally humble, contracting in the rather jejune wedding document she drew up between herself and Jesus to bear whatever he did to her, including treating her with indifference and neglect whenever he tired of his 'plaything'. Such self-reduction may be termed neurotic, may, as has been pointed out, have been intensified by disease, tuberculosis, from which she suffered. However valid those considerations may be in a biography or textbook, they don't concern me here.

My response to her confessional *Diary of a Soul*, which I'm sure was not unique, was compassion and the forming of an imaginary liaison with her, the possibility of which - because imagining the impossible is for minds without discipline and perhaps sanity - I based on her admission that if she hadn't aspired to sanctity she could have become a street girl. That is, I think, lavished herself on all and sundry. But wasn't there something in between? Could I persuade, show, her that what I wanted was not a normal *menage a deux,* which, with a human partner, would certainly limit the fulfillment of her excessive desires. Desires, that is, of self-immolation to another, or to many.

I believed, imagined, and I persuaded Thérèse that because I too had immense desires, though of a far different kind, she would find in me a vessel which could contain a lot of self-lavishing without overflowing. So we set up house in a rather drab provincial suburb, or perhaps in a small industrial town in Northern Ireland, making sure, that is, that we were as isolated from society and its amenities as she had been - would have been - in a Carmelite convent.

Oh, it was a revelation, living with Thérèse Martin! How humble she was, ready to react to my varying demands, which, naturally, I kept to a minimum.

I had to do all I could to make up to her for her having been abandoned - as she puts it in her autobiography - by her divine spouse - as she also puts it. And I suppose it was hardly a drop of balm in the ocean of near-despair from her other, real, existence.

There were times when she reminded me of Emily Bronte, about whom, and our association, I have written elsewhere.
To have been close, imaginatively, to such women even briefly is an epiphany, though perhaps it's laziness that allows me to

use such an over-worked term. It is also a somewhat fearful experience, though that aspect I won't go into at this time.

How do I tie in these extraordinary and extra- or metaphysical events with the actuality of living with Abby? Quite simply, really. By sharing them with her, telling them to her with all their surprising details that - Abby's words - I couldn't have invented. By, above all, relating them to the overall undertaking I was engaged in. The centre of, and impulse toward, the whole project came from the intensity and astonishment, as well as the pain, of our life together.

My mental involvements - if I haven't been up to now convincing readers that they were more than that, it's too late now - were, of course, in proportion to the number of historic relationships very small. And I've no doubt the unrecorded and obscure ones outnumber these in similar fashion, even if what I call 'historic' includes some of the fictional accounts by great novelists. For instance: the love story of Raskolnikov and Sonia, which I've already mentioned, probably more than once.

They meet in Raskolnikov's attic shortly after he has committed the double murder. She has been forced onto the Petersburg streets by her alcoholic father and profligate mother. They exchange crosses, which both wear next to their skin, and read together from the Gospels the account of the raising of Lazarus.

Why this passage is not clear, there would seem to have been others more suited to their situation. Then Sonia tells him he must confess his crime publicly, repent and kiss the earth. It is all feverish and melodramatic. It is one of the great set scenes of literature, very 'set' and too literary, or so it strikes me now.

- She was telling him to give himself up and be condemned to death?

- Not death, but a long prison sentence in Siberia.

- Did they make love?

Dostoevsky doesn't say so, perhaps for fear of the reaction of his readers whom he wanted to work up to a state of spiritual exaltation.

Telling it to Abby I saw the flaws in this famous passage, both as art and as parable. Nor did it do anything to persuade her of the vital influence of the Gospels in these relationships.

To regain the lost ground, the next, this time historic, story I related was that of Jacob, the sisters Leah and Rachel, and their father, Laban. These were Abby's distant kin and, in contrast to Dostoevsky's tale, it was starkly realistic.

I needn't repeat it in any detail. Jacob lived for fourteen years in the household, working with Laban's flocks, first for Leah, and then for the younger girl on whom his heart was set.

Laban had set a trap for him, deluding him into supposing, in the dark of the bridal tent, that it was Rachel to whom he was making love.

- Animal passion doesn't discriminate, Abby, who knew the outlines but not the details, remarked.

I couldn't let this divert me or I'd have lost the thread. Anyhow it was a truism that went without saying.

- During the years he worked for Laban in order to gain Leah, you're not telling me they weren't lovers.

- No, darling, I'm not. It may have been a hire purchase arrangement.

- Or that he never as much as gave the other girl a feel? I've an idea that kisses were dispensed with as frivolous or perhaps unhygienic.

Abby herself was not a great one for kisses, at least not mouth to mouth.

- I don't know whether hygiene was a consideration.

- Oh, far more so than with the Christians, as it was, and is, with us.

- I wasn't going to be deflected.

- They were the first recorded lovers who entered into each other's hearts and spirits, as we say now, shared a world.

- How in heaven's name do you know?

- By reading between the lines, by knowing the code to what at times is a secret language, and then by meditation in the light of our experience, Abby.

- Yes, Joel, I do believe you have some very extraordinary insights, but sometimes you push them too far.

- In what way?

- Don't you exaggerate the historic importance of these

relationships?

- No.

- You won't get many intelligent people to see it like that.

What about Shakespeare? In his exposition of just such a relationship in 'Anthony and Cleopatra', he has the great general and statesman exclaim, I'm quoting from memory: 'Let the wide arch of the ranged empire fall', meaning that the Roman empire, the civilised world, to which he had devoted his remarkable talents, was as nothing to his passionate attachment to Cleopatra.

- 22 -

I took Abby to dinner at the hotel restaurant, the smarter, downstairs one, where I was on my way with Maya at the start of this enquiry. We needed an outing, Abby and I, from what was becoming too academic or theoretical a topic.

- It's not that I don't go along with it, at least some of the way, Abby said - and you should of course make the most of it in what you're writing, but don't let it take over from the main theme.

I didn't ask her what the main theme was. Not that I have too many doubts, though I have a few. There's no harm restating it in alternative terms, indeed the more varied the manner in which a theme is presented the better, in the sense that it gains dimensionally. The Gospels would not be what they are were they not in four versions, three fairly similar, two almost identical.

Inward-turned consciousness, the attribute that makes us human, is both a means of discovering reality and an aspect of reality.

That, then, is another way of defining the central plot - a more felicitous word than theme when considering a work of the imagination.

Back to the outing: special occasions have to be planned and put together. There are certain requisites. They must involve some extravagance, an expenditure that can be ill-afforded. I don't say we were spending our last savings, but our finances were still far from secure. We were neither earning except intermittently, Abby by occasional night shifts at the hospital and I by contributions to mostly women's magazines - most often to the French *Acualite* where they seemed to like my concoctions of psycho-sexual delving and comedy. I submitted my pieces in English and they translated - and 'edited' - them at the office.

Besides financial extravagance, outings to live up to even modest expectations must involve other excesses, such as intimate dialogues. And this seemed to come about of its own - though I suppose it was Abby's - volition. She told me about her past, in particular of the men in her past, on these quite rare occasions.

So it was now. This I appreciated-hardly the right expression because I was on tenterhooks in case I would hear some escapade or orgy which I would afterwards be bound to recall at the moment of our own love-making. But this hadn't happened and, at the risk of lessening tension by forestalling developments, didn't now.

Abby seemed to me a normally sensual woman, which is saying a lot. She told me she loved 'it' perhaps more than doing anything else, that she dreamed of indulging in it day and night, but there were few men who could keep up, and those few were probably undesirables.

- Doesn't it figure prominently in the Moslem heaven?
- Oh yes, and why not?

Why not? I wasn't going to express any views about how a heavenly afterlife should be run. In any case I wanted Abby to continue with what she'd been leading up to. I don't think this was out of an unhealthy voyeurism - nor a healthy voyeurism either, if such exists - but, as I'd already found, it helped me in my putting together of the several Abbys into the one I anyhow only partly managed to fully assemble.

Abby's father wanted her to marry a wealthy Egyptian. Egypt had gained much sympathy in the Arab world after France and England had tried, with bombs and leaflets, to overthrow Colonel Nasser while encouraging Israel to mount an attack across the Canal. Not that Abby had been born at the time but her father, a conservative and traditionalist with some grandiose world views, may have seen the marriage as strengthening the bonds between his country and one of the great kingdoms of ancient times that might regain some of her glory. Abby, she was very young, remembered him talking to her in some such vein, though she couldn't swear that she'd got it quite right. That, anyhow, was irrelevant.

She was sent to stay with the middle-aged Egyptian's old mother, on approval, as Abby put it, while she and her prospective husband became acquainted. She thought, but wasn't sure, that he was a relative, a great grand nephew perhaps, of King Farouk, whose portrait she noticed in his house. For she used to visit him, accompanied by a chaperone from the old woman's household and, Abby soon guessed, instructed by her not to take her role too seriously.

At the very first visit she was left alone with her host who couldn't, or didn't, keep his hands off her.

- Quite considerate, he was, pausing at each cautious advance to see how I was taking it.

- How did you take it?

- Oh, I played the ignorant little virgin.

- Which you weren't?

- That's right, darling. That was probably just what he wanted, but one who could be cajoled and caressed into a passive compliancy. He was patient. Only after a week or so, and I was brought there every afternoon, did it come to the point where having removed those of my clothes that were in the way he tried, very gently, to get me to open my legs, something that the untouched little tangerine - *nolli me tangere* - that he took me for wouldn't have made much fuss about.

- Not that I made a fuss. I just lay rigid and frigid. It wasn't a matter of repelling or repulsing him, but of reacting to what was going on not so much with disgust, which could have been gradually dispersed, but with indifference, boredom and a contemptuous air. Of course, Joel, I don't know how well I managed to express this mixture of alienated emotions, but I put my whole heart into the act which - lying on my back as he'd positioned me, but with one leg bent at an awkward angle - wasn't all that easy.

But with other such approaches on successive visits I

found new ways of frustrating him by never seeming to grasp what was wanted, though I never let him be sure whether my frigidity wasn't the non, or mal, functioning of female glands, hormones or enzymes, or a malicious streak in my very nature.

- I had to think of the most gruesome things, coffins, corpses, tortures, grotesqueries and manglings, not to afford him the slightest physical sign of response.

- Oh, Joel, I was so ingenious that I regretted there was nobody to appreciate the act.

- You can show *me*

- Yes, I thought of that.

- We aren't at home.

- No, but this is a hotel. We could take a room.

- For the afternoon? This isn't that kind of joint, Dove.

- Just try.

- We'll get a taxi.

- Some of the nurses are taken here to lunch and afterwards to a bedroom by their escorts.

- All right. She was daring me and I couldn't not take it up. But I thought to myself these escorts, as she called them, had been staying at the hotel and so could retire to their rooms with a companion without attention being called.

- 23 -

Abby showed me the tricks she'd played on Farouk's distant cousin or whoever he was. They were incredibly life-like, or more death- like, and left even me with a sense of gloom. But what it had left her with - I mean on the original occasion quite a few years ago - was a backlash or hankering after an encounter in which she could lapse into the most compliant and indecorous postures without having to worry about anything beyond the fleeting - how swiftly! - hour.

To cut a short episode a little shorter: she fell into the company of an officer of the British Royal Navy, whose hero was probably Drake, one evening in Alexandria, the very same day that she'd been at the Pasha's - or whatever he was

- palatial dwelling, situated, it turned out, on the Nile between Cairo and the coast. And, to tie it up at the other end, she didn't return to the old woman's house with what seemed to her its numerous *domestiques* who were trained as lax chaperones, but made her leisurely way back to the Gulf by boat, to allow plenty of time for her father's friend to have let him know the projected betrothal was annulled - which required no legal or religious proceedings even in that rather bureaucratically orthodox part of the world.

Marriage being no longer a likely solution - to what? I suppose in that ruling circle the word was apt - at least for the time being, her father couldn't let her continue as a superior kind of stable lass, treated with unnatural and cold respect by the other handlers in the yard. So that was when, of the limited options, she chose to come to our land to train as a nurse. But not without an interlude in Paris to which the Prince was never reconciled so that she had to support herself by menial jobs.

She told me, switching back and forward as was her way, of being aware of the great river even in the midst of her misery on the forced visits to the Pasha. And somewhere near this very spot the queen of Egypt had arrived in her gorgeous barge for what was to be the final tryst with her lover, a great foreign warrior, about whom Abby didn't know much as her information evidently came from older sources than Shakespeare.

Then occurred what she took as an extraordinary coincidence, the coming together of two a-causal events - though separated a couple of millenia in time. Between Alexandria and Suez her ship, a freighter with some sparse passenger accommodation, had passed quite close to a gleaming yacht which she was told belonged to the Greek millionaire, Aristotle Onassis, and on which she later concluded Jackie Kennedy was on board.

Anthony and Cleopatra - Aristotle and Jackie!

In the course of her reminiscences Abby had insinuated, quite accidentally, a consideration into my general theory that, though not unaware of, I hadn't yet dealt with: the degradation of the loving man-woman syndrome. Of course it was equally well-documented and historically verifiable. I was off at something of a tangent, recalling that Aristophanes had made Lysistrata exclaim: "What fun we have and the only problem is how to get rid of the baby."

In another ancient story is an antidote or balm to the above - as soothing weeds are said to grow in the vicinity of nettles - in the blessing they saw it as when, at long last, Rachel became pregnant and bore Jacob Benjamin.

There was big-breasted, sorrowful Ruth. What about her? Only that I imagined her, when I recalled the biblical story at all which wasn't that often, in the image of Abby, which is why I called her 'big-breasted', also 'far from home', though neither tearful nor, as Keats depicts her, amidst the alien corn.

Our life at this time, however, was by no means a matter of outings with, in between, Abby recounting her Arabian tales to while away the hours between love-making. It was an active period, with Abby engaged in getting possession of the mare and foal we had either seen at the monastic farm, or failed to identify, in exchange for the two-year-old colt that her father had given, or only promised, her. While I was in that state of imaginative fertility and ferment in which I write away, not indeed without effort, because there is the sense of clearing a path ahead by disposing of an enormous amount of debris and litter of all kinds, but with the numbers on the top right corners of the copybook pages flickering forward with bewildering rapidity.

There were these cases of the diminishing of the man-woman relationship of which Abby had mentioned the most recent and publicised. Physical pleasure, or fun, as Lysistrata called it, if the only or main purpose of the union, is one of the common causes of the trivialisation, though if both partners are impelled by the same urge it falls short of degradation.

What's this? Why introduce a code of morals at this point? Has it a significance to be revealed later? It has an immediate significance to my way of looking at it, but I won't make an issue of it.

The human brain comes closest to reflecting the overall picture when, its neurons activated by mind or psyche, it achieves an intensity of consciousness that overflows its own thresholds into love of another being. It is then that it reflects reality, as a fragment of an holistic image (produced in the laboratory through laser beams) reproduces the whole picture in miniature.

Having got that clear (I hope) I can continue with my private evaluations. What, as I have mentioned, was one of the first things I noticed about these relationships, actual, privately imagined, and fictional, was that failure was involved. Not, naturally, failure in love or they wouldn't have ranked among my examples, but a curious lack of achievement or success in the more ordinary activities. Thérèse with her boundless ambition remained while alive utterly obscure. As did Emily Bronte, while Charlotte's much inferior work made her well-known. In the extraordinary case - even more so than others - of Jesus and Mary Magdalen, failure was inherent from the start. And, without annotating others, the thought naturally came to me that if it wasn't so with Abby and myself it would be a disturbing sign. That is as much as I need say at the moment.

Returning to why many historic or publicised such relationships didn't achieve a mutual intensity, and leaving aside those in which money or property played a part, which I should have mentioned earlier but didn't, I come to the cases where the woman could not match, or reciprocate, the man's passion.

This had been the case with Lissik and Volodya Mayakovsky, but before going into that, before, that is, I transported myself to that time - the early twenties - and place - Leningrad - and, more importantly, into two or three smallish rooms in that city, and still more importantly, into the minds and hearts of the three protagonists - yes, it was a *menage-a-trois* this time - I had to discuss it with Abby.

These discussions were becoming more and more essential to me. Even when I seemed to dismiss her objections it was a way of clearing a small neutral space in which to take stock. Not that at this period we had much time for discussions. For one thing, as mentioned, there was this business of buying the mare and foal which preoccupied her. When I asked where the money was coming from she said Paul. By now my trust in her was secure against the shock, instinctive rather than rational, that this reply gave me. But I didn't want us to be beholden to him, as the saying is.

- It's more the other way round, Joel.
- How's that?

She explained, by references to dates of foaling, the discrepancy between the thoroughbred breeding season in the Soviet Union and with us, and, I think, other technicalities that went in one ear and out at the other, that when this unnamed foal was a two-year-old and mature enough to be introduced to the race course, it would be the first offspring of one of the stallions exposed to the comet's tail to run.

It was belatedly clear, or fairly so, to me. If this animal should turn out to be something exceptional in the way of racehorses it would be a further confirmation - and I didn't think these were so numerous that any addition would not be very welcome to Paul - of his theory. Another point that had a considerable bearing was that the mare, though herself reasonably well-bred, had not before been mated to a pure-bred stallion, nor had she ever seen a race track. Oh, it would be a minor, and perhaps not so minor, triumph for Paul, and it wasn't surprising that he was ready to contribute a large - probably the whole - part of the purchase money. More surprising to me was Abby's display of business acumen. But then her father was obviously no fool in the ways of the world.

In the midst of these pressures and activities - mine not least, though of a more passive kind - we attended a talk by Cornelius in a lecture hall at the hospital.

It was an exposition of some recent conclusions about the human brain and its functioning. Above our heads, or brains? No doubt, or so I supposed, but for old time's sake, or, more precisely, because we owed our coming together, Abby and I, to the doctor, we turned up.

I cannot report the lecture in a manner that would reproduce its vital arguments, or correspond to the notes that I saw several nurses and doctors in the audience taking. It is, once more a question of translating the expressions of one discipline - neurology - into those of another - literary art.

Considine started by quoting an article from a medical

journal on the effect on the brain that 'even a small quantity of alcohol' can have. By 'effect', he went on, the eminent author of the article, whose name he mentioned, meant a damaging one. Anything that interfered with what was called the normal functioning of the brain cells or neurons was considered, by this highly influential school of thought, to be self-evidently detrimental.

The reality was, however, that it was largely through interventions into the smooth running of this structure that it had evolved and increased in complexity. And a large part of the interventions had come through viruses of probably extra-terrestrial origin as well as drugs, including alcohol, though less significantly than certain others. There was some laughter and also heckling.

- Are you suggesting, Doctor, that the lack of evolution in animals beyond a certain stage is due to their non-use of drugs?

- The Professor is asking one of the trick questions for which he's so well-known and popular with his students. I'm sure he is too well-informed on this whole matter to have put it seriously. But for those who expect a reply, let me say that any animal that would of its own volition take a drug would, by that, have forfeited a vital part of its animal nature.

Laughter and some applause, started by myself and Abby.

- More decisive in the growth of the cerebrum with its twin hemispheres, is intense nervous stress. In responding the neurons create increasingly complex patterns, very much as a composer, painter, or writer has to push his art into new and more subtle forms to express his on-going experience.

- Life is sucked into the cerebellum at one open end and is ejected at the other as art. And the raw experiences most likely to be transformed into the finest musical scores, paintings and fiction are of love and pain, twin emotions inevitably conjoined.

At this point, we couldn't contain ourselves and not only burst into prolonged clapping but, with a shout of 'Bravo!' from Abby, instigated an enthusiastic response from a section of the audience, mostly, I noticed, nurses, some students, and a couple of the younger doctors. Those who I took to be professors and senior consultants, as well as the middle aged or elderly laymen and women, appeared unmoved or even somewhat embarrassed.

To return to my attempt at osmosis or assimilating into my own sensibilities events taking place not far short of a century ago in the Brik's - Lissik's and her husband Osip's - apartment and at Mayakovsky's dwelling in a lane not far distant, it became clear that Lissik (one of Mayakovsky's various pet names for her) was not among those women to be enshrined in my Compendium. Not, that is, an angelic creature, fallen to earth - I'm speaking metaphorically in case among my audience there are those as obtuse as there were at Cornelius's lecture - without loss of passion and self-immolation, without a diminution of the precious balm - the 'ointment' in one version of the Mary Magdalen story - that they brought with them.

I asked Abby to read a biography of Vladimir Mayakovsky (1893-1930) which she did faithfully, despite her difficult business dealings with Paul and with the farm manager at the monastery. A complication that I hadn't grasped and which she now mentioned was how to identify beyond doubt which of the several mares and foals we had seen were the Canadian importations?

For my sake, she put those anxieties aside - a considerable loving achievement - and concentrated on the five hundred page long volume.

- What may have bothered you, Joel, she said - is that with your wonderful gift of imagining far-away and mysterious events as present reality, you lose sight of the wider setting. While you've been peering through half-open doorways and eavesdropping in dark passages in long-demolished Russian dwellings you didn't take into account that the very private events you were following were taking place during one of the greatest revolutions in history. You, Joel, who lived through the last war at one of its foremost centres learnt, as you told me, not that lives are unlivable at the very personal level, but that on the contrary are increased in intensity, though those involved don't realise it at the time, to a kind of abnormality.

Yes, where I hadn't insinuated what she'd called my 'wonderful gift', was into the Communist Party office where

Volodya and Lissik had worked frantically far into the night printing posters and leaflets as fast as Mayakovsky could compose them. They had even received a congratulatory message from Stalin.

But Abby had something more to say, and it took my breath away.

- Don't you see the strange thread in the pattern, Joel? The madame at the 'Firmament' whose funeral we were at had Mayakovsky's Lissik for an ancestor, though I think I heard that the connection was through a sister, Elsa. And one of the girls from the brothel she ran, Rebecca, has dedicated herself, body and soul as they say, to a lonely, despairing old man. Doesn't that do something for your faith in the overall dispensation?

8

24

And then an extraordinary event took place, a phrase that may by now be familiar and will come as an echo to students of Dostoevsky. I say students because even devoted readers will have read his novels between hard or soft covers. It was when they were serialised in his own periodical or *The Russian Messenger,* and it's *Crime and Punishment* that I'm thinking of in particular, he often ended an installment with this sentence to encourage readers to order the next issue. This was when he and his young wife were living at a German spa and he was spending hours at roulette in the casino gambling away his meagre earnings, not to mention Anna's wedding ring and pawnable trinkets. Of course, he had no idea of what the event was going to be, but he was taking a minor risk in comparison with the sums staked nightly.

Need I say that my use of the phrase doesn't constitute any risk and is for a purpose not dissimilar to the injunction before an aircraft takes off: Fasten your seat belts and extinguish your cigarettes. A warning, in fact, that I am going to increase the tempo. The event, it may be objected, is the commonest, present and on-going at all times, everywhere. Yes, it's time I'm thinking of. A considerable portion of it in human terms, two years, take or add a month or two.

What I needed to ascertain was happening so gradually, secretly, daily, hourly as not to be noticeable, as the growth of the grass, that I failed to notice the vital changes. And the way to do that was to choose a quite arbitrary date in the future when I would awaken and take stock of the changes that had come about. Not that I could lose the time in between, annul or forget   the days when 'nothing happens', the Wednesday afternoon, say, that prolongs itself, turns back on itself to start all over again while we drink cups of tea in semi-desperation, because to start drinking alcohol would spoil *l'heure de l'Aperitif* which is all we look forward to. No, there was no question of lapsing into a catatonic state, or coma, but to balance two aspects of time inside the consciousness: the past revealed in its effect on the present, and the gradual, subterranean movement that is a continual present. I did not suppose I would come up with any information about time to rival or even qualify Proust's on the subject in his great novel, *Revelations of Things Past*, and, in particular, the final part: *Time Regained*. My modest hope, as I've said, was to try to understand some of the secrets of growth, change, decline.

The most pressing, and, as I saw it, the most frightening of the situations - relationships - to be checked for change was that of Rebecca and Margraves.

I couldn't, imaginatively, as I must stress is how this part of the commentary is being composed, I couldn't present myself at their apartment to pick up the signs. Perhaps, for I had to forget temporally what the gradualism of our fairly constant contacts with the couple had told us over the period, and try to detect whatever change for good or ill had taken place at the end of the period I'd chosen, and that in constant contact would have been imperceptible.

We would invite them to a meal. But supposing the phone was answered by a stranger who said they had rented the apartment from an agent more than a year ago? Am I straining the faith of some of my audience in my seriousness? Well, have patience, I'm engaged in a legitimate if difficult exercise in perception.

To be brief: They answered the phone and came to a meal a few days later. For the first half hour or so, over an aperitif - one each, and not more, until we, Abby and I, had reached at least a tentative conclusion - all was in the balance. I was nervously ready to interpret the least words or even expressions of our guests in the negative.

But then, soon after the start of dinner, the extraordinary event that I heralded at the start of this section really did take place. The old fellow - Margraves, that is, lest there should still be some hope in the minds of the sceptic or two that may have persevered as far as this that the dark girl had switched to another, perhaps wealthier, old man.

I saw him - Margraves - put a hand on some part of Rebecca hidden by the table, the belly as it turned out.

- Get up and show them, darling, he told her.

She pushed back her chair and rose. I don't know what I expected, and even for the first moment or two I waited, as I think did Abby, for something to happen. Nothing did, though the 'nothing' was one of the momentous events that take a time to sink in.

Rebecca was pregnant, and had been for some months, as Abby surmised.

This was a justification for my 'experiment' beyond what I could have hoped for.

The lunch at Paul's and Nicole's, though far from joyous, also confirmed me in my 'experiment'. At the first glance I took at him in my new imaginary role as having returned from a distant voyage after a two-year absence, I saw he had wilted. Some of life's flow had been diverted from him, from his person. Nicole, on the other hand, was in late bloom, like an autumn crocus, as Abby put it. But she seemed unaware of the change in Paul.

When I mentioned it to her, she took it lightly.

- Look, Joel, we'll arrange a situation where his clowning is called for.

- What do you suggest?

She came up with one or two ideas which struck me as a bit of clowning on her part. I suppose having been with Paul day and night over the two years that I had put imaginatively between myself and him she really noticed nothing.

Finally Nicole did make a serious suggestion.

- There's a professor here on some academic mission or other to whom Paul's treatises are anathema. We'll get him to call on Paul by pretending that he has had second thoughts and this will be just the stimulus he has lacked lately to provoke him.

Before, however, relating what followed on the first changes I registered in our immediate circle, there was one, a natural one which required no prophet to foresee and which, on one level, was of the greatest importance: the foal had become a two-year- old colt.

9

25

Not only did the colt have an importance for Abby, the complexities or subtleties of which I didn't yet grasp, but, as she pointed out, it could be a main factor in the salvation of Paul. That's what she said: 'salvation', as usual not balking at the biggest words. Paul's decline for her was linked to the mysterious law of general decline - turning tepid, losing clarity, polluted, innocence fading - that had its scientific equivalent in the Second Law of Thermodynamics. Don't ask me to give a summary of this, I'm not compiling a physics textbook, though I think I've caught whispered suggestions to this effect.

In a word, as we say, if the colt, called Abby's Gift, (not to be confused, as I did, with the original animal of that name), and anyhow a misnomer because she had acquired the animal by a devious method that I have not time and space to go into, turned out to have acceleration and staying power considerably in excess of what might be expected from his breeding, what a boost that would give to Paul's theorem!

And now a brief comment on the lunch, because it all ties in. All that is, in fact, ties in, and, to the single eye, is a seamless garment, and woe on me if I leave loose ends, patches.

There was chicken stew. I thought Nicole had mentioned *coq au vin,* but not having breakfasted in anticipation of a French repast, may have misheard her, when she had gone to fetch the vegetable, which turned out - if taste is anything to go by - a dish of braised cauliflower leaves, Abby whispered; in memory of Soutine's scrawny old hen.

It was, in fact, hardly a whisper. She had evidently concluded that Paul wasn't picking up our chatter.
I asked Abby - not then and there, but a bit later - what was wrong with him. She said: - Oh, Joel, wasn't it obvious? He and Nicole have fallen out.

- You mean, that's all there is to it?

- Isn't it enough for God's sweet sake? Allah's, come to that. What looks like the end of the world, no matter how tiny a one. Surely that's something you know about.

Oh, I 'knew about' a lot of things, but if I couldn't tie them together, get a glimpse of the pattern, what was the good of that?

Paul has always hankered after a state of enlightenment, a heaven on earth, with this planet becoming part of the celestial harmony. If that came about there'd be no need for loving consolation. I think his clowing came partly from his belief in this higher state, a rejection of what he saw as temporary palliatives.

I was fascinated when Abby got going like this, clearing a path for us through what I'd seen as an almost impenetrable jungle.

The kind of earth we have, she went on, and always will if you ask me, though getting gradually worse, is part of a great disharmony. A pestilence of fear, isolation and desolation has descended on us but which love makes bearable, as the deathly poison and the antidote grow side by side. Or, you see, Joel, because this is what it adds up to, the more desperate our condition, the more miraculous is the gift given us and then is added the pain without which we wouldn't have known how to use it.

What we hadn't discussed - it didn't rank high on the evening's agenda - was why Nicole, not mean or thrifty by nature, had served such a miserable meal.

- When she and Paul fall out perhaps she starts dreaming about Soutine and their days of degradation and poverty.

- Degradation, darling?

I didn't see this as one of Abby's more inspired comments.

- It's not always the purest of pure loves you try to see everywhere.

When we'd got home we were both hungry. Abby, in her leisurely way - but I knew by now that what struck me as leisurely was something else, a stateliness that came from a different time scale (and which made her indecorous love-making the more sensational) - padding around, undressing, taking a shower, partly dressing again to go into the garden for, I think, chives to put in the salad.

- 26 -

Abby and I might have reservations about a heaven where there was no marriage nor, presumably, extra-marital relationships. What about the Koran's depiction of that particular environment? I haven't yet gone into it with her.

With Thérèse Martin there was no such problem, though, of course, there were a daunting number of other ones.

We were married in the Norman town of Besancon where her mentally ailing father had moved. Neither he nor her older sisters, who were Carmelite nuns, could attend the simple ceremony, even had they wanted to which Thérèse was doubtful about. She had letters from them, one enclosing a small silver crucifix that had belonged to her mother, the receiving of which had made her weep, but only briefly.

She had extraordinary courage as, of course, I had known ever since reading the last chapters of her autobiography.

I've disappointed them, she told me. Ah, in one way how easy it would have been to have followed them into Carmel.

- But Thérèse, it turned out far from easy, according to, in obedience to your Prioress, Mother Gonzaga, what you say about the years of dereliction.

Oh, how warmly she embraced me! I thought I felt her heart beating through the rather stiff corsage. 'Thought'! Wasn't I sure, and disturbed out of all my habitual attempts at composure? It is one of those never-to-be-effaced moments. Language isn't entirely adequate for these imaginative events, even though they be verities too.

He has brides to cling to him unrewarded just as faithfully. What he needed was somebody to send out into the streets, not as a missionary, nothing like that, but to immolate herself in a fire of love for whoever was in most need of her.

We had the third floor of a house on the outskirts of this town that wasn't quite large enough to have suburbs, sharing bathroom and toilet with an old couple on the floor above.

We had only the royalties sent me by my publisher, plus what I could write in the way of stories and poems - for the latter I never received more than a couple of pounds - three of them for Thérèse, who wasn't yet twenty. Though, of course, her age had nothing to do with it. But we weren't that poor, or if we were it didn't bother us. Not until the one great fear that was at the back, with frequent intrusion to the front, of my mind was realised.

What happened is one of the most shattering - how inadequate a word - events in this whole report and I need whatever gift I have to describe it.

I have the feeling it was three or four in the morning, daunting hours, I was going to say at the best of times, but then one sleeps through them.

We weren't asleep. Lying in my arms, Thérèse coughed. With a deft movement - I'm trying my best to reflect the quietude that came from her - she pulled her handkerchief - it was long before the time of tissues - from under the pillow and spat into it.

I felt for the matches.

- No, she said - don't strike a light.

It was the first time I faced the fact that our little dwelling was built on sand. In the morning when she unfolded it the cloth was bright with arterial blood.

We were still in bed where I was planning to keep her while I called a doctor. I took her in my arms and at that moment recalled and became aware of the unthinkable import of Christ's promise in St John's Gospel that she applied to herself: - 'If anyone loves me, he will keep my word, and my Father will love him and we will come to him and make our home with him' (John 13 XVIII).

Feverish, uninhibited ravings? Not like the outpouring of human passion though. This was a secret language to be decoded by someone already beyond the pull of earthly gravity. A neurotic in common terms, but it was also her illness, as yet undiagnosed, that disposed her - again the word is clumsy - (a) to belief in such a mystical extravaganza, and (b) to apply it to herself.

I tried to clear my head: what it came to in sober terms, but of course it didn't come to much in sober terms; no such concept as sobriety - spiritual, neurological - could exist in the heart of that fiery star.

I was going to bring a cup of coffee in bed to her in whom

dwelt - in no symbolic or equivocal fashion - the creator and sustainer of all that is, if one of the great spirits of our time has not been duped by the very passion that made her so unique.

I brought the doctor. Thérèse insisted on getting up later in the day. For six months she carried on with her household tasks, as well as loving and consoling me.

- When I die, she said, you'll know that what I said was true.

- I believe it now, Thérèse.

- Yes, and it's because you do that afterwards you'll be left in no doubt.

Nor was I. Such gifts as I have, and in some few ways they're considerable, I owe to her. It strikes me now, though not immediately at the time, that we aren't left, or not for long, without comfort, even without what is vulgarly called proof. As with the colt who, as I have hinted and shall relate, turned out to be something quite out of the ordinary for which there was no rational explanation in terms of breeding or conformation.

These considerations may seem a sharp decline or comedown from what went before, but I have never lived for long on such heights as at the time of my imaginary association with Thérèse Martin. And afterwards, whatever I have gained, it is not immunity from the allure of the world and certain - though not the most common perhaps - of its prizes. It wasn't, however, the business of the two-year-old racehorse that we were immediately involved in, though when Abby came home that afternoon and after, in her unhurried way, while taking what she'd bought from the shopping bags, told me what had happened, she was well into the story before I fully grasped that it wasn't about the colt at all. As I think I've mentioned, when a suitable seed falls into my imagination it finds such nourishment that it shoots up and for a short time takes over.

- For heaven's sweet sake, darling, I'm talking about Maria.

- Yes. All right.

I had to make the adjustment, and, quite irrationally, felt a slight resentment.

- They're turning the old place into a club house.
- What old place? The monastery with its stud farm?
- Partly, I imagine, because of AIDS and also to make it even more profitable. Oh, the new proprietor hasn't the flair of Madame Lissik.
- 'Flair'?

  Let it pass, or I'd never catch up.

Maria was invited to attend a conference there at which the more trusted and wealthy clients were asked to contribute either a yearly subscription or a lump sum that made them life members. Among the gentlemen attending was this Philip somebody, well-known in this town it seems in some civic capacity, who also owns horses, and a highly valued client of the brothel when run by Madame Lissik, who always asked for and was regaled by 'the dark girl' on his visits.

So what more natural, Abby went on, than when the conference was over and a toast to the new Club Firmament had been drunk he and Maria retired to the top floor bedroom that she knew so well?

Outpaced in the early stages, I at times can accelerate and end up ahead of the pacemaker.

She didn't seem to think much of it. It meant so much to him, it always had, and, although she admitted she didn't have to let him, there was no point in putting on airs. In the end she said she really had to go, or he'd have kept her well into the night. A depressing thought: was he the cause of her pregnancy?

I asked her if she felt ashamed and guilty towards her 'old fellow'. But no, not at all. It's nothing to do with what I have for him. These were her words. It's not a big deal, though better than nothing, to spend your youth giving men what the nicer, more generous ones, call the thrill of their lives. When I was given a chance to show I could do something more important than that, that I could make another being happy - not just from time to time excite and satisfy him - then I'd be crazy to let anything interfere with that.

I asked her wasn't she afraid of her carry-on with this former client of hers getting to Margraves? Yes, she was, because one of the girls at the Firmament was jealous of her and might take it out on her by some such nastiness as a letter to him, either anonymous or on the new Club Firmament note paper.

Having thought it over - by which time Abby had finished unpacking, storing food items in the fridge and drink on the shelf of the dining room dresser - there was one point I needed clearing up before coming to a conclusion. Not, of course, that I had to come to any conclusion, nor that Abby was telling me with any such purpose.

- What about Maria's own response? Did she enjoy it?

- She said that to be honest she wasn't all that keen on Margrave's love-making, or fucking as she called it, being in the mood, I think, for the plain words. She associated it with worms and even his penis - or cock as she called it - was like an engorged worm.

- So what?

I had an idea, as I suppose she hoped I might. I told her that she should see whether Margraves was above temptation before a situation arose where he'd cast the first stone. She hadn't heard of the biblical term - it comes in the Koran too - and I explained it to her, and then suggested she get one of her friends at the 'Firmament', a girl she could trust, to call when she was out, and at a propitious time, and see how vulnerable Margraves was to her sophisticated allurements.

No doubt Maria had used the plain words that Abby repeated, and possibly the cruder ones that Abby reported. But by then she had finished putting away the commestibles and, without any hiatus, pause or hesitation, in what struck me as the same placid rhythm, hitched up her skirt and sat up on the metal draining board. Then she lazily leant back and waited for me to do the rest (my interpretation). Maria and Mr Philip X, Margraves and his temptress, Tony joining Cleo on her barge, for which the draining board was a substitute I dare say - these, and other couplings or pre-couplings, were in our subconsciousnesses, but, if so, that didn't delay the final effacement, the washing away of the musings and imaginings into a simultaneous - as rarely happens - oblivion. Oh, how quickly!

And just as well. For we were hardly reassembled and

with our feet back on earth, or the red kitchen tiles, than Abby started telling me what I guessed from the tone - I was beginning to grasp the relative importance to her of our various activities by how her voice was pitched - was more crucial than Maria and her escapades.

- We'll have to auction the animal.

No, I didn't enquire what animal. I knew by now - perhaps I'd known before; I wasn't at sea in these matters - that in racing parlance horses sometimes became just animals ('that's a useful animal').

- Why?

The explanation either wasn't all that clear or I wasn't in that crystalline, attentive frame of mind to take it in. It had to do with her father and the strings that were attached to the gift. One of which was, I'm half guessing, that we get married in a Muslim ceremony.

The big annual sale of yearlings and horses-in-training for which our country - because of its limestone pastures, the best in Europe for raising thoroughbred horses and other livestock - is famed, was shortly taking place and, for a late-entry fee (exhorbitant it seemed to me) she had put in the unraced two-year-old.

- We'll buy him, Joel. He'll go cheaply, there'll be no reserve, I've had a word with the trainer, because neither his looks nor breeding will catch the eye of the leading local or foreign buyers.

Before I get to the auction, another few words about the Club Firmament will not be out of place as we shall see. It would be open to a restricted number of women, not, naturally, wives of members, but to selected women who could use the amenities in the day-time and who would not be charged a subscription.

10

There was a large international attendance at the two days of the yearling sale and a number of these remained for the auction of horses-in-training that followed, on which day the two-year-old colt appeared in the catalogue under the number 254. That meant he would be led into the ring shortly after the start of the afternoon session.

Abby, dressed in her Arab garb which she seldom wore these days, and I attended the morning session. Noticeable among those in the famous 'pocket' - a portion of the auditorium on ground level that opened directly onto the rows of loose-boxes and open air rings where the horses could be inspected before being brought into the stadium - there in a wheel chair and wearing dark glasses, panama hat flopping down over his forehead as if for added privacy, was the well-known English trainer who had been much in the news lately because of what the racing fraternity considered his shabby treatment by the British Queen concerning the non-renewal of his lease on the training establishment owned by the monarch.

- What can have brought the Major here? Our colt's trainer - he was also one of Prince Ahmed's - asked, hurriedly looking through his catalogue. I say 'ours', for we supposed he soon would be.

- It's Paul, Abby whispered to me.

I really was dumbfounded.

- You don't think he'll take it into his head to bid for the colt?

We hadn't discussed the matter with him, indeed hadn't seen him in the last few days. He probably thought that we had decided to sell the animal for the best price we could get and was here to boost it. (There were several trainers and owners who, seeing the famous Major, who had only this year won the Epsom Derby, bidding for the colt, were sure to follow suit.)

I was about to go - it meant leaving the stadium and walking round it to the 'pocket' entrance - and explain matters to him when I suddenly doubted if indeed it was Paul. Could he really assume such a marked resemblance to the once dashing Major, now paralysed by a hunting accident?

I looked at Abby, hoping she'd tell me to sit down again and wait a bit. There was plenty of time. If the figure in the wheelchair bid for any of the earlier lots, then it wasn't Paul. But Abby didn't share any of my doubts.

Until I was actually beside him I wasn't completely certain. I recognised a girl from the institute, as we called what was really only a laboratory, one of his students, who was leaning on the back of the chair.

In a low voice, and attracting the attention of several well-known members of the racing fraternity around us, I explained the true situation, which didn't appear to surprise him. It was I who was surprised by his lack of surprise.

- Yes, I know, old soldier. You and your Muslim maiden plan to have the colt trained with next year's classics in mind, and that means not letting him on a race course till the back-end of the present season.

That was too long for Paul. Maybe he was still up to clowning, but now it was for a serious purpose. I saw that far from being his old self - not that I had ever quite known what that was - he was nervy and distracted. He evidently meant to buy the colt - was somebody else behind him? - and run it as soon as possible.

He explained what we were only too well aware of, that this was the only racehorse that had come, albeit in the dam's womb, under the direct radiation. Whether the effect, if any (this is my proviso, not his), could be transmitted through the genes, as Prince Ahmed and the Russians supposed, was extremely doubtful.

- Naturally, Paul, this is something I'll take your word for. But don't you realise, if you start bidding for the animal in your present get-up, what effect it will have on the eventual price he fetches?

- What an old muddle-head you are, Joel! That's what I've

had to put up with most of my life - muddle, and fear of clear, simple thinking. Here's a heaven-sent chance, and I mean that literally, of putting a thing to such a test that few innovators in the history of cosmology have ever been granted and you and Abby are still thinking about a gala day at Epsom or Chantilly.

- Even if we were - I was trying the conciliatory tone - I do see your deep interest in the business. All I'm saying is why spend much more than you need, or can perhaps afford?

- Oh, the money is there.

- You mean, the Prince's?

- I was quite at sea.

- Christ almighty, what has the Prince to do with it?

I took the circuitous route back to Abby and told her as much of the foregoing as I thought relevant and could present in a rational manner.

No need to continue this blow-by-blow commentary up to the denouement, which, in fact, as far as we were concerned, didn't take place that afternoon but a day or two later.

While we sat through the early part of the afternoon sessions and, in some cases, heard sums that I couldn't envisage in any familiar sense (by estimating, say, what we could do with such a fortune) I began musing on the situation that we, using 'we' this time to denote the civilised world, had arrived at in regard to money. My thoughts wandered, long-forgotten memories came from nowhere - the subconscious? - and presented themselves in vivid pictures.

I recalled an antiquarian shop-window in a northern seaside resort when I was a boy. There was a sign there which I stopped to read whenever I passed: 'Nothing displayed in this window is for sale'.

I had a lot to puzzle over. One part of me, the innocent one perhaps, wasn't at all surprised. This was as it should be. Here was laid out a display of treasures of various kinds, all with the mysterious patina of coming from another, ancient world. Added to which, though this I only later mulled over, was that they were not there to attract buyers or to put it another way - and there were all sorts of fascinating ways of putting it to myself - they had no part in a society of consumers which even then - and in a way more noticeable because it was a comparatively new phenomenon - we were becoming.

Now, consumerism, the marketing of commodities of all imaginable kinds, for most of which a need had first to be infiltrated into the minds of an up-market section of the community, had completely taken over. In some cases the need was genuine, in many it was a matter of stimulating a dormant avarice into an obsessional hunger.

Nothing was considered above being used, that is trivialised and degraded, in what is a frenzied attempt at persuading, principally by the television commercials, though also in large- scale, static advertisements lurking wherever the weary eye rests in the hope of repose.

Take the case of motor cars. To anyone capable of a rational approach to this form of private transport there are two or three preliminary considerations: do they need a car? And if so, the security - I don't say 'prestige' - of a new one, I'm still supposing a degree of common sense. If the answers come to them in the non-pressurised interior of their home, a room, say, without a TV set or where it is not switched on, then between the enormous number of makes and models, European, American, Asian, the only practical consideration is price, which, for vehicles comparable in performance and space, varies little. Which is why the automobile commercials are the most brutal, unrealistic and frenzied. The gangsters who devise these, which in all but the perpetration of physical violence is the group they emulate, desperately attempt to picture one particular make as obviously superior in operation, comfort, speed, appearance and value to all others. (If this is so evident why do so many prospective new car consumers, by no means fools or they wouldn't be earning a salary that enables them to be customers, buy other makes?)

Of course it is not only motor cars. Sometimes a monologue is conducted in upper class accents that have suggestions of advisors whom the viewer has come to consult of his own volition, with suggestions of a trusted family doctor or solicitor say, gently recalling that their special knowledge, which they have spent years in acquiring, is at the service of the viewer, or, at other times, dismissing all such sophistication for crude and intimidating harangues, delivered in a tone of near-hysteria.

Supposing a firm of television makers put a set on the market that automatically switched itself off at the commercial breaks and, for the extra price of a video, replaced the advertisements with a short film, sporting, educational, erotic, according to choice?

Beguiled by such distractions - if such they were - before I was fully prepared for it lot 254 was led into the sales ring. The young auctioneer who'd just taken over from a more sedate, old-world gentleman started by asking for a bid of five thousand pounds, a modest enough figure. There was a longish pause as the colt stepped delicately over the freshly-raked gravel of the arena, at moments breaking into a few side steps and even a miniature trot.

- Well, then, four thousand. Will somebody bid me a mere forty hundred pounds for this well-grown two-year-old colt, broken, but not yet put into training.

This, as I understood it, was not strictly true, but he presumably did not want it supposed by a clientele than which there is none warier - in contrast to the average TV viewer - that the trainer had, after galloping the animal, advised the owner to dispose of him.

Abby, attired for some reason that I didn't fathom in her Arab robes, started with a bid. At once Paul/the famous Major made a sign from his wheelchair and the whole stadium was agog.

Though I tried to restrain her, Abby raised her catalogue, indicating a bid of by now how much I don't think she had any idea. Immediately a new bidder appeared. Yes, if you haven't guessed, it was Philip Weisberg, recent founder and presumably chief shareholder in the Club Firmament.

- Now we're getting somewhere! the dark young man in the rostrum exclaimed, stabbing a finger in the direction of Philip. - Forty thousand I'm bid. Thank you. Forty thousand for this extremely interesting, untried colt.

An imperceptible gesture from Paul.

- Forty-five thousand on my left. Surely we are only starting to get to the value in realistic terms of this exceptional colt who with careful handling could be on the racecourse within a couple of months. Thank you. Fifty-five thousand on my right (it was Philip raising the bid by a cool ten thousand).

And so it continued. I heard later that the bids included some made by agents of the Maktoum brothers. At a hundred and eighty thousand pounds the colt was sold to a buyer on behalf of a syndicate. That was the only information available at the moment.

- 28 -

It took a couple of days to establish who made up the syndicate, or cartel, as Abby, unconsciously voicing her upset, called it. And then the information came from what is called an unexpected quarter: Maria. Heading the group of a dozen or so citizens - all were our own nationals, mostly even from our city - was the friend-client of hers, Philip Weisberg.

This Mr Weisberg, she told Abby, had bought the colt, on behalf of a consortium, shareholders in the newly-floated company, and they were donating him to the Club Firmament in lieu of their life subscriptions to race in the club colours, which were being registered that very day, of silver stars on a dark blue background for jacket, silver and blue sleeves, blue cap with silver tassel, the last decoration being Paul's idea to suggest, perhaps, the tail of a comet.

While Abby and I were still discussing these events an invitation arrived from the club itself asking us to attend a reception to celebrate its formation, or re-orientation, which crossed my mind - one by now trained in finding precise definitions - as being the appropriate term. And with the impressive card came a personal invitation, almost an appeal, to me to make the opening address.

I was all for declining with a show of appreciation of the honour, but Abby wouldn't have it - if only for the sake of the animal.

By now she was reconciled to its loss; she quickly accepted the irreversible, but wanted to have some, however nominal, part in what she saw as its coming triumphs.

The position of 'Madame', unofficial but traditional, had not so much been abolished as let lapse. The old lady who had run the place after the death of Madame Lissik and who'd asked me to deliver the funeral address on that occasion was now, it seemed, the receptionist-hostess. She was greeting the guest-members, perched on an upright, period (what period I'd no notion) gilt chair in the middle of the entrance hall.

When the civilities were over, we were transferred to the care of a woman in her forties, obviously - but not too obviously - belonging to the local social upper-crust and, I took it, one of the *Belle-de-jour* members of Club Firmament who spent a few hours there on afternoons when she was not herself preparing for an evening's entertaining.

She - she told us to call her Lily - conducted us to the upstairs room where I recalled the corpse having been laid out on that other less festive occasion. There were still the signed photographs of Vladamir Mayakovsky, Lili (Lissik) Brik, her husband, Osip, her sister, Elsa (Triolet), and several others that I failed to identify, on the walls.

Chairs had been placed in a semicircle and a little back from its open end an armchair - a considerate touch - and a table on which was a glass, a jug of water and a decanter containing a golden-greenish fluid, which turned out to be Calvados - the powerful apple spirit from Normandy which I hadn't as much as sniffed for I don't know how long - and what I took to be a bottle of wine, though actually a concoction of fermented pear juice, popular - so I heard later - as an addition to the fiery Norman liquor.

I settled, almost sank, in front of this improvised bar on which there was just room for the notes I'd given much thought to preparing. Yes, I was proud of what I had composed. After some soul-searching, if the expression will be allowed to pass, I'd decided not to compromise and compose some sort of anodyne in keeping with the somewhat ambiguous occasion. So here is the gist of what I said, take it or leave it.

'Throughout history there are recorded cases of statements of great significance having been made which were largely, if not totally, unappreciated. The time was not ripe. I could give you examples from Kierkegard, who most of his contemporaries looked on as a crank, to Freud, who although admittedly with his patients as a captive audience didn't go quite unregarded, was mostly misinterpreted'.

'My own case is rather different. A composer of original fictions as parables for our own time, I have not been without followers, all the more faithful in that they are in no way captive'.

'The lady who introduced you mentioned me in connection with the Nobel Prize for Literature. In case there should be any misunderstanding, let me say in passing that I believe I have been long-listed for this prestigious award. I was told in fact by a secretary to the Swedish Academy or Committee that I was twenty-seventh on the list, but that among those before me in the queue are several names that you, ladies and gentlemen, would at once recognise, belonging to persons of advanced age or who are (and I don't think I'm betraying the trust placed in me when telling you) suffering from terminal afflications of one kind or another.'

I paused to take a first sip, mixing a measure of Calvados with the pear liquor. This was taken by the audience of perhaps a couple of dozen as, mistakenly, a signal to applaud, quite incongruously as I had reached a rather lugubrious, though quite incidental, part of my talk.

'I don't for a moment suppose it has escaped you that within the last few years, within the lifetime of the older among you, the cosmos has taken on a different look which may at first appear somewhat strange to those of us used to its well-defined outlines based on mathematical equations involving space and time.'

Of course they hadn't bargained for this, but were taking it with an air of good humour, based on the 'it-takes-all-sorts' attitude.

I wanted to tell this small gathering, among which were several individuals known to me, two or three - Cornelius, Maria- Rebecca, Nicole - even close, what I saw as part of reality. What they made of it I left to fate, or, let's say, to whatever breeze blew it in the right direction. Or, put it another way, I believed I had been entrusted with a few germinal seeds, not to hoard in a sealed packet next to my breast. Scattered, some would fall on fertile soil, etc.

Abby wasn't present, as we had agreed. I'd have been inhibited by her, afraid she might have thought this was some kind of showmanship, of which taint perhaps it wasn't quite free.

During the next pause for a restorative refreshment, there were one or two interlocutions.

- Excuse me, Professor, but if you're so far down the queue lined up for the big lollipop, why not shift over to the scientific one where you'd surely be somewhere up at the top?

- Hear, hear! Bravo!

A few giggles.

It was time to survey them. Anyone with experience of giving talks knows that if you get so intent on what you're saying and keep your eyes fixed on a point just above the last row of listeners you're at a serious disadvantage from the start. They are surveying *you*, in some cases to the point where what you say goes in one ear and either out of the other or dissolves somewhere into vapour between the two.

With a reading it's worse, for there you tend hardly to look up at all, particularly if you wear glasses which, if you did look, would reveal nothing but a blur.

I took an unhurried gaze, recognising several of those present. Philip Weisberg (who, though I'd never met him, I knew by sight from the auction) wasn't, I was pleased to see, sitting anywhere near Mary-Rebecca ('Mary' makes a better-sounding combination than if the twin names both end in 'a') but was sitting by himself at the end of a row - it was he who had shouted 'Bravo!' just now. Several of the girls were well scattered, delegated to attend, I imagine, by Madame Lily, and told not to huddle in a group. Finally, of those I could place, a couple of the society dames I've mentioned as being 'day-members' of the club. It was one of these, surprisingly, who had suggested that, failing the big prize for literature, I might qualify in another discipline.

Perhaps this was meant as comic relief. Oh, these suburbanite women, at least in our city, are sophisticated to the point of not being beyond a bit of farce, encouraged - who knows? - by Paul's example.

Lastly, there was Maya, sitting in the front row next to a

young man who could well be her latest protege.

'No, I don't have any other qualifications other than literary ones.' I took up the thread again, or one of the several loose ones. 'All I have is my imagination, ladies and gentlemen, and although that is in short supply among astronomers, not to mention astro-physicists, it hardly entitles me to a welcome among their ranks.'

'I shall quote a sentence from Sir Isaac Newton, one of the greatest of them all because he came nearest to combining the pure scientist with the artist. The fusion of the two, however, put too great a tension on even his complexity and unique capability of holding two causally unrelated patterns or images inside the consciousness simultaneously, and he crossed the threshold into what we see as outer darkness, but is, no doubt, something else. But from where communication, as in death, ceases.'

I took what I saw as a necessary breather, but was almost at once reminded that I had been about to quote the great scientist.

- Let's hear what he had to say for himself before he went bonkers, one of the young girls, evidently intoxicated, exclaimed impudently.

'I seem to have been only as a boy playing on the sea shore and diverting myself in now and then finding a smoother pebble or a prettier shell than ordinary, while the great ocean of truth lay all undiscovered before me.'

- Truth, ah truth, the haunting conundrum! (This was Cornelius, evidently also quite drunk which, as I've indicated, required a prodigious amount of alcoholic spirits.) - Pontius Pilate, to give him his due, which he seldom gets among churchmen, was aware of this vast ocean.

By the pocket watch which I'd had the prescience to place on the table, or temporary bar counter, it was time I was beginning to wind down. I well knew that there are several ways of ending these talks, such as by reaching a climax followed by a dramatic curtain, or by a deft summing up of what has constituted the main argument or theory. Neither of these I much favour, certainly not in the present circumstances.

I risked a bold move, though not all that bold, given the

nature and mood of my audience, most of whom, I guessed, were ready for anything that I might come out with.

I reminded them - or more particularly myself - of the occasion and expressed my good wishes for the opening - or re-opening, I was on slightly delicate ground - of the Club Firmament, and wished it well in its ambitious task of preserving its reputation for providing eternal delight while gaining a new one as a prestigious meeting-place for our distinguished   citizens.

11

29

I don't know what proportion, if indeed any, of my listeners heard me say something to them that activated new patterns in the brain cells or neurons. I do know that it affected me, the talk, that is, transporting me back in time three hundred years or so to a lonely sea shore, which, to the eye at least, had changed much, and to a garden which may not have changed at all. And that, in turn, brought me to within a few steps of other gardens, some green and fertile at this moment - Abby's and mine which so far I've neglected to comment on, and one, at least, far more ancient than Newton's mother's, a favourite of Jesus's and his disciples. It is wrong to suppose, and comes from an inattentive reading of the Gospels, that Gethsemane or Golgota was in itself a sinister place to which he only led them as a prelude to his suffering and death. More likely he went there in the hope of gaining some tranquility before what he foresaw, though how precisely we don't know, as the crisis or final epiphany of his shortish life on earth.

Which, belatedly, and, need I say, in all consciousness of the disproportion in all ways of the two events, brings me to my solitary retreats into the small garden at the back of our dwelling.

Only this morning, the morning of the talk, I noted the serrated dandelion leaves protecting the yellow buds and traced the spirals of seeds with a finger on the dark faces of the sunflowers. (Yes, it's autumn, which, if it comes as a surprise, is my fault for failing to keep track of the seasons.)

In the silence that is part of the earthly patience these trellises and whorls, snail shells, inhabited and empty, as well as convolvulus and ivy, are being presented to me as minute blue-prints of reality.

Here our temporal measurements are arbitrary. What we call the four seasons could as well be a dozen, studied more patiently. Not that I am trying to excuse my poor sense of chronology in this report.

I shall take the talk as a static point from which to obtain a fix, in nautical terms, on our present position.

New acquaintanceships were being formed, old ones renewed as the evenings shortened. Philip Weisberg sought Abby and me out and consulted us as to which of the big two-year-old events towards the back-end of the season to run the colt in. A graceful gesture on his part? Yes, and perhaps more than that. He himself confessed that he was not deeply versed in the lore of horse racing and, I think, Abby's blood connection with members of the Arab racing fraternity, now so dominant, impressed him. Besides, although he didn't say so, I imagine that he was determined to resist Paul's impatience to run the animal at the first opportunity.

Who owned the colt? He smiled at Abby's question and, before answering, asked her to whom the sum that he'd fetched at auction was being paid. She surprised me by saying that it was divided half and half between her and her father. (This was not so, but I hope to go into the financial side of all this when it becomes clear to me myself.)

As to the present ownership of Abby's Gift - yes, the name was being retained despite it being a misnomer - it was registered as belonging to the four-member committee that ran the Club Firmament.

If all this was somewhat complicated it did'nt cause us any surprise. But, to use a phrase that had become a private joke between Abby and me (as I mentioned we got it from Dostoevsky, at his wits' end in some German gambling resort) - 'And then an extraordinary event took place!'

Philip - we were soon on first name terms - confided to us that (a) the Zapodeki comet was due to return in early summer (why had I supposed that many years passed between cometary visits? Because the only such heavenly body I'd heard of till then was Haley's?); (b) he was sailing to the vicinity of Cap Breton at the northern tip of Nova Scotia and into Northumberland Sound, which would then be free of ice and navigable; (c) so that Paul and an Indian colleague, Deva Brata Mukerjie - Abby was taking notes - could study the effects on the local environment, in particular the flora, without any ulterior motive. It seemed that Paul had come belatedly to resent what he now saw as the exploitation of pure science, represented by himself, for the commercial or, at least, personal prestige of Prince Ahmed. (d) Abby and I were invited on the voyage.

There would be seven or eight passengers and a crew of five. We made a quick unspoken calculation: Philip - but did he rank as crew or passenger? - Paul (Nicole?), the Indian astro-physicist, Abby, myself, which left two or three strangers. Though, come to that, we didn't know whether they mightn't turn out to be old, or more recent, acquaintances.

Philip was telling us about the ship, nothing very technical, but giving us two landlubbers some notion of what life on a smallish, privately-owned vessel was like. We each took the factualities, a word I use to denote reported rather than imagined facts, and, turning them this way and that to see how they caused a flicker in our fantasy.

Long before the spring voyage, as we thought of it though it was scheduled for early summer, there was this two-year-old contest in which Philip and the colt's trainer decided to run Abby's Gift. It was the main supporting event of the Autumn Derby meeting, and the five supporting races were all prestigious. We studied the list of entries when it appeared in *The Racing Calendar* some weeks before the event took place. I won't go into the technicalities. Although not a handicap, the colt was set to carry, along with three or four others, the lowest weight, because, never having won a race (he hadn't run before), he was not liable to the penalties, in terms of pounds - the extra weight being calculated in proportion to the value of the prizes won. But whereas the other two-year-olds with the minimum weight of 8 st. 11 lbs had failed to win their previous contests, Abby's Gift and one other animal were the only entries seeing a course for the first time. He must have been an exceptionally promising two-year-old or, as Abby said, be an exceptionally bold trainer/owner to put their charge in at the deep end.

Philip invited us to his private box but when the day came Abby, shortly after waking, felt for my hand in bed, pressed it as though imploring patient understanding, and said she couldn't go.

- Not going! For C.... But I broke off in time, ashamed at even the momentary break in emotional communication.

So we stayed at home, but as all the races that afternoon were televised that didn't mean, as I'd immediately concluded, that we couldn't watch what happened. But before the race was shown something shameful and demeaning, at least to those responsible for organising this year's Autumn Derby, and, I believe, reflecting some trace of the supine in our community, took place.

What it came to was a long commercial for a firm of American brewers, with a horse race televised live thrown in. It started ominously with, to every mention of the Autumn Derby, the trade brand of the brewery being pre-fixed. In the end it replaced the 'Autumn' and there were only repeated reiterations that something called the Cadwallider (I'm using a substitute) Derby, sponsored, subsidised and staged by Cadwalliders, was being contested. Furthermore a plot of heath on the opposite side of the race track from the grand stands, a place where the public could go for nothing, a slight hollow traditionally known as Casey's because of a famous bare knuckle fight there in the eighteenth century, had been rechristened 'Cadwallider's Green' where plastic mugs with the firm's slogans were distributed free.

Abby pointed out, despite her state of distraction due to fears for the colt, the fact which I shall, with her help, soon examine, that though the English and French Derbys had their sponsors too, these big businesses had not taken over the events as an exercise in publicity. They were still called the English Derby and the *Prix du Jockey Club*.

The Autumn Derby, which had always ranked not far below these others, I won't comment on. Too conscious of the desecration to one of our national institutions, we sat through it dispirited, though our resentment was obliterated as the time for the big two-year-old race over six furlongs approached.

Abby was valiant, the word 'tough' would not be inappropriate as long as it was understood not to imply any trace of insensitivity. I'd seen her, single-handed, in the dead hours before dawn, deftly dressing an open and suppurating wound. I knew, from what she had told me from the past, such as how she had dealt with the Egyptian who'd been her father's choice as husband, that she had exceptional determination and endurance.

Now when I laid a hand on her I felt the vibration that, coming from her nerve-centre, reached the surface of her body in ripples.

- What is it, Abby? He's only going to have to gallop as he often has on the training ground that is quite close to the actual course, pushed a bit harder, it's true, than he has been before. But he'll be ridden by this Australian jockey from France, not just among the half-dozen best in the world, but, like all Australians, never hard on their mounts, and, in this case, he has been instructed, as Philip told us, to treat him very tenderly.

- It's the world, she said. - It's not easy when you're up against the world for the first time.

- How do you mean, darling?

- The ruthlessness when it comes to money, the awful indifference to the small natural joys and reassurances. Animals are especially dependant on a habitual daily routine, on dusk and dawn, the seasons, the changing environment. Even thoroughbred horses, perhaps even in some ways they're more conscious of their roots in the earth, the far off sandy soil.

Galloping over the desert the Arabian steed feels the winds of heaven blowing between his ears. That's from a Moslem poet.

12

30

There are several ways of describing horse races, from that of the course commentator, the TV commentator, the radio commentator, to the journalistic write-up in next day's papers.

Before introducing mine on the 'Autumn Futurity' for two-year-old colts and fillies run over six furlongs, here are a few words about sport and games in general to set the perspective.

These are trivialities, as the more objective of the life-long addicts are well aware. But trivialities have an important place in the overall metabolism. They provide space and the equivalent of oxygen for the verities to burn in and with.

The outward and visible sign of an advanced community is not its art, which evolves in isolation from - if not in opposition to - social progress, but its architecture and its games. I imagine that among some at any rate of the inhabited planets with a more highly developed communal consciousness than ours this will be evident in their buildings (artefacts) and in their sport.

It isn't just a matter of devising games requiring more skill to play, though with golf-, tennis-, cricket-, base- and football the imagination hasn't come to the end of its flight. These distant communities I'm thinking of must surely be preoccupied with games which come closest to involvement in life itself: games that last for days or perhaps weeks and whose outcome is seldom clear-cut and which thus are only distinguishable while being played from the pressures and hazards of living because the rules are man-made. It may be that in some cases they are played in specially constructed buildings containing, besides arenas and stadiums, living quarters and training grounds, temples too - for these are mystically and not technologically-minded societies. Thus, in my dream of them, the two most evident ways the passer-by -

which is all I can hope to be - can measure how they have out-developed us - in architecture and sport - are combined.

Now, by this rather circuitous diversion, I come back to horse racing which for me is the nearest we have yet come to deliberately reproducing on a microscopic scale some of the intense sensations that are experienced by what we call 'chance'. The 'laws of chance' operate, but not totally or to the exclusion of other partly unknown ones, on the race course, and not mechanistically as at a casino either. It is possible to feel an emotion on the race course not without its affinities to love. And this no doubt was what Abby felt as she had tried to tell me in relation to the colt and the test devised for him.

Yes, once again, an almost incredible thing happened. And, as I think, without checking, a large percentage of these have been purely interior events, so is this. I'll hope to perceive the best words available for what I am trying to put across. It's not a matter any more of interesting those in the audience uninvolved in or indifferent to racing. We're here at the point where either directly or by sleight of thought one of the partners has to see the other, with all the qualities he or she admires so much and fears for, exposed to the powers and principalities of the world. This Mark Anthony must have known during the naval battle when his and Cleopatra's joint fleets were sunk by the emperor Octavian at Actium. And it was my lot to identify Abby with the colt, Abby's Gift, so that it was she who was up against more powerfully equipped opponents.

There was to me nothing forced or fanciful in this shifting the images of woman and animal towards each other across the field of interior vision until they slipped into one. For I was aware of their sharing much that was precious to me. Both came from parts of the world that were still unspoilt by 'development' and unpolluted, the animal from the far north of Nova Scotia and the girl from Arabia Deserta as, despite the hidden lakes of oil, it could still be called.

Love is encompassed by fear and compassion. We try to make our love a shield for the beloved but outside intervention, for which there is no earthly defence, comes between. I saw Thérèse struck down before my eyes and in my arms, and now there was this contest when all was loaded against the animal that for me had become the woman.

The race was run in a downpour, and I recalled what Thérèse had told me about how the weather had seemed to match what was happening to her. The cold Norman nights through which she shivered and the chill rain that fell into the convent garden on those fearful mornings of dereliction, I would always remember.

Now, though, the immediate question is: how did the colt acquit himself? Not spectacularly, far from earning a bracketed note in the record such as 'impressive' or even 'showed promise'. However, he did all that was asked of him, that is the expression the young French-based Australian jockey used when I telephoned him back at Chantilly that evening. I didn't enquire into it further, for that struck me as entirely appropriate. I mean in relation to Abby, who, I believed, would always acquit herself well in a test or crisis, not spectacularly either, not dramatically. But come to that neither had Thérèse in her lifetime.

As for Paul, he was downcast but blamed Weisberg - he dropped his first name - for running the colt before he was ready in the hope of gaining some quick publicity for the club,

Note to the above: The history of almost all the lovers in the Compendium is an obscure and secret one. They had very minor parts in the earthly scenario, in particular perhaps the women. Cleopatra was the great exception and, although I have included her and her Roman Senator in my list, I am not entirely at ease with them.

To serve its, and my, purpose a Compendium such as I envisage must contain a very high proportion of the obscure and unknown. How then can this contradiction be overcome? By a canvas carried on in various communities, a house-to-house questionnaire such as formed the findings of the various Kinsey reports? That, however, was recording sexual practices, not the imponderables of loving relationships. It's a dilemma that the advertisers overcome by having a paid agent come on the air to report: 'More and more of the people I meet are putting their money into...'

Publicity, political, commercial, cultural, is based on

deception and fallacy. To keep ahead in the competitive world requires gaining the attention of the largest possible number of voters, consumers, readers.

Obscurity, at the very other end of the communal spectrum, is essential to the growth of love into a consoling power that embraces pain and worldly defeat.

Though this sounds like quotes from a lecture delivered to an extra-mural audience at a small university, it is in fact a summing-up of several discussions with Abby between the race and the next outstanding event in our normally quiet existence: the voyage on the yacht.

A high-powered, sturdy boat that can take a lot of bruising and come up again, resilient and vigorous. I'm quoting its owner. When we were taken to see the vessel it struck me as smallish and quite unimposing, but that was probably because it was docked at a wharf where freighters were being loaded. It was only gradually, several days after sailing, that I began to take in the life at sea and our habitation.

It was, away from the cargo boats and the buildings across the street, larger than I'd thought, and there were more of us on board than I'd expected. Besides Philip, Paul, the Indian physicist, Abby, myself and a crew of half-a-dozen, including the chef and cabin boy, there were, surprisingly, Maya with a man companion (her presence I'll come back to shortly), a couple of young women whom I supposed were from the club, and, for once, had supposed correctly, and an individual whom Philip referred to as the ship's doctor.

Among the more vivid of the new impressions: a lift, although there were only three stops, or floors, or decks (I was slow in adapting to nautical terms), the library, some of the contents of which I'll have time to describe and even comment on, the bar at one end of the dining saloon, open at scheduled hours, and, displayed in the library and on a table in the dining saloon as well as in the cabins I'd been shown, including our own, a brochure about the Galapagos islands with glossy coloured photos and, on the cover, the caption: 'A fascinating opportunity to follow in the wake of the survey ship, HMS Beagle, and to ponder on the origin of many species you will see at close quarters.'

This, I took it, was a relic of the last voyage, but, reverting to the normal pattern of my suppositions, was wrong.

The half-absent-minded - as if part of her was still on land - unhurried, almost stately approach adopted by Abby to this new life is the one that I'm following in my own words. I'll begin on the evening of the second day at sea - the first was hard to grasp or clarify even in retrospect - and much of the second Abby and I spent in our cabin coming to ourselves, which included making love. Then, at aperitif time - kept with the more ceremony for there being not a speck of land in sight - most of the passengers and the captain gathered at the bar.

After a drink or two the conversation that at first was self-contained and private between the couples, as most of us were, began to spread and merge. Boyd Robertson - this was Maya's friend, I won't at this stage say 'protege' - addressed the captain.

- I heard the pumps last night, Skipper, spotted them beneath the drone of the diesels. Just a routine precaution to see that all is ship-shape, eh?

The captain dismissed the suggestion but Boyd Roberts - I had the name slightly wrong first time - insisted.

- I spent some time afloat, know what I'm talking about, Skipper.

I already disliked him, as is evident I imagine, and was delighted when Paul intervened.

- Afloat on the Grand Canal and the Cam, wasn't it, Mr. Boyd-Roberts?

I glanced at Maya and regretted, for old times' sake, my spitefulness. It was then I realised that it was Paul who had distributed the Galapagos brochure and that some of the guests - Maya and Boyd-Roberts among them - thought that this was where we were going.

Later that evening, the third - I want to keep strict track of time which on a ship, as in a monastery, is divided into watches and *horae* - Philip asked, on the intercom, whether he could have a talk and, if so, should he come to our cabin.

Philip wasn't nervous, diffident perhaps, though that isn't
the word either. Not that it's important enough to spend time
looking for the right one. He kissed Abby - one, two, both
cheeks with the lightly ash-dusted sheen, pressed my hand
and said:

- A pity this trip hasn't started that well, and paused as if
to give us - me - the chance to contradict or at least demur.
But I'd no intention of doing so.

- You must be wondering about some of those on our list of
guests.

'Our?' But let it pass.

- We haven't had time or cause to do much criticising as
yet. It's more a matter of pleasant surprises: a library in the
middle of the ocean - we had a look round it after dinner - the
bar, and the sea itself, though that's in a different category.
Abby who wasn't saying much, was, I think, a little
apprehensive at my flow of words.

- I wasn't entirely free in my choice. Maya, as you probably
know, is a sponsor, responsible, that is, for all the overheads
on the voyage.

What did that amount to? Everything apart from the fuel
and the crew's wages?

- And that meant taking this Boyd-Roberts punter (on the
Cam! Ha! Ha!) along. Then there was a quite unexpected
intervention by the Nobel Prize Committee requesting we
take an official of theirs who was to remain incognito, though
I'm sure you had your suspicions when I introduced him as
the ship's doctor.

- Need I tell you, Joel, he'd be very welcome if he was
checking up on you instead, as I believe is the present state
of play, on our Indian friend.

All this was strange, and I foresaw it would engender
much discussion between Abby and me.

Perhaps you're also disappointed at some absences, Nicole's
for instance. And, of course, your friend - he looked at Abby -
Rebecca and the old man, and I, too, would gladly have
offered them the last available cabin in place of the two
birds, or rather pigeons as they'll turn into if they forego the

strict diet imposed at the 'Firmament' and guzzle as they are doing.

- Oh, and by the way (Abby remarked later that when a type such as Weisberg adopted a casual air it was a screen behind which to indulge his malpractices) take no notice of the Galapagos business, just a bit of Paul's clowning, though for a purpose.

Yes, his renewal of his sex with Rebecca had been casual and incidental, as she'd told us about it. Almost the identical 'take no notice of it' to her as to us in reference to the Galapagos islands, which we were still utterly in the dark over. Not that it was one of our first concerns, nor had it for us as much of a curiosity value as, say, had the presence of the two Firmament girls, Lisette and Anne, (one of them appeared to change her name later, I'm not sure which) who, as by now we'd grasped, were the special guests of Philip.

Here I'll interpolate some reflections, based on notes I took at our departure. There was a farewell party on the after-deck, to which the bar had been transferred and from which the gangway led to the quayside. (The yacht, unlike the freighters, was moored by the stern.) Some people, mostly middle-aged to elderly gentlemen out for a stroll round the harbour, had stopped to look on. And among those whom they took to be seeing us off - how they distinguised these from the passengers I don't, of course, know, perhaps from their attire, though none of us, except Boyd-Roberts, was got up in anything like yachting gear - were the girls.

When the gangway was pulled in and, instead of tripping down it, they disappeared, with a wave, through the door into the deck house, these old gentlemen out with their dogs had a thrill of envy and regret. I know, because I've been in the same situation: outside, looking in.

There they were, Lisette in miniskirt, Anne in new-type, non-tight, pale blue denim, voluntarily captive for God knew how long, a lunar month at least - a suggestive phrase - never more than a few yards away, say forty feet at most. This they mulled over, no doubt, as they returned to their secure but dullish habitats.

Later that evening Maya called us - we saw that we must decide to leave the intercom off its cradle if we were to keep to our habit of early hours - and invited us to her stateroom, that's what I think she said, though it was just like ours to which it was next door.

At least she was alone. I imagined her latest protege in the bar, if it hadn't closed, relating his seafaring adventures to whoever was doing duty as barman - certain of the crew took this on. Maya herself wasn't quite sober, not that that was noticeable to anyone who didn't know her well.

- Do you remember the evening it all started, darling? she asked me.

I nodded, There was no point in asking what she was talking about, as I would hear soon enough.

- When I pointed out Paul's dimly lit window, the electricity cut off, and told you there lives a genius in obscurity and penury, little did I think that in three or four short years he would be famous (he had been famous then) and that we'd be involved with him in this voyage to Galapagos to carry out tests which may refute Darwin's theory of the origin of species once and for all.

Yes, this took my breath away, though not to the point of speechlessness till she said to Abby: - I'm so glad to see your charge well on the way to recovery, nurse.

I'm not giving a verbatim report, but the gist and tone. Was this a joke? But Maya wasn't much given to comic remarks. No, there was always a deposit of gossip in our city from which numbers of the circle to which Maya belonged could collect information which they believed was 'inside', confidential and accurate. And in this case 'common knowledge'.

This particular rumour evidently had to do with my state of health, very possibly my mental one. I made a rapid survey of recent incidents, aware that quite trivial ones could, in Maya's circle and some adjacent, be seen as evidence of what had only been suspected. For instance, my talk at the opening of Club Firmament, an occasion which itself had aroused some unfavourable comments.

- He'd got through a half-bottle of spirits by the time I slipped out.

- An Asiatic lady who I heard was his day-nurse was in attendance.

- Three people out of the forty present claimed to have been able to follow him.

- Would any writer of his standing who was in his right mind have agreed to make a public appearance at such a disgraceful occasion?

Remarks made independently at the time, suppositions I admit, but in accord with the majority reaction.

Maya wasn't malicious. I don't know what she was except wealthy with a motherly sexuality, and the need to feel drama all around her while remaining cool, wise, sympathetic and uninvolved. Like one of the women of days gone by, whose salons were frequented by all sorts of people, mostly men, none of them entirely obscure, seeking moral or physical sustenance.

Back in our cabin; darkness and desolation. I don't think I'm given to dramatisation - though the poet - to use the term in a general way - is often blind to his or her worst flaws. It is not that we were suddenly two strangers trapped, say, in a stalled lift. I've experienced sudden loss of temporary (though I couldn't foresee this comforting aspect) communication with a person close to me. This was different.

It is over-bold and spiritually arrogant to suppose that there are no counter-flows, currents in the black waters under the earth, to reverse the illumination and heavenly transports of our union.

Had we been able to ask each other what had overtaken us, we would have been saved, spared, that is, what ensued which will try my descriptive skills to make convincing. If even we could have touched one another, but touch, contact, physical, emotional, was utterly beyond us. (Imagine that! I couldn't have a short time ago.) Perhaps I've been negligent or too indulgent in this compilation in not drawing attention - my own as well as yours - to being puzzled by certain twists some of the love stories had taken. It's only now I begin to see that they were the outward signs of the couple falling apart, of a fission between them causing psychologically - but atomically too possibly, because we are also molecular in structure, disruption.

When this happens, as now came back to me in my reinterpretation of what at the time I hadn't grasped, all conspires to aggravate the horror.

They hide away, these stricken lovers, not so much from one another but from the new person he or she is, with its sense of loss of all that it - and I use the pronoun deliberately - was composed of.

We couldn't flee. We were on a small vessel where every corner was occupied, in the middle of an ocean. Did it occur to me that while these circumstances increased the torment, they also offered a simple way out? Yes, in a sense. To climb on deck or take the lift one floor, if I was capable of operating it, and jump overboard. For which the resolution - energy - wasn't there. If it had been, even a slight trace of what had once seemed a rich deposit, I, we, could have used it to raise a groping hand above us to ascertain whether there was any grip on the sides of the pit.

We crawled into bed and I lay in a kind of cold stupor, partly self-induced to stop me thinking of the days, and weeks perhaps, ahead on this ship with all the outward observations and social niceties to conform to with this puncture in a ventricle of the heart through which was draining away the life blood.

Some sentences, not visually composed nor spoken either, but seeming to be drawn together, word by word, out of the surrounding chaos, entered my mind:

'With cheerful confidence I shall stay gazing at the sun until I die... If thick clouds hide it and if it seems that nothing beyond the night of this life....' Here she breaks off before committing what she would have seen as a blasphemy. Yes, the words are from the last couple of pages of *The Autobiography of St. Thérèse of Lisieux*.

She continues: 'I stay away from you and soil my wings in the dirty puddles of the world. if you remain hidden I shall just stay wet and numb with cold.'

Poorly written, probably when numb with the physical cold of her cell - the French is somewhat better - I realised that she was trying to describe this very condition that had overwhelmed Abby and myself. And furthermore that - despite all contrary indications - she believed it was not only an essential part of the intense experience of love, but, once survived....

I put out a hand and touched Abby.

13

Abdallah Consolatrix: one of my more solemn names for her.
It wasn't that she had taken Maya's words, spoken not in jest
but in ignorance, to heart, nor that my failure in the earlier
part of the previous night to lift us out of the pit had, apart
from the terror of the desolation, worried her as indicating a
diminution of my usual spirit, but I think a trace of these
and other oblique incidents had a part in her surprising
suggestion next morning.

Before I come to that, though, I can't leave out how the
night ended, though by then it was almost dawn because
after a very active - would 'violent' be going too far? - bout of
love-making, we sat up in bed, sweaty and appeased and saw
through the window - it was more than a porthole - a slightly
tarnished silvery gleam along the far edge of the ocean. Not
spread smooth in one long stroke but, as if falling on the
scales of an enormous fish, in separate quanta. Later, I heard
that this was a sign of bad weather to come.

- The seafarer next door will think he heard the pumps
being operated again last night, Abby remarked with her
innocent- lecherous look. What sort of look is that? Oh, it
would take a visual artist of considerable talent to depict and
it would be nothing like Mona Lisa's.

What she suggested was that I spend the day in our cabin,
reading (she would fetch books from the library down the
companion-way), bringing these notes up to date, meditating,
and giving her a thought now and then, as she modestly put
it.

So there it was again: world history, sacred scripture,
repeating itself personally. The dove soaring out from the ark
to take stock of the situation, though there the parallel
ended, for I hadn't, need I mention, any trace of this first
great navigator in my blood, wasn't in fact an explorer at all,
but more of the hermit *maudite*.

The weather worsened. The fast, small, sturdy ship (over-powered for its tonnage, one of the know-alls had remarked) took the waves head-on, or so I concluded from the bucking of the cabin floor, each fall ending in a crash that was more of shattering hardware than watery collision.

I wasn't incommoded, a discovery that boosted my morale, not that it was low this morning, though I was beset by the usual temptation to disbelief, my intermittant lack of firm resolve.

At lunch-time, as if he kept to his habitual timetable - surgery 9 - 12.30, visiting patients 1 - 2.30 pm, 'the ship's doctor' called to see me. Sent by Abby? I wasn't sure, and he didn't say so, simply introduced himself as Soren Wangel, an admirer of Ibsen (he probably didn't announce this straight off, but it certainly came up later in the talk). I was rather discountenanced - as if unexpectedly under some disadvantage, at least health-wise - by his appearance.

- Tell me, frankly, Mr Samuel, would you care for a thorough check-up, as thorough as I can make it outside my consulting room? It's an opportunity that I suppose doesn't often arise in your life ashore, as I know from some of my patients who postpone coming to me till it's too late because, as they say, they hadn't a minute! Though what they lacked was courage.

- Very kind of you, doctor.

I needed a moment to think this over. Was it purely altruistic? Was he just keeping his hand in, so to say, on a tedious trip? If so, why had he come on it? What made me agree was the possibility that Abby had asked him to look me over. And, to a lesser extent, his half-aside mutter that there was no question of a fee.

He used the intercom to ask the seriously-overworked cabin boy to bring his case of medical supplies and instruments from his state-room to mine.

- I didn't want to alarm you by appearing with all the paraphenalia.

No. But he alarmed me by sending for it now after he'd had time to take a good look at me. Well, perhaps I'm joking, but not to the extent of being overcome by a sense of the comedy.

The mobile laboratory arrived, not actually wheeled in as I half envisaged but intimidatingly large. I undressed and lay, face upward at first, on the bed, the movement of which didn't appear to discommode the doctor.

He asked me whether I was suffering from any particular disability or ailment. Was there a difference? I didn't ask, wishing as rapid as possible a conclusion to the whole business. As for his question, I didn't mention my sinusitis, which I haven't mentioned either in this report, waiting to see if he would detect it on his own.

Cardiac, respiratory and metabolic monitoring, though what this entailed in regard to the latter I didn't determine. A prolonged pressure on the left side of the belly with his fingers, a plumbing of the flesh. Had he discovered a distended liver, could he actually determine a high degree of sponginess without the evidence of X-rays? Or was there an occlusion - no that wasn't the clinical term - an incipient stoppage in the bowel? Incipient because I hadn't as yet experienced the symptoms. (Straining at stool, a few drops of blood?)

- Turn over, Mr Samson, and at the same time relax.

Had I been tensing my muscles in a crazy attempt to prevent possible fatal discoveries?

Then, out of the blue, or, more precisely, the lower intestines, the investigation changed its clinical aspect into a cultural one. But gradually.

- Mr Samuel, I can give you a clean bill of health as the saying is. Apart, that is, from one or two comparatively minor matters. (Like what, for God's sake, cancer of the ...?) Such as chronic infection of the sinus cavities. (Ah, a skilled practitioner, despite what I'd heard, or misheard.)

As you may have gathered - a shipboard community is not bound by a vow of silence, not the other monastic ones either - I happen to be a member of the *Svenska Akademiens Nobelkommitte.*

A pause. Should I express appreciation? Come out with, say: - An august body, Doctor Wangel (having retained the name in my mind despite the recent distraction). However, he was resuming: - There has been some misapprehension. I'm not a member of the committee that collects information from around the world and evaluates the work of scientists as, it appears, somebody told our Indian fellow guest.

Paul, no doubt, had been behind whatever misapprehension existed. Very likely a mix-up had occurred earlier as well, which I reconstructed (- May I dress now, doctor?) while putting my clothes on: the doctor had visited the Firmament brothel during one of the international cultural conferences held in our city. Madame Lissik, with her eye for even minor celebrities, had got it out of him, or one of her girls, that he was a distinguished Dutchman, inventor of a component for, and here of course vagueness and loss of curiosity had intervened.

When the voyage was being planned, quite a time ago, though Abby and I were unaware of it, Nicole had recalled Madame Lissik's confidential account of 'an internationally famous scientist' who was one of her clients having, in the course of an absorbing conversation, told her that for him our city had two outstanding claims to fame: the Firmament itself and as the residence of the great controversial physicist, Paulus Keller.

So the invitation had gone to Stockholm, sent, in this surely not uningenious reconstruction, by Nicole, without Paul's knowledge. Had Paul been consulted he probably had enough information on the membership of the adjudicators for the prize for science to have realised the mistake.

Mistake or not, he was pleased to be aboard, he told me, with such delightful company. He surprised me a little by mentioning the two girls, calling them Lisette and Enala, of which Ann, the name by which I'd been introduced to her, didn't sound like a diminutive. However this had no great significance - the Firmament girls often changed their first names or added, like Rebecca-Maria, a second one.

No, I'd never imagined that he had accepted the invitation when hearing that I was one of the guests. I don't sponsor extravagant flights of fancy when it comes to myself as a writer.

But now that he was on board, and in my cabin, I didn't mind indulging him in his other, non-medical, calling which I guessed was his principal preoccupation.

Yes, I'd known W. B. Yeats quite well, and had also had a

youthful friendship with Mr Samuel Beckett though later our
paths had divided, even quite dramatically.
- And never crossed again?
No need for a reply. What if they had? It was a memory I
didn't want to air. The doctor was off on an easier tack,
sailing with the wind.
The woods of Arcady are dead
And over is their antique fog -
Naturally, I didn't correct him.
Of old the world on dreaming fed
Grey truth is now her painted toy.
- Not only profoundly true but beautifully put? he
commented.
Who was I to disagree?
- What a master!
Of dramatic attitudes. But why be manoeuvred into the
position of nagger or niggard? Let sleeping dogs lie and dead
poets rest either in glory or obscurity, both are hard to come
by.
The doctor left with a warm handshake and a nod that
might have meant anything, the sort that seems to signal:
Make what you like of that. But, having developed a certain
discipline in these ways, I didn't entertain for more than a
brief moment the thought that what an adjudicator for this
year's destination of the Big Lollipop was very discreetly
intimating was something in the line of: This visit wasn't
merely to carry out a physical examination, as I'm sure
you've guessed. It would have been inappropriate,
embarrassing even to us both, to quote from your work, but
I'm familiar with it, as our host will confirm, and when it
comes to making my submission to our conclave, besides my
own conclusion, I shall cite some prestigious critics.

- 33 -

Between the doctor's departure and the return of the dove
with her news, I had a brief interlude in which I gathered
news of my own. Not, naturally, immediate developments

and events in life on board, but news from the past of a not-unsensational kind. News in fact of the *Tour de France*, irrelevant as that may seem.

It was long ago and I was watching it pass from a hotel room in Nice. I remember there was a green jersey in the leading group and I'd always had a sneaking regard for the Irish, though not claiming a drop of Celtic blood.

I was with my very first girl, though it could be said an exaggeration to call her that considering I hadn't penetrated her - though intimate in almost every other way - and never did.

A knock on the door and *le patron* came in followed by a young man in dark glasses and a local *poule,* her face a mask of bizarre make-up. Would *monsieur et madame* permit *monsieur et madame X* to view the great sporting event as regrettably their room looked onto the courtyard?

The man was Paul. Why have I only mentioned this now? Didn't I recall it to him at our first re-meeting? My silence in the first instance and failure - if that's what it was - to tell Paul - who evidently had not taken much note of me at the time - was behaviour that in, say, a criminal trial in which I was the accused could be made to weigh heavily against me. Supposing, that is, I claimed that I was watching the *Tour de France* in Nice when the prosecution suggested I was battering almost to death an old lady in Paris and I produced a friend of mine, claiming our first meeting had been in the circumstances described on the day in question. And, in the witness box, he, terribly distressed, admitted that though, yes, he had seen the famous contest from another room than his own, he didn't recollect its being occupied!

That mightn't alone have been enough to ensure I was found guilty, but an alibi that is demolished does a lot of harm to the accused. What I'm getting at is that my neglect to mention the incident earlier in this report or to Paul at all, I don't suppose will make any reader think I'm inventing it, such lying for one thing being motiveless, and, for another, I having gained, as I hope, a considerable degree of trust from my audience.

Vive la France! It was a French victory that year, the same one, and the same day, in which an old woman was found severely injured and robbed in the St Denis suburb of Paris. The difference between the two events being - apart from the more obvious - that one reported and transformed fact and the other imagined fiction, though both unite in the art of the novelist.

These absorbing musings were broken off by Abby's stately entrance, just as she used to enter the ward. She didn't bring back any startling gossip, not that I expected her to, gossip was not a feature of her quiet and rather narrow street. What was up it were confessions of a sensual sort, such as Maria-Rebecca related. So I asked her if she'd come across the Firmament girls or were they keeping to their cabin as, it seemed, most of the voyagers were.

She'd run into them, if you could call it that because it happened at the ship's social centre, the bar. Before that, she'd had a conversation with Maya in which, as can happen with women and is perhaps why their fallings-out are not as nasty or have less malicious connotations than those between men, they exchanged enough intimate confessions to efface the unfortunate turn the trialogue had taken the day before.

- I told her just enough of why we were together to make her see how silly she'd been about us.

I'd heard that women had a secret language and shared a coded communication system, such as oppressed and subjugated people develop, in which it is very difficult to lie. This is because, as distinct from the dire necessity to prevaricate and conform to expectations in the men-and-women world, it, like scripture, if in a more personal manner, could only deal in verities.

- And what did Maya tell you?

- Mostly what I might have guessed, though there were one or two surprises.

- Go on, darling.

She usually waited for me to have to ask before telling me what she'd learnt in strict secrecy (which her confidante knew did not apply to a lover).

- She doesn't sleep with her sailor.

- What *do* they do?

- Oh, I don't know. Copulation isn't the alpha and omega for women as it is for most men. That's biologically understandable.

I could pick up a lot like this about matters that psychologists have devoted volumes to and then not got it right. But I sensed that my dove had flown back with more than a few green twigs. She was weighed down, and at the same time, lifted up by what she had to tell me in her own time, which was never in a hurry.

Reverting to the expedition that she was partly, largely, financing, Maya mentioned the Argonauts, but didn't develop the comparison, probably for lack of historicial or mythical knowledge.

It was in Abby's head that the symbol glowed with the invisible rays that recalled a much more recent quest: the golden fleece; the comet's tail or coma!

In the ancient story the symbol fitted uneasily at its heart, unassimilated, ambiguously depicted and, in the end, a treasure whose seeking was more important than its possession.

Where did this new leap leave us? Or rather Paul, for neither Abby nor I were inextricably committed to his theories. But I realised that from where we now were we could, if we wanted, trace patterns, follow what, in physics, would consist of new arrangements of atoms into traditional or classic molecular structures which, under close scrutiny, turned out to have one minute deviation, a mysterious link with - and prophecy of - the future.

And with the past. Coming down to solid earth and the hot streets of Nice on that July day many years ago, had Paul seen the yellow jersey, worn that morning by a Frenchman, as an objectivisation of something in the subconscious symbolising the never-ceasing quest?

No, he had not. For one thing he was too preoccupied with his little *Nicecoise* whom he soon drew from the window to the bed.

What about you? Abby asked.

I told her about the doctor's examination and his diagnosis of sinus infection, but not of my anxiety at what he might discover. I didn't want her to have to make an adjustment, a toning down, in the image she had of me: if not the bravest of the brave, which could only go with some poverty of imagination, but intrepid in the face of the daily threats and aggression of fate.

An altogether different fear has just struck me. A sign of the lessening of associative awareness in the brain, which I've seen happen to once competent novelists. I have never mentioned that this ship is called the Argonaut! And on Paul's suggestion. To forestall any nigglers, though such types are unlikely to have stuck it out thus far, their vessel was the Argo.

What were heroes? Jason and his band just hadn't known what was ahead of them when they set out. One day I would confess to Abby my wretched inner deportment under the doctor's hands, but not now, not, I thought, till conditions were right and I could set alongside this, by then, distant failure of nerve some casual-seeming - oh, nothing showy - act of valour.

Abby hadn't run out of surprises, each of a different sort. She had had a long conversation with the captain who, it turned out, was Russian, Chaim Magressen, in his quarters directly beneath the bridge.

- Didn't it strike you that he might make what's called advances once he had you there?

She paused. To consider this in her unhurried way? To find out how to put the fact that he *had* tried something on while making it clear to me that she had not wavered for the briefest heart beat on the other side of that indefinable threshold beyond which clouds gather and the star of faithfulness, a binary one, is obscured?

- I was prepared for that, Joel. There are so many things always to be prepared for. But I knew by the way he closed the door and hung his cap on it that there'd be nothing like that. He'd overheard us at dinner, last night was it?, talking of Soutine, a namesake of his, and he said, yes, Russian artists meant what they said and mean it in a way that has little to do with art or literature. They had something that foreigners couldn't at first make out, a quality that they've never come across in other cultures. He asked if I hadn't felt it, and if you, he knew you were a writer, hadn't. I said yes, we had. Do you know, Joel, what he said it was? Purity.

Yes, and he knows what he's talking about which is fine for

you and me, but to those engaged in the free-for-all ball game being played in the big world what he told you about having skippered the Onassis yacht when Jacqueline was on board is of far more interest.

But, at the risk of seeming to try to reactivate a possibly flagging interest in the audience, I can announce that: then a most extraordinary event took place.

No, not perhaps dramatic or sensational in the accepted sense, we weren't in collision with a Russian submarine that had been tracking us all the way.

That night in bed, long after Abby, as I could tell from her breathing, was asleep I was visited by demons or spirits of enlightenment, depending on my own response.

Oh, it wasn't a simple visitation, preceded by a knock on the door of consciousness, but an infiltration through, at first, my obsession with words. Neuropathetic, egomaniac, infantilism, erotomaniac, *folie de grandeur*. Was there, I wondered - with my liking for parcelling and tying up - anybody, historical or fictitious, to whom all these clinical diagnoses applied? And then, gently and tactfully, a name came to mind: Thérèse Martin, St. Thérèse de Lisieux.

From then on, the outer defences stormed, this new theory completely took over. The childhood incident when shown a packet of trinkets and she and her sister, Celine, were told to choose something from it. Celine selected a piece of braid but Thérèse announced she chose the lot.

She was cossetted and spoilt. her secret ambitions were unmeasurable. There was no outlet for them in a middle class suburban household in a middle-sized Norman town. She must enter the Carmelite convent which was part of a large and famous congregation and astonish it with her piety. But once a professed nun it wasn't so easy. She was treated like everyone else, even, she thought, with less consideration. Her patience, self-effacement, pious practices were getting her nowhere. Very well, if her dream was to be dashed on earth, it would come true in heaven. After her death she would be revered as a great saint. But even that wasn't enough, so in her autobiography she took into her own mouth the words of Jesus Christ at the Last Supper (St John Ch 17) addressed to the Father.

'I have glorified Thee on earth, I have finished the work which Thou gavest me to do... I pray not for the world, but for those whom Thou has given me, because they are Thine, and Thine are mine, and I am glorified in them... I will that where I am, they also who Thou has given me may be with me, that they may see the glory which Thou hast given me...'

Pathological self-glorification induced by the frustration of her actual situation? On this earth the last and the least but afterwards a godess to whom the devout would turn in their small miseries.

And so they did, and what's more, they had their prayers answered. What a farce! No wonder that Paul, who had a knowledge of human, as well as of cosmic nature, went in for what we called clowning, by way of getting out of his system, perhaps, a sour sense of the tricks fate played on us. He wanted to have the last laugh, prove that his sense of the comic was at least up to the universal one.

Thérèse, I couldn't long evade her by thinking of Paul, had no sense of humour. She sent out a wedding invitation with a graphic design of the coat of arms of Jesus and her own (customary on such occasions among the nobility of nineteenth century France) to the other nuns and her relatives outside the convent.

It was touch and go. If the demons had turned out to be spirits of enlightenment then somebody who had been guide and inspiration to me, beyond that of any great writer or philosopher, would have been debased and accounted a pathological, if harmless, fake. As in fact a large proportion of those who had heard of her took her to have been.

But hadn't I known her intimately, lived with her in the same rented room? Only imaginatively, yes. But, as this report attests to the point of boredom, imagination is, in its true, disciplined, painful operation, the highest achievement - except love, which is hardly an achievement - of the human brain.

It was this precious faculty that saved me from losing faith in her, and I did not care to think of all else, with such a deprivation, that would be undermined.

Ah, Thérèse - I have made this section of the report, hiding or keeping back nothing of what could, and has been, said about you. For that increases your unique place, not just among saints, but among women. Do you recall the bare-foot pilgrimage I made to a shrine of yours in a distant part of Paris from a smart hotel I was staying in, taking my shoes off once out of the foyer, but returning with bloody feet staining the carpet? And which will be later repeated.

Here I will add an extract from a book I read lately - from the ship's library - about sacred and profane love.

Of the dark night of the soul as experienced by mystics (commented on by Thérèse) the author writes:

'Since the Christian mystics are so prone to make use of the imagery and phraseology of human love when speaking of the love of the soul, it may be permitted to reverse the simile and consider how improbable would be a comparable occurrence in the love of the heart. Jealousy, quarrels and suspicions, those human failings, we may disregard since they have no counterpart in man's striving towards God; but is it conceivable that a happy love, a love fulfilled and reciprocated... should undergo such intervals of utter blank, when the thought or presence of the beloved should bring no stirring, no excitement, no transport, no response, no glow?'

Not only conceivable, dear madame, but we have been through it, Abby and I, as I have related. Which ties up the kind of men-women relationships that I am researching in this Compendium with those between certain human inhabitants of this planet to the Being from whom they receive intimations that have the unpreconceivable lineaments of truth.

I woke Abby up to tell her all was well.

She murmured something I didn't catch. Then she felt under the pillow.

- I meant to show you the menu.

But she fell asleep again before she had found it.

14

34

Who said Thérèse had no sense of humour? What about the time I asked her for the winner of the 1950 or '51 Prix du Jockey Club and she told me *Tantieme,* which many people at Chantilly that afternoon, including his jockey, was sure had passed the winning post in front, but the judge without a photo-finish camera gave the race to Scratch?

Perhaps she acquired it in heaven. As for this planet, things are becoming deadly earnest and, simultaneously, banal, and there's little room for comedy in between (all the more credit to Paul!). When the first computer laughs it'll be time to apply for an exit visa, because it won't be laughing at itself.

She - yes, I'm on about Thérèse again - once asked me if in the city I came from there were many street girls. I said I thought there were quite a few and also some brothels.

- If I'd entered a brothel instead of Carmel I'd have put my whole heart into pleasing the clients and there'd have been two or three, say one in every twenty, to whom, when we talked afterwards, I'd have put in a word that would have borne fruit in his heart.

How simple love is! And, to those who know the ways of the world, heartbreaking.

Which is why contemporary spirituality is so depressing. Everything is horribly difficult, God a negative entity. Karl Barth who, after his death, was made a spokesman of this school, declared: 'If anyone supposes God is waiting for them at the end of the road, it isn't God.' That Barth ran foul of the Nazis did him no harm posthumously, of course. Nor Dietrich Boenhoffer who, though, was a saint. Though neither were great prophets, of which we have had three in our time: Einstein, Wittgenstein and Heidegger, two Germans, an Austrian, two of them Jews.

Supposing I asked Thérèse to send us a storm. In her

whole-heartedness it might well be one to sink our ship, without loss of life presumably.

Discussing God with Abby, she said the Muslim divinity was a cousin of Jehovah's and that Mohammed, unlike the Gospel Jesus, hadn't done much to make himself companionable. But that was the official and organised version. She spoke of, and even quoted from, Muslim mystics such as Ibn Araki in the thirteenth century, a book of whose aphorisms her father had given her on her thirteenth birthday.

However, I'm not compiling an anthology from the sayings of prophets, hermits and anchorites throughout history.

The weather got worse. Had I said that prayer inadvertently? I'm joking, of course.

Then, one late summer afternoon, eight or nine days after we had set out from our city, the M.V. Argonaut sailed into the deep-water sound, or estuary, between the Canadian towns of Halifax and Dartmouth.

Rooms had been booked for us - some of us, others were remaining on board - at the Hotel Nelson, the only old-fashioned hostelry in probably the whole of Nova Scotia. I mention this not because it has any obvious relevance to what I'm about to relate but simply because after a fairly detailed depiction of the yacht I don't want to leave our next habitat, a brief if unforgettable one, up, so to say, in the air.

We have been - the excursion formed, from several angles, a considerable earlier section of the story - to the new continent before, but that was different. For one thing it was taken up with the strange and sensational events I reported at second hand and was not involved in. This time if the continent was about to once more be brushed by the comet from outer space it was, to my private knowledge, going to be enriched from inner space, from the treasure trove I bore in my consciousness. Of course the continent was unaware of both these prospects and would almost certainly remain so after they had taken place. Though, as far as I was concerned, to carry here a consciousness so absorbed in love relations and adventures, must brush off into other minds and nerve systems now and then, or here and there. That, though largely unrecorded in history, is what took place with the early colonisers. As well as the effects of their rapacity and, usually, brutality, they brought and left traces of modes of living, suffering and consoling quite unknown in the new lands, which is not to deny that these new lands had their own ethos, myths and scriptures which suffered as a consequence.

Above all, however, it was between Abby and me that there was an upsurge, and insurge.

It was *as if* we had been separated on the yacht, meeting at meals, but not sitting next to each other, catching each other's eye across the table, once or twice standing aside to let her pass in the narrow companion way, exchanging a half smile that, on my part, may have turned into a half frown of frustration. Now, I say 'as if', a mysterious phrase though not quite mysterious enough to express what is experienced sometimes in very close and intimate relationships. We are in need of a new   word, perhaps more than one, to keep up with the evolution taking place in thought and instinct.

'If', 'as if', introducing alternative situations, real and imaginary. 'If you hadn't missed the plane', 'If we'd met five years ago', 'if only you'd be patient'...

If it had not been for my previous experience before meeting Abby, for my fear of impotence, that is, I would never have become so sex-conscious. As long as I was in youthful animal health there wasn't the time or the necessity for sensuality. Abby, like many women, was sensually aware to start with.

So these two near-strangers who had been denied the hour alone together they'd have given the world for because of the cramped conditions on the small ship, but nevertheless, for the same reason, were in daily sight, and almost touch, of each other, were now let loose together in a room with bathroom, toilet and a lock on the door. That is how it felt, not only to me, but to Abby, an 'as if' situation which only from one angle, that of objective factuality, did not take place.

Note: You don't have to be contaminated by one of Paul's comas to host the passion virus. It is there in the human genes even if it lies dormant. In rare cases it combusts in a passion for power or conquest, but for the most part psycho-

Francis Stuart

physically in sensuality. In most long-standing relationships, having flared briefly, it wanes through lack of fuel - a sketchy explanation but I don't want to be side-tracked - and seeks new partners with whom it can be revived, though again short of a great conflagration. This last only happens gradually, or rather in the by now familiar small leaps or quanta, and requires a stable relationship, a faithfulness.

A high degree of imagination and energy, with a few lesser chemical and spiritual ingredients, coming together in the one human receptable, sparks off the fiery sequence. Even at this late point I should stress once more that what I mean by imagination has nothing to do with flights of fancy or day-dreaming. It is one of the only two modes of experiencing. St Paul - who knew this and expected his correspondents to when describing the great event in his life which happened on the road to Damascus - writes, 'Whether in the body or out of the body, I know not', using the phrase 'out of the body' as the equivalent to 'imagination', a word not available to him, or familiar to those to whom he was writing.

Abby and I had come to the newer continent not with a bible, like the earlier settlers, nor, need I say, with any idea of conversion, but with our privately engendered passion that illuminated one room at the Nelson for the two nights and days we spent there.

As I've indicated previously, there's no need to set down the sensual details. Words won't burn up the page and therefore though they might titillate, they would be in danger of being interpreted in the light of similar words and phrases recalled from pornographic books and video casettes.

Not that it is a simple matter: what to try to say and what to leave unsaid. Because, as every inspired poet and prophet knows - and as did the composers of the Gospels - writing such intense experiences down gives them added validity, seals their truth. In physics, according to Heisenberg and others, a particle isn't there until it's observed.

I have tried rather clumsily to suggest that Abby was, in a sense, a stranger with whom I was sharing the hotel room. What I mean is that a new, or more developed, insight into her womanhood, and womanhood itself, dawned on me.

The best I can do is to compose quickly, without too much

pondering, especially brain-wracking, a poem or paean to Abby herself.

Man appeared first in the ancient tale and then woman, and it is to me unthinkable to reverse the order. Man had his purpose no doubt in his relation to his creator and in other solitary ways. But the appearance of woman changed the whole plan - if there had been one on the basis of the primal creation.

She - Eve, in this first and seminal confrontation - was there not to satisfy man's - Adam's - desires and in doing so propagate. She was, so to say, the source and fount of those desires, structured in a very cunning, if not actually miraculous, manner, to arouse, in quanta-like succession, ever more sensuality. And yet, as in the cosmos itself, the basics were few and simple. Many were indeed dual-purpose. Each part of her body can be envisaged according to its distance from the sexual centre to which all, once this particular function of imagination is operative, lead.

Her foot, for instance, which in high-heeled shoes becomes more evident perhaps. Her hands, that cupped can stimulate the male genitals and are thus dual-purpose.

We still approach her with awe as well as excitement, as Adam must have at his first sight of another being. Man starts off with the idea, despite whatever he may have heard or read to the contrary, that his as yet imprecise longings would strike her as extreme, or even outrageous. I am thinking both of an individual couple alone for the first time, and the man-woman relationship in general and in history.

Dostoevsky says that the man who as a youth hardly dares kiss the hem of her robe, ends in the grip of the lusts of Sodom and Gomorrha.

Leave aside the robe and its hem, it's more a matter of her pulling down her skirt that has slipped above her knees. But of course, whether she knows it or not, this doesn't impose a frontier or limit to what she reveals. On the contrary, it is a signal to his imagination to take over where his eyes no longer serve.

Not in its totality, not in a blinding flash which would confuse and incapacitate him, even, who knows, cause a shock of revulsion from her whole system of ducts, apertures, mucus-secreting glands, draining outlets, all situated in the same zone, or valley of flesh, an inch or two deep and a few inches long. His inner eye roves up her legs, lingers on the inner thighs and then the veil of the ultimate goal and treasure, looming larger than life in the powerful lens of his imagination.

We are only at the fringe. She - Abby - knows, if the man - I - am still lingering at this first opening into her, that in her structure one thing, that at first seems the ultimate, leads to another, more ultimate, or at least less obvious or natural, though, God knows, the previous erogenous organ wasn't that obviously available before its discovery.

She's well aware, if only subconsciously, that she could have been made very differently. Supposing the creator had been, was, more of an idealist, an academic, a Platonist even, he would have placed her genitals in the vicinity of her eyes and ears, the more spiritualised organs, which need not have been in the head.

Leaving speculation aside, she is composed of undreamed of fleshly devices (undreamed until she herself reveals them one by one, keeping pace with her lover's responses).

His dual-purpose penis has several choices, a moist, padded, deep recess, on the way to the womb, a narrower, drier one with the accent on local friction, her mouth with the tongue that caresses, consoles, stimulates, delays, postpones and brings him to an orgasm more sensational and perhaps shameful, or shameless, than the others.

Now I have introduced the word shame, and I'll try to interpret what I mean by it. In all this, as is surely evident, I'm putting our seal, Abby's and mine, on this universal experience. So I'll continue in this way by suggesting that the impulse to what is shameful comes not from any desire to defile or subjugate the woman, but to subvert and counter the whole polite social conventions and usage. This is why animals are shameless, or, as we say, innocent. Young children too, possibly.

They have no experience of a society with its phoney respectabilities and chillingness.

When he thrusts more and more actively into whatever of her orifices, it is, partly and hardly consciously, to - in her name and his - renounce and decry all social behaviour, not to mention its offshoots in the business, religious and political worlds.

15

35

After that there comes, not so much a let-down, but a change of mood. With the psycho - and neuro - and plain brute sensuality dissolved, though I didn't actually bring my brief essay on Woman to its natural conclusion in orgasm, we were into other realms of private and social, not to mention scientific, activities.

As regards the latter, the ostensible reason for our being here, we weren't, had never been, all that taken with the project, or task, or whatever it was.

One aspect of it which we had now time to consider was the, to us, surprise that if it was the Zadopek comet whose return Paul was going to welcome, in the space of the few years since its previous appearance it would hardly have had time to travel very far through the solar system before turning back. Whereas we'd assumed that these heavenly bodies invariably made long trips into space.

Back on the yacht, her bag full of souvenirs from Halifax - designed for tourists but of a higher quality than those to which we are accustomed at home - they ranged from minutely and accurately rigged barques and old whalers in bottles to beautifully naturalistic lobsters that raised a fighting claw at the press of a concealed button - it was Abby who brought up the subject to Deva Brata.

It was, he thought - wasn't he sure, for heaven's sake! - the same comet. The little Indian, himself with his dark glow and partly-uncoiled inner spring struck me as comet-like, but that may have been an associative conclusion.

We were sailing along the eastern coast of Nova Scotia, three hundred miles or so from the North Cape, beyond Cape Breton, not, for some reason that I, nor even Abby with her habitual enquiries, didn't find out, not taking what appeared a considerable short-cut through Canso Sound into George's Bay. Possibly we had time to spare until our unilateral appointment and it was probably pleasanter sailing on the smallish, well-appointed vessel in these waters, always within sight and easy reach of land - we put into several small ports for fresh vegetables and lobsters - than anchored off the rather barren land, though we'd only seen it (at one remove) under thick snow, on the southern shore of Northumberland Strait.

What Abby didn't take kindly to, though that's putting it in too homely a way perhaps, was Deva Brata's assurance. Indeed the answer wasn't crystal clear, as I was beginning to learn they never are on this level of astro-physics, just below where it becomes a matter of equations. From what I could grasp of what Abbey told me, with my untrained mind, coincidence played a large part in the timing of all speeds below that of light, combined with the relative positions of the objects involved (whether sub-particles in test tubes or bodies of considerable magnitude in outer space) and it might not be the same comet after all.

Somebody had got it wrong, either us or Deva Brata Mukerjie. And it could hardly be he. I shall add a note in exoneration from a treatise on the thinking process:

'In the evolution of ideas it may be necessary to go through a wrong stage to arrive at a useful one. The most fundamental difference between lateral and vertical thinking - one of the author's themes - is that in vertical thinking one is not allowed to be wrong at any stage, whereas in lateral thinking one is allowed to be wrong on the way to the solution... There is also the possibility that one is wrong only in the current frame of reference. It is by being prepared to be wrong that the frame of reference itself eventually gets to be changed...'

Which, at a lateral angle, brings us to Darwin's evolutionary theories and the planned later voyage of the yacht to the Galapagos Islands. But this too was ambiguous. We still weren't sure if it was one of Paul's jokes, though of a somewhat different kind of humour. In any case Abby and I had no intention of joining that expedition if it really took place. We would fly back to Europe at our own expense - expense of that sort was still a consideration - by the same airline, Air Canada, as I reminded her that she had travelled on alone on the previous occasion and had had the passive, on her part, sexual encounter with the strapping, as I envisaged her, hostess or stewardess. What was she called?

- Milly? (No, Melly)

What about us, as we sailed in leisurely fashion through calm waters for two or three days - we berthed for a night at a small fishing port - the name, New Harbour, struck me because of its banality? Well, we lolled about on deck in the company of the others, eating sparingly, especially Abby, of the delicacies provided at lunch, which had become a more elaborate meal than on the Atlantic crossing, and dinner. There was a mobile bar on deck and we drank white wine at all hours, Abby and I, that is. Neither of us are sippers, as I noticed were some of our deck chair neighbours, while others stuck to spirits, notably the skipper when off duty, Boyd Roberts, permanently intoxicated and by now openly shunned by Maya, and Maya herself. Deva Brata never drank alcohol, while neither did one of the Firmament girls, while the other, I'm not sure which, I hadn't come to clearly distinguish them, made up for it.

Eating and drinking, guzzling and sozzling, is one thing, lovemaking, fucking, is another, to which I'm getting round. It was, as I've hinted, in abeyance. Which doesn't mean that we never felt like it, which, in turn, doesn't mean that we never did it. But, I think, only once, though 'only' in a period of, roughly, seventy hours is not all that abstemious. And, although I'm accelerating the forward tempo of the narrative to get there, I may as well leave this matter of our intimacies, at least for the time being, by going into the circumstances of, and reason for our only copulation, I think, between Halifax, Nova Scotia, and Northumberland Strait that stretches between New Brunswick and Nova Scotia to the south and Prince Edward Island on the north.

It was a hot night and we lingered late on deck, sleepy as we were, or I certainly was. The arch of the sky was a dark, stretched membrane that could have been inside my own brain as seen by a minute eye situated outside a cluster of starry neurons.

Captain Magressen, whom I saw descend from the bridge, came forwards where we were at the bow and gave me a radio cable. Ahead there was, just above the horizon, a pale violet streak. I opened and read aloud the message that was from St. Bride's hospital and addressed to both of us. Dr. Cornelius had died there after a car crash.

Below deck, in our less oven-like cabin, we undressed without a word and embraced, made love I suppose, though I don't recall the physical details. It was our spontaneous and intuitive response to the death of somebody who had been responsible, via destiny, for bringing us together. It is, perhaps, the instinctive response of two lovers in the face of sudden death.

Towards the end of the following day we sailed round North Cape, that could well have been Ultima Thule because of my premonition that we were sailing beyond the ken of much that had been familiar and precious and into, not just another hemisphere (which was, anyhow, not strictly the fact) but a new world.

Yes, what love, what grief! Not just at the loss of Cornelius, whom we had seen little of in the latter years, but for the accumulated loss that I had suffered - Abby considerably less - in my life, even if mostly of animals, and not by death, of Noona. That she was grievously there too didn't astonish me, as I believe it would have a short time before, even the day before. So let that serve as an indication, however shaky, of what I mean by a 'new world'.

As I say - though I may not have - we dropped anchor in the Strait midway between Pugwash on the southern shore and the much larger town of Charlottetown on Prince Edward Island, where it - the Sound - is about thirty kilometers wide.

Abby, always on the look out for the unexpected, suggested there might be another foreign visitor: a Russian submarine.

- But hadn't the one that time come by arrangemennt to transport your father's stallions to the Soviet Union?

- Would it have been let make the long journey with its very tricky last bit of navigation if there hadn't been Soviet submarine commanders who knew someting about these narrow waters?

Perhaps. But this seemed to me irrelevant, and I said so. The next thing she'd be suggesting we were here by appointment with another Russian sub, or the same one. Hadn't we a Russian skipper, and hadn't her father (though, what he had to do with it, she didn't say) an inherent distrust of, if not hostility to, the western world?

In the end she had to laugh too when I said that if so I might as well compose quite another kind of compendium containing up-to-the-minute top secret international information.

- 36 -

Whose idea the fancy dress ball was originally I've no idea. Abby suggested that Chaim Magressen and Maya had thought it up between them. The Master, as we were now calling him, had friends, or at least contacts, in Charlottetown - which Abby took as a confirmation of her earlier suppositions - and Paul would look up some acquaintances from the previous visit on the southern shore.

Nobody was supposed to know what the others were coming as, but naturally Abby, who was thrilled, and I, somewhat less so, consulted together. From the first mention of the project to her by the Master, she made up her mind to be Cleopatra, and, I've an idea though she didn't mention it, leaving it up to me, that she hoped I'd get myself up as Mark Anthony. This was a role in which I didn't see myself, knowing little or nothing about him but the passionate declaration that, anyhow, was Shakespeare's. Captain Magressen offered to take me to Charlottetown where he had friends in the business - what business? But I didn't ask - who would fit me out. The shore excursion attracted me after what I thought of as long days at sea - our couple of nights at the 'Lord Nelson' had hardly been a shore excursion!

In the bar, one of the few in the place, because of the strict ethic in regard to alcohol in this part of Canada where drink flowed freely, he asked me what I thought of Moby Dick. The unexpected question startled me. I partly misunderstood it, supposing he was starting a literary discussion and asking for an assessment of Melville's great classic. Whereas, as soon was evident, what he meant was how did the idea of my going to the festivity as the White Whale appeal to me.

- Very imaginative, Captain.
- Chaim.
- Pardon?
- That's my name.
- Oh, yes. As was that of your semi-kinsman, the great painter.

I would have been happy to talk about Soutine instead of the work of the other artist in which, if at a tangent, he was involving me. But he wasn't to be deflected.

He took me to what at home I'd have called a ship's chandler, of which the place seemed fuller than of licensed premises. In a yard at the rear were lobster pots and the spherical buoys which float above them as markers. The proprietor and Chaim - might as well get accustomed to first name terms - greeted each other in Russian. A scenario supportive of Abby's passed through my mind. The marker buoys could also be guides to nuclear submarines entering the Sound.

By cutting, with a blow lamp - the old Russian had doubtless a range of sophisticated equipment (I was letting Abby's fantasies take hold, largely to evade, for the moment, the reality of what I'd got myself into) - the small iron balloon was adapted to accommodate flesh. There was an aperture at the top of the buoys - for some electronic communication device? - large enough for my head to emerge. It was the lower part that had to be cut open. Sprayed white, and with fluke and fins painted on the spheroid, it would cause much amusement and not be inappropriate, Chaim declared. Self-assured, perhaps pig-headed, in more important ways, I'm quite malleable and persuadable in trivial matters, and was talked into agreeing to the Captain's 'inspiration', as the shop owner, now speaking a mixture of Russo-Canadian-Cockney - he must have been for a long time in London (naval attaché at the Soviet Embassy?) - called it.

Of course, the worst was yet to come. That was breaking the news to Abby. Nothing could persuade her that a completely rigid marine mammoth, leviathan or whale (she hadn't heard of Moby Dick) was anything but a disaster as a companion and playmate - leave out a dance partner - to her dusky Queen of Egypt.

And when I think of how tenderly some of the men have planned their costumes in relation to the partners they wanted to please! The doctor, hearing that one of the Firmament popsies was coming as a lobster pot, is, at great expense, so Paul told me, getting himself up as a lobster.

What Paul evidently didn't tell you, Dove, was that it was he, Paul, who is making a fool of the learned Swede. The girls are coming as two competing comets. And that too, for he doesn't restrict himself to making fun of others, is Paul's suggestion.

Before going any more deeply into it, I'll clarify the pre-ball situation as, to my knowledge, it stood at the time of our talk. Many of the disguises, if not all (such as mine) were convertible into alternatives, which I note in brackets.

The two comets (vintage party dresses sprinkled with stardust)	Lisette-Eulalie and Ann
Abraham (the significance of this will be explained in due course)	Philip Weisberg
Cleopatra (Queen of Sheba)	Abby
The cosmos (with addition of top hat, Pop Star)	Boyd-Roberts, in competition with Doctor for the girls
Lobster (incontrovertible)	The Doctor/Academician, victim of Paul's pleasantry in his erotic expectation
Charles Darwin (convertible into several distinguished figures of last century)	Paul, still clowning of course, and now with himself as butt
Two or three unrecognisable persons or objects (convertibility doesn't arise as there is no initial identity).	Worn by some of the guests

Correction

I'd got this far with list based on confidential information
from Paul when he rang me on the yacht's intercom to say
that the ship's doctor had a second disguise in reserve which
he might decide to use and which consisted of large pieces of
hardboard, representing the covers of books attached to each
other by elastic spines on which were printed the titles: *The
Spirit of Pure Science* and, when reversed: *The Spirit of
Literature.*

Why was Paul keeping me so well-informed? He evidently
wanted the occasion to be fully recorded. More enigmatic is
why he was giving what I saw as a lavish end of term kind of
party such importance.

Now I come to another unexpected but key event. I was
given, or rather offered, the answer that I was beginning to
resign myself to foregoing.

Deva Brata Mukerjie, small, dark, insignificant-seeming,
appeared in our state room - Abby was on shore getting the
few extras she needed for her part - and plunged right into it
with:

- Mr. Samson, I've got something to tell you: an
announcement that from experience I take to be ominous.

And in the brief pause before he continued, there was
ample time - what a wealth of it there is when it comes to
inner forebodings! - for me to form the next sentence or two.
Abby had had an accident, fallen from the launch - a large
motor boat, actually, which the yacht towed - and in which
she'd crossed to Prince Edward Island. Word had come from
Prince Ahmed forbidding his daughter's further association
with an infidel who refused to marry her.

- I've come to explain on Paul's behalf the real purpose and
import of this voyage, and, incidentally, of the coming
festivity.

Relief, relaxation, miraculous, instantaneous answer to
prayer - had I prayed? Very possibly, without registering it
(God of Abraham, Isaac and Jacob, do not let my Dove
perish!). If so, I'd appealed directly to Jehovah, not just on
the principle that, where possible, go direct to the highest
authority, but because if this stern and jealous Deity who
had tormented his nearest and dearest, humanly speaking,

by commanding he sacrifice his son (the nearest I could identify with the old man's anguish was if he had told me to kill the cat that I, and Noona, had doted on).

- There have been, which, as a student of history, you well know, a few momentous events in man's comparatively short stay on this planet. Looking back they can be seen as keys to the mystery of his presence. Leaving aside the early legends, and disregarding - while according them profound respect - the prophets and avators, Judaic, Muslim and Hindu, the first such shift or leap out of one phase of man's evolution to another was the Incarnation of Jesus Christ.

Must he spin it out so wordily? Possibly, in my recalled impatience, I'm exaggerating. naturally it is not a verbatim rendering, I had no concealed microphone, though how I wish I had! What a treasure the tape would be. To whom would we bequeath it? These are idle speculations, indulged in later.

In the new phase, covenant or psychic dimension - that of the early Christians, the Fathers of the Church, St Paul above all, Jerome, Augustine and the amazing Tertullian (never raised to sainthood for very good reasons), there was the all-pervading expectation of the Second Coming.

(I am now paraphrasing what Deva was saying.)

Man, however, even in these examples of his, till then, highest spiritual flowering, had mistaken his destiny, his place in the eventual harmony, and instead of a not-long-delayed Coming there was to be a Going.

What it came to was that it wasn't man's destiny to play a purely passive part, to live out his days on earth awaiting heavenly graces and visitations. He himself, fashioned in part from the burning core of distant stars, distant in time and space, had not been composed of this passion, daring and energy merely to produce an occasional genius, in art, science, or sanctity.

Yes, I was responding at last, as always with me, it takes time.

Then, Mr Mukerjie, this voyage is, in Paul's eyes, a 'Going', perhaps even a practice run.

The last expression may have puzzled him, but no matter.

He told me that, yes, he had been commissioned - that's the word he used - by Paul to explain all this to me, in my capacity as reporter, record-keeper, witness, recording angel.

I intervened to point out that, as I understood it, this voyage had not been Paul's doing but had been planned and undertaken by Philip Weisberg with the financial backing of Maya and, possibly, other sponsors. Paul was on board as a guest, very much as were Abby and myself.

- Is that not the beauty of it, Mr Samson?

I waited, hiding, as best I could, my incomprehension.

- It happened, it took place, not just out of the blue, but because of ostensibly some very unworthy causes. I think one of the purposes was to advertise a notorious brothel. Nothing, to my mind, could be greater proof of metaphysical intervention than when a momentous event has its origins in the gutter.

- So far, so good.

I didn't actually utter that popular cliché, but waited, less impatient now, sensing some rhyme and reason, even if more of the former, in what the Indian was saying.

He suddenly switched to computers. It would take several generations of them to come up with the correct equation, the algebraic formulae. For what? For the voyage, the Going, of which this was a token or symbol. But it would take more than that, more than algebra, it would take inspired construction of artificial intelligences. I demurred at this point. Artificial intelligence was something I was wary of.

- So am I, Mr Samson. So, of course, is Paul. but all types of calculus have been artificial through the ages. And here there is a curious analogy: the artificial - non-human - signals sent into space by contemporary astronomers return with equally artificial - non-human - information. But no non-artificial signals cross outer space, we have had no communication with intelligences on other planets. And this could well be because personal, that's to say communications tinged with emotional, mental, neurological or non-artificial meanings cannot survive such sub-zero temperatures. These signals are automatically rejected as we find most transplanted organs are by the human body, though I admit that the analogy is not very apt.

- And now, the fancy dress ball. In the envisaged, or better, visioned landing on an inhabited planet, the first few hours may be the vital ones. How to make contact with that race of possibly supermen and women?

By a shared festival in which the unexpected visitors introduce themselves by mime. Of course the roles taken will be very different from those this evening. They will depend on what man has been able to glean about this distant body in space.

It may come as a surprise, it may be hard to believe, but Deva and I embraced.

An addition to the list of trivia noted earlier: Philip Weisberg was coming to the ball as Shylock. Oh, he had his own brand of humour!

What about the comet? I took advantage of our warming to each other to ask Deva Brata. He was not a comet-man. That was very much his fellow-countryman's territory - he mentioned the famous Asian astrophysicist, a close colleague of Paul's whose long name I don't at the moment recollect but that I remember transcribing earlier.

16

According to academic gossip - the most unreliable - I've been promoted to thirteenth on the Nobel short list for literature and twenty-seventh on the one for pure science. Having gained that ranking as an intuitive, which, after all, was what Einstein was, rather than as a brilliant and indefatigable researcher, it should confirm my idea of myself as anything but a social commentator. So I won't attempt to describe the revelry naturalistically.

However, as a rough guide for the scribe selected to record the space voyage in, say, the twenty-second century of which this was supposed to be the prototype, I'll jot down some notes and also elaborate imaginatively. The latter comes easily to me, and one of the most absorbing images was of this future expedition ending in failure. But as failure is often an extension of triumph on another plane, even if a major disaster overtook the craft and those on board, the same number (with a slight adjustment) as we are, and seven men and six women, vanished from earthly ken - that is to say no more signals reached this planet - their voyage may have been diverted rather than interrupted. Where they eventually docked was perhaps where the dead land and among the first to greet them were myself, Joel Samson, and Noona with our once-beloved Minnie in her arms. Why once-beloved? The time-sense becomes confused, and I'm unsure of the tenses. A more serious question, even objection. What of Abby? There is no problem where there is neither marriage nor giving in marriage, which does not exclude intense and even, possibly, spiritual-sensual relationships of a sort unthinkable to us at present, though Tertullian had a shot at it, which lost him any chance he had of a sainthood. (He was probably on the Church's short-list till then.)

This prediction of mine had salutary repercussions on the present and immediate, which, according to theologians, is proof of the 'vision' being from 'above'. It brought Noona back, imaginatively, into my daily living.

Back to the revelry: Of course I in my lobster buoy was an easy target for jibes. Equally naturally they all failed in comic effect. At the heart of comedy lies incongruity, hilarity is induced by the funny or farcical confronting the solemn which is thus reflected in a distorting mirror. The farcical object, which, belatedly, I was well aware of being, is not a suitable object for distortion, the figure of fun and the funny remark cancel each other out.

Sallies such as - 'You should have a flashing light on top of the contrivance in case you fall overboard' and 'It'll be awkward when nature calls' were, as I knew, pallid in the face of the ludicrous spectacle.

Generally speaking, I don't think the ball was a great success, though some of the locals enjoyed it. Am I biased? Yes, but being self-alerted to this probability I took counter-measures, cutting short sour and critical appraisals of my fellow guests.

To put the festivities in proper perspective I shall not devote too much space or time to them. But as they shouldn't be dealt with too casually - for the reason, already mentioned, that for Paul, Deva, and, possibly, for Wickramsinghe, the famous astrophysicist, who had remained in Cardiff, it was a rehearsal, or, more precisely, a guide to a select company of future astronauts, instead of devoting several uninterrupted pages to the affair, I'll break it up with welcome interpolations.

Let one, the most vital, be a declaration, lest some doubt may have arisen, that whatever Paul's, Deva's or anyone's impression, I was here not primarily as a chronicler of their bold pioneering, but as the equally intrepid composer of my *Compendium*.

How, it may be wondered, does accepting the invitation to join the expedition further this enormous and fascinating task? Were there a couple on board worthy of the close scrutiny that the voyage offered? No. The only relationship that reached the higher intensities was ours. But for new insights into that, the voyage - I had been about to write 'the cruise' - was well worth it. In particular, the couple of days and nights at the 'Lord Nelson' in Halifax and the night of desolation at sea.

Two of the company were not dressed up: Captain Magressen and Deva. The Master was on duty and, as he told us, in the unlikely event of an emergency such as a freighter bound for the St Lawrence (surely far out of its course) running us down, or at least looming up at an excessive speed, his handling of the incident would be made the harder if he was got up as an eighteenth-century waterfront floozie, as Paul had suggested.

- Freighter, my arse! commented Abby afterwards. She still had Russian submarines on her mind.

The Firmament girls, whom, as I have mentioned, Paul told the Doctor in confidence were coming as lobster pots, were elegant in their trailing dresses, especially when they danced, with their trains draped over an arm. The doctor-academician, probably not unaware of Paul's propensities, made his appearance, not as a lobster - a difficult transformation which I doubt whether, his temperament and background being of an essentially sober nature, he'd have pulled off - but as previously noted.

I won't describe the locals, many of whom were wearing masks, taking the last minute invitations to be something like a Halloween party, which some ethnic groups I believe celebrated, in a bizarre fasion, as a surviving link with their homelands.

Philip Weisberg told Abby that, as the only two Shakespearean figures, they should stick together for the evening. That's what she said, and although Abby in all vital ways was, as they say, the soul of truth, she could give a twist to a trivial incident when it suited her, and she was still upset by what she called my buffoonery.

Late in the night, or in the early hours of morning, I was alone on deck, or the forward part of it, divested with difficulty of the ridiculous get-up when Deva joined me. We had, as I've said, parted affectionately earlier, and at first I thought he just wanted to confirm that, if late in the trip, he had made a friend. However, though it may have been that too, it was something else. It had to do with Paul and perhaps with bringing his old and his recent friend together, that is: in his own mind. There is also another association that, in what I'm coming to, I'll have to be careful about narrating because it involves Chandra Wickramsinghe, who is alive and well though unlikely to get round to reading this report.

- It's a lonely quest.

We were standing by the rail at the bow and to the north, over the long dark shape of the island, far, far away, it seemed, above the North Pole, the sky was glimmering with a cold pallor.

For Abby's sake, still puzzling over the comets, I made another attempt to clear things up.

- Who keeps track of them all?

She was wondering much more than that, but I supposed at that stage we'd have to proceed a step at a time.

- The B.A.A. handbook.

While I was working out what the initials stood for (British Astronomical Association) he had pushed on deeper into his theme. It was for me a strange sensation: to sense that, yes, we were now at the heart of the matter, while still not being sure what the matter was.

There was passing mention of the two bright Arend-Roland comets of 1956, of Alcock's two comets of 1959 and of the one discovered by Biela in 1826. (I put this down in the copybook that never left my inside pocket during the voyage, and whose cover is rough by being in constant contact with the teeth of my metal comb, by the faint light of what could be the Aurora Borealis.)

- Much of this information, you know, Joel, comes from Paul. Does that surprise you?

He was testing my belief in his other close companion, and, in this case, guide.

- From Paul and, I imagine, other astrophysicists.

- Most astronomers are more at home with calculation machines than with telescopes and radar.

Here I'm shifting away from the verbatim, to present what Deva told me in my own words.

In the valley of the Nile at the time of Isis and Osiris, around five thousand B.C., there were mystery rites expressing the wisdom and science of antiquity that, had

they come down to us, might well have taught us everythig
that we now know, and much earlier.

- Outside of love and pain, I put in.

There was, at the back of my mind, along with the
knowledge that Deva, and Paul, saw me as chronicler, or, to
put it at the lowest, travelling correspondent, I'd been chosen
as recorder of a more ambitious chronicle.

- We aren't concerned with the prophets, Christian, Hindu,
Muslim, or, if it comes to that, your Incarnation.

He meant, naturally, Christ's.

Instead of Isaiah, Daniel, the Psalms of David,
Mohammed,
Buddha, Lao Tse, he was naming Heliopolis, Memphis,
Abydos, where the temples had carvings depicting solar
barques used by what he called 'initiators' (I think a
translation from the script itself) who came from outer space.

Similar carvings and inscriptions exist on Indian shrines,
where there are graphics of the craft, powered by snakes and
eagles (these may have been understood figuratively).

What Deva was explaining was that these days the quest
was a rather lonely one, but that it had not always been so. If
I assimilated all the data correctly, and I am still thinking it
over, there was this widespread tradition that man had
reached this planet by a series of planetary stepping stones.
Had, possibly (but I can't go into the surviving indications for
such a seemingly wild - to me - supposition) arrived here and
then left on several occasions.

- 38 -

Yes! As the floozie exclaims at the end - at the start too? - of
Joyce's outpouring of comic-tedium. And also the 'No!' that
the exhausted - he was tired throughout - Fignon whispered
as he semi-expired at the end of one year's *Tour de France*.
Or rather some word, not yet coined, incorporating the two
and with cryptic intimations of a third. 'Almost... not quite...
never.'

The afternoon after the fancy dress ball, when all on

board, apart from some of the crew, were in deep slumber, Abby and I got the Master to take us across to Charlottestown and there we booked a room for a couple of nights in a small hotel in Vespers Street.

After an early dinner - clam chowder, lobster stew, coffee - we strolled out in the warmth of the evening and round a corner, into Vespers Lane, came on a narrow two-storeyed house built of pale wood that a notice said was for sale.

- Do you think we could buy it?

I'd opened my mouth at the same time as hers but she got the words out before me.

- We might, with some support from your father.

Then came the tangential thoughts and emotions that follow on an important decision or prospect.

- The flowers of home beckon.

Only Abby could have had that reaction at that moment. if, as I fear, I haven't made that evident, I've failed in my evocation of her.

- And other things, and people, too.

- One thing for sure, Joel, we've come to the end of the cruise and aren't going on to any volcanic islands, are we?

- No.

This time an unequivocal one. Why did she suppose they were volcanic? The aftermath of the ball?

- Let's do our accounts.

We'd strolled out, but we hurried back to the Melville Hotel Melville here, Nelson in Halifax. (Had the great writer had a wife, a mistress? What had been the illustrious admiral's relationship with Lady Hamilton?)

After booking on an Air Canada flight to Europe, we had almost a thousand Canadian dollars in travellers' cheques.

A belated thought, evoked by Abby's reference to the islands: Deva had pointed out that no convincing link had yet been discovered between Homo Sapiens (what a misnomer!) and any lower form of life.

I spent three or four days in an Arabian night (nurse) ambience at the hotel. We didn't join the committee, or group, to welcome the return of the comet, but returned to the yacht the following day to take leave of our fellow voyagers, in particular Paul and Deva Brata Mukerjie. Nor could I leave out Captain Chaim Magressen without a pang of disloyalty, though this I couldn't rationalise.

Just before we left, with the yacht's motor boat waiting under the rope ladder, Paul said: You don't believe it's either the pure scientists or the imaginative artists who are nearest to grasping reality, but lovers of a rather special kind.

He was addressing us both, and clasping each of us by the hand. I - or Abby - might have corrected him on a minor point or two - but that would have been niggardly.

- One of the prophets, said Abby, halfway back to Prince Edward Land, speaking for the first time since the farewell.

Back at our hotel she was still thinking of prophets and prophecy, this time from her homeland, in particular about an old woman in the city, though at that time it hadn't been much more than a settlement around the royal residence, who told fortunes at the turn of the century or thereabouts. She had a large clientele of poor folk and her reputation gradually spread and seeped into the royal apartments, perhaps first the harem, and then to the vice-regal tent - I imagined richly emblazoned tents in the desert, whose canvas was almost as solid as brick, associating what I'd imagined as our small tent in the wilderness when Abby drew the curtains around my hospital cot with what she was now saying.

Anyhow, the fortune teller, now become a prophetess, was summoned to Prince Ahmed's father - it might have been granddad - and told him that all his worry about keeping up with the legendary Arabian princes, riding out on their fleet-footed steeds of an evening with a falcon on their wrists and the Koran in its enamelled leather pouch, was unnecessary because there was only a thin, almost, if not quite, transparent screen between his highness and a bottomless black cistern in which was stored treasure untold. Or was the treasure itself black, making the prophecy even more singular?

While listening to Abby I was beginning to see that, if I was to round out the Compendium and make it as complete as was possible, I would have to include some love letters. And this would entail research, a prospect that didn't appeal to me.

I had, tied with string and put away somewhere, a small bundle of notes and longer scrawls from Noona sent to me in the early days of our on-and-off courtship. I had, besides, two letters from Abby composed when on night duty at St Bride's and brought to me by hand - hers - during the day. But these I would not include, though deeply relevant. And, of course, I could, and probably would, compose some myself.

If I made use of Noona's I would have to ask her permission. This would provide a good reason for getting in touch with her which I had been half-intending to, and had consulted Abby about.

If my contention that through the experience of intense love and pain which - apart from certain individual spirits in and outside contemplative monastic houses - is confined to one-to-one relationships - and for my somewhat particularised purpose, to the man-woman situation - wisdom (even prophecy perhaps, now that we're on the topic) is gained, then these lovers, or ex-lovers in cases where one of the partners is dead, are what somebody - Shelley or Keats, perhaps Plato - called the unofficial arbitrators of the world. Not just unofficial, but obscure and unremarked.

Then came a really incredible event or incident. At 6 p.m., just after we had put down the phone after asking for aperitifs from room service - Canadian Bourbon, soda, no ice - it rang and at the other far - oh, how far! - end was Prince Ahmed.

How on earth had he tracked us down to our hidden retreat in this town on the fringe of the northern wastes? Not by any supernatural means - I was, we were, still in the throes of prophecy and the likes - but, having reached the yacht by radio, and, from the Master, got our address, found the phone number through, I suppose, some large international handbook - I was half mixing it up with the B.A.A. handbook mentioned by Deva - that listed, continent by continent, the numbers of every licensed hostelry on the globe.

What had he to say? Why this rhetorical question? Because, at first, it wasn't so clear. True, I was only hearing Abby's part of the dialogue, but even from that I could tell that she herself was somewhat at sea.

- Oh? ...Ah! ... No, Daddy... I do and I don't...

A distinguished, distinctive, figure, Prince Ahmed, upright (in posture), with a short black garland of beard around his jaw and coming to a point below the chin, dark-suited, bareheaded, grave. A widower, have I mentioned this? Her mother died when Abby was a child. Hamdan al Ahmed, the last of a long lineage, unless Abby had a son, and autocratic ruler, but by no means despot, of an oil-rich state.

He had two animals, a three and a four-year-old, in the Arc de Triomphe. This was the first thing he said when Abby passed me the receiver. The four-year-old was the filly, Abdal, of which I'd heard, though without being *au fait* in respect of her triumphs on French and English racecourses.

How devoted he was to his only daughter - only child in fact - I was reminded by the filly's name.

He was telephoning us - or at any rate me, he may have had other things to say to Abby - to invite us formally to his box, or reserved accommodation, high up on the stands at Longchamp for the great occasion, still six weeks or more distant, on the first Sunday in October.

Much more immediate were the love letters. Or, as it now occurred to me: love poems. These were easier to discover and, if my intuition and instinct didn't desert me, would express the same intensities. Not that this Compendium can be devoid of those sealed and secret missives, awaited with fear and longing, unexpected, half-dreaded, wholly welcomed, delivered by hand, post, courier, underground tube, express delivery, slid under doors, left under pillows, concealed in the spines of prayer books passed by a warder from the women's section to one of the cells in the men's wing of a penitentiary.

First the sonnet John Keats wrote to - in memory of - Fanny Browne in February 1819, at the age of twenty-four, on the sailing ship which took him and his companion, Mr Severn, to Italy in a belated attempt to prolong his life.

Bright star, would I were steadfast as thou art,
Not in lone splendour hung aloft the night,
And watching with eternal lids apart,
Like nature's patient, sleepless eremite,

Francis Stuart

The moving waters at their priestlike task
Of pure ablution round earth's human shores
On gazing on the new soft-fallen mask
Of snow upon the mountains and the moors.
No - yet, still steadfast, still unchangeable,
Pillowed upon my fair love's ripening breast,
To feel forever its soft fall and swell,
Awake forever in a sweet unrest,
Still, still to hear her tender-taken breath
And so live ever - or else swoon to death!

Fanny wrote him a last letter to his lodging in the Piazza di Spagna in Rome, not in answer to the poem which, of course, she never read till much later, a farewell letter which Keats told Severn to place in his coffin unopened.

This was after an event that precedes by some eighty years the similar one that happened to Thérèse Martin at roughly the same age.

One night he had hardly lain down, as Severn reports, when he coughed slightly and said, not waiting as she had until morning: - There's blood in my mouth. Bring me a candle.

Keats thought long and in anguish over what Fanny's letter might contain.

A farewell, yes. But there are many forms. Passionate, despairing, the one that is a self-holocaust, a near-hopeless promise to the beloved in the certain knowledge that his or her death will soon follow. Then, at the other end, deep in the waters under the earth, the cool farewell, uttered in relief, and perhaps an attempt to persuade the recipient that all is for the best.

Nobody knows what Fanny wrote and, although tempted, surely I would be wrong to compose some sentences from it in imagination.

Think of, too, the love poems written by Emily Bronte, about halfway between the time of Fanny's to John Keats and Thérèse of Lisieux's last few years of torment. To whom isn't certain, but, as I think, to her brother, Branwell.

No later light has lightened up my heaven,
No second morn has ever shone for me;

All my life's bliss from thy dear life was given,
All my life's bliss is in the grave with thee.
But when the days of golden dreams had perished,
And even despair was powerless to destroy;
Then did I learn how existence could be cherished,
Strengthened and fed without the aid of joy.

Then did I check the tears of useless passion -
Weaned my young soul from yearning after thine,
Sternly denied its burning wish to hasten
Down to that tomb already more than mine.

And, even yet, I dare not let it languish,
Dare not indulge in memory's rapturous pain;
Once drinking deep of that divinest anguish,
How could I seek the empty world again?

'Memory's rapturous pain', 'divinest anguish': phrases so wonderfully precise, as anyone who has ever reached the fringe of such states of consciousness well knows. And of an intensity possibly only reachable by a mind whose material (physical) structure is breaking down through the ravages of tuberculosis.

By day my eyes, by night my soul,
Desire thee and I'm weary of my own
   - quoted by Abby in one of her letters.

    What chance has this Compendium of mine against the powers that it seems are going to take over?

Here is a prediction from *The Mysterious Unknown* by Robert Charraux:

The development of a new form of existence in which the laws of necessity will compel us to eliminate everything concerned with the old system of love.

17

On the flight home on Air Canada there was no sight of
Melly, the stewardess who had taken up with (to lean to
understatement) Abby on that other flight, an incident that
had she told Paul about he would surely have supposed it
another indication of the embelishing effect the comet had on
those exposed to its path.

Though not almost empty as on this occasion, I was aware
of the big dark barn of the Jumbo cabin that Abby had
described, and of a predominance of couples huddled together
under the discreet dark blankets distributed by the cabin
crew.

It must be evident from this report that we were never at a
loss for things to talk about, and mostly what seemed to us
very important matters. So it was now. After the miniature
bottles of Canadian rye with accompanying minerals were
placed on the hinged tables we turned to what, during the
packing, bus ride and wait at the airport, had been on our
minds. At the forefront was the yacht and its continued
voyage with our friends and acquaintances on board to the
Galapagos Islands. 'Galapagos Archipelago'. Which of us had
called them that? It doesn't matter. But how significant was
the term, reminiscent of Solzhenitsyn's *Gulag Archipelago,* a
copy of which we had noticed in the hotel at Dartmouth, that
refers to the prison camps throughout the Soviet Union
during the Stalinist era and beyond, that had been so many
islands of torment and hopelessness.

We did not make any logical deductions about the ultimate
effect of Darwin's theories of evolution - though nor did he,
but rather the neo-Darwinists - but, as so often before, found
Paul's comets comforting as a counter-current to the image of
a self-contained, closed-shop planet, a speck of dust
momentarily caught in the cosmic light as it drifted through
space.

Not that we based our faith on laboratory tests or probes that discovered living particles at a height that precluded an earthly origin. Nor had the disciples believed in the resurrection because of the empty tomb nor even of the women's story of angels and a ghostly figure. They had gathered together in one room in Jerusalem before any such rumours or reports after having fled and scattered in doubt, fear and disarray at the arrest of Jesus. Nobody could have brought them so soon together, none of them could have restored their faith in the loving communion that he had shared with them but Christ himself.

The later reports, which is all there is to go by, are halting and composed in an idiom to which we are unaccustomed. To complete, or to really grasp them, we need to have some, however dimmed, experience comparable to the disciples themselves. And, allowing for all intervention and distraction, that is what we had, Abby and I. It is also something attested to by those other lovers who had left poems or love letters. It is about all there is, a fragile Ark in which to survive the coming flood.

Not that we only had serious discussions. Far from it. We talked about all kinds of subjects, even those that are commonly called trivial. There was never anything that we could not say to each other, nothing was too embarrassing, too sublime or too silly. With most people, especially with women, I can think of all sorts of things - and what a lot I think! - but of course can't come out with a fraction of it. And I don't mean because of decency. It's by no means only sexual musings that the woman behind the counter, say, arouses. I wonder about what she eats for breakfast, if she drives a car, is married, sleeps alone, has a cat and so on.

There we were, my Dove, my Pigeon (when she becomes that I sense where we're headed), side-by-side in the big, dark, barn afloat amid the stars. It's inevitable. What is? Did the more perceptive of the designers of the big, long-haul planes not have this in mind when they allowed a few inches more leg room between seats and the backs of those in the next row, besides providing a number of twin ones along the windows?

The film on the big screen isn't a distraction, indeed by

focussing the attention of those alone, the very old and the very young, it removes the risk of being watched, not that we wouldn't have taken it. I won't go into details, not even in a footnote. Nor how long, how quick, how sharp, how often.

Finally we slept, every part of our bodies comatose and still melting together where the flesh touched as did my hand and her belly. We were in a semi-trance when we arrived, where tiredness and the aftermath of sex are one, as I dare say, were several other couples. Though so persistent are the powers of recuperation in the neurological economy that by the time we were back in our city we had almost fully come to ourselves.

Among the letters on the hall table, put there by our neighbour when she came to feed the cat and clean her tray, was one from Noona in answer to mine. Did I note that I wrote to her care of a firm in which she once worked as secretary before we started on the cruise? I didn't open it at once, nor any of the mail, come to that. There was an incredible amount of sorting, rearranging, unpacking, plant watering, throwing out, getting in and heaven knows what to do as there always is even after a few days absence, let alone weeks.

To revert for a moment to our never having time to talk about all we had to, though this awkward to and froing of the narrative may well be exasperating: To have someone to talk to without let or hindrance is why many men resort to brothels. It may, naturally, often end in coitus of one sort or another, but in these not infrequent cases that is not the primary goal. Of course, the conversation is normally limited, the other, deeper or darker end of the scale, metaphysical, scientific or cultural territory remaining unexplored. Not that this is always so. it wasn't with Madame Lissik and one or two of her girls in the heyday of Firmament House - or House Firmament as she liked to call it with the stress on back-to-front - nor, I imagine, between Vincent Van Gogh and the girl in the bawdy house at Arles to whom he gave his severed ear. When she called on him in his room that he painted so tenderly with its rush-seated chair, wooden bed and window that opens in an impossile inward perspective, to thank him, it wouldn't surprise me if she'd added: 'But I'd sooner have your cock.'

The first letter I opened contained an envelope addressed to Paul and a note from the famous - alive and well - astronomer, Vishnu Narlibar, asking me to forward or give it to Paul as soon as he returned from wherever he was. Then I read out Noona's without first reading it myself.

She was living in Switzerland, in the top floor of a chalet in a small, though fashionable (I had often heard of it) mountain resort, alone perhaps, or indeed probably as she did not mention a second husband or lover, and described the couple who owned the house and lived below as her closest friends. She sent her love undifferentiatedly to me and 'your wife'.

I had hardly come to the end when Abby said: - Shall we ask her here?

- On a visit?

As usual I lagged behind. I was moved by Noona's letter, I suppose I'd been moved to write to her in the first place. I was also aware that the grace of love between Abby and me was to be both treasured and extended. Not shared, because its source and intensity was binary. To be back after how many years was it - twelve? - with Noona in the same habitation! This thought was disturbing, and it wasn't now purely an imaginative one but one out of which actuality could emerge.

However, this, and indeed much else, was being postponed until after our excursion to France for the big race at Longchamp early in October, a formal invitation to which, following the phone call to Dartmouth, had been among the letters awaiting us. There was an accompanying note from the Prince's secretary enclosing air tickets and telling us that reservations had been booked at the Hotel *Georges Cinque*. This brought back memories to me of events which I have recorded, one at least, in this narrative and others elsewhere. Between our homecoming and embarking for Paris events remarkable enough to have a place in this story were few and far between. That is, of course, according to my judgement, whose unerringness however I occasionally have doubts over. We had Rebecca-Maria and Margraves to lunch and all seemed well with them, which was confirmed by Abby after she had had a private talk with Rebecca who told her, among other intimate confidings, that the old fellow had taken to getting her to recount her experiences at the House Firmament and at the Geneva establishment which she had entered at sixteen. She enquired of Abby whether this wasn't an unhealthy preoccupation, as she put it, and if she shouldn't discourage it. Conversely, if she agreed to it, should she come úp with the more shameful details, miss them out or tone them down?

I only learnt later what Abby's advice had been because of the pressure of immediate events, none of them, according to my afore-mentioned scale, being in themselves of much significance. We visited Nicole to tell her about the voyage and give her the latest eye witness news of Paul, although she was in touch with the yacht by radio telephone.

She didn't, as we had feared, take what might seem our desertion from the expedition badly. Indeed, I had the feeling that she thought the whole thing a waste of time and money.

- 40 -

Our first outing in Paris, if outing it can be called, was to retrace the pilgrimage I had once made to a shrine of St. Thérèse in a northern part of the city, to a church in, or just off, the *rue du Poteau* to be precise.

Looking back, I see that to have repeated the barefoot walk was an indication of nervousness. For I was sometimes beset by doubts about my bold behaviour in taking, in the world that was no less real to me than the factual one, Thérèse Martin to live with me.

Though I hadn't specifically invited her, Abby accompanied me, not, of course, barefoot, but, I noted, suitably or sensitively garbed for the private occasion. And, I guessed, the spirit of pilgrimage - albeit to shrines such as Mecca - was not at all alien to her.

It's a long walk even shod, and this time the pavements of Paris were rougher and more thickly strewn with sharp objects than I recalled. Despite my recent claim of there not being enough time for all that we had to tell each other, conversation lapsed; as I limped along beside Abby, I could hardly respond to her remarks, most of which I interpreted discouragingly. 'It'll put your mind at rest, Joel' I took to mean: 'Better give in to your superstitious observances if you haven't the resolution to dismiss them'.

In the dimness of the small church I couldn't make out the tawdry statue. I supposed I was dizzy, but neither could Abby. It wasn't there. I sank, as they say, though sinking is pleasant compared to my awkward collapse, onto a bench. It (she) was gone. What more unmistakeable sign could I be given of her displeasure? When she had written that if she hadn't become a Carmelite she could have been a street girl she hadn't meant to be taken up on it. And yet, she had never posed, attitudinised for effect. Abby had disappeared. Had she also fled from me and was already on a bus back to the Place Concorde?

I knelt, not to pray, but to take the weight off the soles of my feet which, leaning backwards, I dabbed at with tissues. Then she was beside me again - Abby, not Thérèse, and telling me she had sought out some old woman - a worshipper? A cleaner? - who had said that the statuette had been removed for cleaning and redecorating, the paint having worn off some parts through the constant touching by rosary beads, hands and even lips.

Did this console me? Why should it. There is usually a good reason on the rational plane for what the recipient believes are spiritual communications.

There was nothing for it but to accede to Abby's suggestion to buy some socks and shoes and return to the hotel by taxi. I didn't go into the shop with her and, as usual, she seemed to be taking her time - using the opportunity to fit herself out with footwear for the races? She emerged at last with a pair of bedroom slippers, socks, she said, would have stuck to the abrasions.

Back at the hotel there was a message from her father that he would be calling for us after lunch to take us to visit a friend of his.

My obsession - to call it that - was to get to Lisieux, this time in actuality. To think I'd been there once before in a state that may have been a mixture of hallucination and psychic projection - a meaningless phrase, really, but at the moment I was in a desperate state - to ask her, of all things, what would win some horse race or other!

When her father arrived Abby explained to him, without any hint of my condition, that I had to make an urgent trip to Normandy by a train that left the Gare du Nord that evening.

Prince Ahmed, standing to attention, as was his way I'd noticed at certain moments, turned his face, darker than Abby's, but that might have been because of the black fringe of beard, to me and gazed, as nobody else except women, and not so many of them, ever did, into my eyes. Then with a slight expulsion of air from his mouth, as though he'd been holding his breath - I'd also noted his habit of sighing, once on the racecourse and another time, I'm not sure when - he turned to his daughter and said: - you've time to call on Benedicta and be wherever you have to in Normandy before you'd arrive by train. Either I or Ali will drive you.

I read somewhere that the so-called ypsilon areas of the brain make no distinction between waking reality and dream. (I'm harking back to that other journey to Lisieux.) If these areas exist I take them to be on the threshold of the unconscious.

Prince Ahmed's friend, whom Abby had met once before several years ago, had an apartment in a street near the Place Victor Hugo. She turned out to be an old lady, one of those French ones that it is hard to imagine having ever been young.

This visit, which I had agreed to endure because it seemed by doing so I would get to Lisieux sooner than by train, was in itself extraordinary. I am not going to try to report it in cool, precise sentences. I was too disturbed to register what was happening in an objective, orderly fashion.

After tea, which beverage I declined for a glass of *Marc*, was served, but I don't know how long after, our hostess sat down at an instrument that I think is called a clavicord and began to play. Nor am I sure how long she was playing when I began to listen and absorb the strange sounds, strange to me, that is, who am not what is known as 'musical'. I had no idea what she was playing, though it struck me that the notes were lighter than those of a piano (I don't know the technical expression) or required a lighter touch, yet the effect wasn't in itself lighter, airier perhaps is the word, than the serious piano music I could recall. At some point Abby, who was beside me, took my hand that, she said afterwards, was trembling. She may have also whispered, not knowing the depths of my ignorance, something about five, or five-and-a-half octaves, though it may have been Benedicta herself who mentioned this in a brief introductory comment.

By the end of the session, I was no longer in a hurry to get to the shrine at Lisieux - or had it been the convent and Thérèse's cell that had drawn me? - and, in fact, didn't see the necessity to do so at all. I was reassured and at rest as in the calm aftermath of a fever. I believed, and always shall, that this was Thérèse's way of re-establishing the line of communication that had been shattered by the absence of the statuette.

Footnote: Later, Abby told me that what Benedicta played had been, firstly, a piece by Beethoven called 'Variations' and, then, some of his last compositions for the piano, or clavicord. On a later occasion, because I think he saw that I wasn't in a state to take anything more in, Prince Ahmed informed me that, not just in his estimation but in the opinion of respected French music lovers and critics, this old woman was one of the three or four greatest living interpreters of Beethoven.

It was in his box at Longchamps, high above the course, the ancient windmill and the Bois de Boulogne, that Abby's father made this assessment which didn't surprise me. Such excellence had been evident to me, if obscurely, somewhat as was the excellence of at least three or four of the horses in the big race.

I'm not going to reproduce the pages of the race card devoted to the *Prix de l'Arc de Troimphe* with a list of runners, owners, trainers and jockeys, real, imaginary or a mixture of both. Prince Ahmed had two runners, a three-year-old colt called *Ibn Saud* and a four-year-old filly, *Benedicta,* presumably named after the great pianist and breaking the traditional Moslem series. A cousin, also of the royal household, had likewise two animals in the line-up, one, *Mirage,* which he had bought only the day before and was among those being quoted at fifty and sixty to one on the Pari-Mutual electronic screen. An item of late news that intrigued me was that the Irish jockey, the season's champion in the UK, whom Prince Ahmed's cousin retained as his first, and had had the choice of the two horses, elected to partner the recent purchase and complete outsider.

How long does it take, the one and a half mile race for which research (the studying of videos of previous runnings for instance), plans, bookings, training, started as long before as a year or more and continued until the last minute with a word from trainer to rider as he gives him a leg-up? Roughly two and a half minutes, electrically timed, longer or shorter on different individual time scales, whose variations, could they be compared, would show astonishing divergences.

There is a copse or coppice that hides the runners from those even high up in the stands briefly after about a quarter of the race has been run and there are circumstances where these few seconds impose a greater sense of endurance on an observer than the whole visible spectacle.

There have been times when I was more dependent on the outcome of this race than now, although in a somewhat confused way I felt that an epiphany doesn't manifest itself in isolation but is followed - if not preceded - by lesser signs and wonders and that thus the outcome of the race had to be a success for the Prince. (As usual, even when I was right in my rough inner grasp of these vital if nebulous matters, I was limited in the envisaged range of possibilities.)

This year the Prix de l'Arc de Triomphe result was as follows:

1 Mirage (Sheik Mohammed Ahmed)
2 Ibn Saud (Prince Hamdan Al Ahmed)
3 Girodeaux (Mme de Valliere)

The Prince's cousin had won with the colt he had bought a day before, the less fancied of his two runners, though chosen as his mount by the champion Irish jockey at odds of approximately forty to one (a considerable sum of money had evidently been staked on it shortly before the off) by a head, in a photo finish, from Abby's father's animal, that had started second favourite for the race.

The Prince, whose demeanour fascinated me, and who had discarded his binoculars soon after the horses had turned into the straight and watched the last three furlongs or so without them, murmured something that was more a long sigh than an exclamation, though I just caught the whispered word, 'excellent!'.

He gracefully declined the invitation to accompany his cousin to the President's box for congratulations, though suggesting to Abby that she and I take his place, which, of course, supposing we'd have been intruders, we did not. It was then that I recalled that during the few seconds that the race was obscured by trees it was the thought of Noona and her arrival here in Paris the next day that had crossed my mind.

18

41

I suggested Abby coming with me to meet Noona at Evry airport but she said, after a few moments' thought - No, Joel, that might set a wrong tone.

I knew, as I almost always did, what she meant: something not easy to put into spoken, even less written, words. For us both to have met her might have suggested that for me the past, mine and Noona's, the best of it as well as the other times, was cancelled and her position, place, situation during the visit was one of welcome outsider.

In the bus to the airport I had no idea of how she was going to fit in, but surely she would. She was the only other human being I'd ever loved, for more, that is, than, say, twenty-four hours in which cases it had been a matter mostly of infatuation. I was apprehensive, excited and sad at the prospect of the first sight of her: a middle-aged, prematurely elderly, artificially youthful-looking - at first glance - woman? She'd be a bit - more than a bit - over forty, still girlish were she American. But Noona wasn't American. Would I recognise her as the passengers emerged from the customs hall? She would know me, probably even from afar.

The plane was late though not as late as I'd expected, or more likely I was so absorbed by thoughts, memories, speculations, that the time flew. I glanced a couple of times at one or other of the several clocks but a moment later forgot what was recorded there.

What a crowd of people were emerging who weren't, couldn't for a moment, be Noona. What a large - jumbo jet? - plane it must be, though I didn't think these flew on this comparatively short journey. And then there she was! That's to say: there was the first person who she could have been and become and, a moment later, was just as before.

Among all my imaginings, hopes, fears about the meeting, I hadn't considered how we would greet each other, so that when she was in my arms and our mouths pressed together, I drew mine back and kissed her on both cheeks and then on - no, not a third - but a third kiss on the first cheek, for good luck, as the French custom is.

We, Abby and I, had come from Longchamp with considerably more francs than we had gone there, and there was no question of extravagance in taking a taxi back to the city. Sitting side by side, the initial shock over, I was composed and assured. But was I? Here was another shock: I had an erection, or a partial one, it's sometimes difficult to be sure without investigation.

At this first real test, was my faithfulness to my Dove in danger of faltering? If so, why wasn't I overtaken by a sense of guilt? Answer: because while experiencing this sensual tumescence it is difficult, perhaps impossible, to simultaneously register painful sensations such as remorse or anxiety. Or else it requires a more complex cerebral and neurological structure than mine to do so.

Mine is a fairly simple, not necessarily primitive, organism, capable of harbouring only one idea or emotion at a time, but these with great intensity. Did I want to take Noona in my arms and on the drive, which was quite long enough, make up for those latter times of hurt and fear and reach a point, a peak, in which the achievement seemed complete enough to outbalance whatever consequences? No, I did not. Did I think about doing so? Yes, of course. What came, in fact, of these emotional and physical excitations? What came, I mean, that would have been noticeable to a third party, or fellow passenger, if not to the taxi driver? Very little, and, in the way of non-noticeable, surreptitious gropings and touches, none at all. For a few moments before our arrival at the Hotel *Georges Cinque,* I held Noona's hand, more as a reassurance that the meeting with Abby wouldn't be an ordeal of any sort.

Nor was it. Abby took her in her unhurried stride - I still retain the image of how, almost majestically, she walked slowly along the ward with some clinical apparatus. She had more than a trace of the majestic bearing of her father, which made her lapses into the most indecorous love-making the more exhilarating.

We had a light meal - all I took in of it is luscious globe artichokes with a dark golden sauce and a sparkling wine, I think it was the glasses that sparkled. After which Noona retired to her room to rest and unpack.

I had to tell Abby about my physical reaction at the reunion. She took it, as she did most things, in her leisurely stride. She even gave me a short, informative talk on marital, or the popular concept of, faithfulness.

- It's all palaver - sometimes her English seemed to fail her, or else she used a word she'd lately heard in her own sense - an orgasm can't be bad no matter who you have it with. And what's not bad is hard to feel wrong, at least at the time. But orgasm isn't everything, Joel darling. You can even give it to yourself in loneliness and sadness.

- I couldn't bear you to have it with someone else.

This wasn't an illuminating or necessary interjection and she ignored it.

I can best go further into this, not by extending our discussion but by relating what Abby told me later of the long talk she had on the subject with Noona.

Who had brought it up? She wasn't sure. It wasn't such a coincidence if Noona did, the subject was in the air, had been in the air at the airport, hadn't it?

According to Noona - and what she said I took as an indication of the life she had been living - the orgasm, that's to say the importance given it in our society, especially in male society, was a mistake. She was into something called Tao, of which I had of course heard but wasn't too sure about.

According to this philosophy, or religion, orgasm was to be shunned but not copulation. The longer the lovers could remain cojoined the stronger the bonds between them became. For some couples it wasn't that easy, it meant not moving the genitals, or at least very little. And, to ward off involuntary spasms, it might be necessary to think of entirely different situations: gloomy, drab or painful ones.

Noona showed Abby a portrait of herself that the painter with whom she had lived after leaving me - I had met him once at our house previously - had made of her. I saw it the next day. Noona wasn't just nude but exposed, or 'presented', because, I think, of her startlingly white skin and the necklace of diamonds (they were actually paste) that hung to her breasts against which she clasped a black cat, that I recognised as her beloved Blackie, and which her lover had painted from a photograph.

It was a remarkable picture, but then I was closely associated with it. However, Abby was impressed too, and not only Abby but her father to whom Noona showed it when, at a phone call from his daughter, he came to lunch. He'd be delighted to have an acquaintance of his, a Paris art dealer, who, incidentally, had had a runner in the race the other day, have a look at it. It turned out that Noona was short of money.

And what about me? Who would support my project that I had resolved to extend to, some might say, the borders of fantasy? I was going to include imaginary love stories - were not my novels composed largely around them? - into which I would introduce those elements - of pain, failure, the cruellest of contingencies and, in particular, those that appeared most irreconcilable with any overall fate or harmony. I shall, when I come to it, quote one or two of these situations in which spirit and nerve are tested to their breaking point.

But now I told Abby of my sense of isolation and neglect. Even the typing of a first rough draft would cost more than, once back at home, after foregoing the luxuries and genuine sense of 'excellence' in Paris, we would have over from living expenses.

- Another thing: have you invited Noona to come back with us?

- I've asked Daddy to invite her to the royal guest house that he converted from an ancient palace for visiting personages. He'd invite us too if I asked him later on. You'd like it, with its view onto the Gulf.

A relief, though one that diminished me in my own estimation. Abby knew that our earlier idea of a welcome for Noona, and after a stay with us, the possibility of her living in our city, wouldn't work. Why not? Because of my sex-obsession, crude, demeaning, unloving, that's why! Noona and Abby were blameless.

Could somebody so basically flawed complete such a work

as I had started on? One in which purity of purpose, single-mindedness and self-forgetfulness were vital?

When I asked Abby about this, without telling her the reason for this onslaught of doubt - which she may have guessed - she reminded me of what appears the ironical manner in which destiny, or the Creator, goes about preserving its handiwork. King David, whose sensuality drove him to murder, was none the less, according to tradition, the author of some of the great psalms.

Noona had hung her portrait in our hotel bedroom - a gesture that gave me a further pang of contrition in what seemed its innocence - and in the early light of autumnal dawn its whiteness was intensified.

Ah, I had even been jealous at the Prince's plan to show it to his friend who owned a well-known gallery!

However, consoled by Abby's loving words, I felt a lightening of heart as if the same pure, pallid light that bathed the portrait was also shining on my pre-visioned labour of love.

Not that, on the practical plane, the difficulties were not piling up. How present lovers from the past whose experiences, I believed, fulfilled the main purpose in this planet's existence, and yet about whose existence I knew nothing?

Never one to decline a dare, as children put it, or draw back from a precipitous brink, I resolved to imagine - no, not invent - them. I would quote from their secret vows and avowals, from whispers in the dark dragged out by anguish, employing whatever skills and inspiration I have as a novelist, that themselves weren't granted for nothing, by which I mean they didn't come at a bargain price.

But then, despite my attempts at casuistry, it would be, like it or not, an invention no matter how ingenious. When I put it like this to Abby, she said: - So are your Gospels, at least in most people's estimation!

A call to meditation!

- Yes, darling, and it is only those who in their consciousness can substantiate the promises made there that believe that they contain aspects of truth.

We left it at that for the time being, which turned out to be considerable because of our return home and all that involved re-settling in.

No need to sift through this for any small events that might have significance in shedding light on what has gone before or is still to come. If I seem to be in a hurry and leaving too much up in the air, that's because I'm anxious to relate, albeit at third remove, the latest totally unexpected quantum-like leap in the development of this narrative. At third remove because the events concern Philip Weisberg and to a lesser extent Paul, were reported by Maya and are now being transcribed in my own style.

Maya can scarcely have been off the yacht when she phoned and asked might she come round. Expecting the usual chit-chat, Abby suggested the following afternoon but, sensing Maya's urgency, said: OK, make it this evening.

The Galapagos Isles are one of the bleakest, most inhospitable spots in the world, no matter what the season. The arctic and antarctic scenes are tranquil by comparison. Even though storm-force gales rage there on occasion, they do not affect the overall picture.

Yes, I'm into Maya's report, at least the preface to which all I had to add was that Gander, New Foundland, in a snow storm couldn't be far behind, especially if you were in a jumbo jet on the tarmac one of whose engines that were being revved up appeared to be vibrating excessively.

Maya wasn't attending, just waiting for the sound of my voice to cease so that she could go on.

There had been a cruise liner at the islands, apparently a popular place of call for the more serious types and wealthier holiday-makers.

Here Maya's tale took a short diversion to comment on the added enjoyment of, say, dining on board, with a view from the saloon of huge black crags rising from the perpetually stormy water, enormous waves and circling sea birds of various species that, through binoculars, she couldn't identify.

A pause. Was this all? I mustn't seem to be expecting more. If this was the full extent of the news she couldn't wait to impart, and of which I'd seen a visual replica on film, she was somewhat more naive and less sophisticated than I'd taken her for (though I'd been aware of a certain naivete too).

She was continuing. On hearing that there was a well-known astronomer on the yacht, whose presence had intrigued the organiser of the cruise, he radioed to ask whether the famous biologist - he had got it wrong, quite understandably I suppose - would honour him and his clients by giving a talk on the liner. Paul, equally understandably, had declined but suggested Philip go instead. What he, or the part-time radio operator on the yacht, whom I recalled as not without humour, introduced him as Maya didn't say, probably didn't know.

Now came the central point of her news, to which all had been leading, as I could tell by a subtle shift of tone, as when, towards the end of a race, the commentator's voice rises an octave and the words come in rapid succession.

- It was simply magnificent!

What? Philip Weisberg's discourse?

- What was his chosen subject?

Or had the passengers on the cruise ship suggested it? Did they, still under a misapprehension, suppose he was an authority on Darwin?

Not that I asked. Anyhow it would have been hard to get a word in.

- He told them about the Jews.

- He did?

I tried not to show surprise. After all, I saw myself as merely the recorder. But I did enquire if she had also been transferred to the liner. No, but the Master, Chaim Magressen had, at the invitation of the liner's captain. Perhaps they were acquainted, or possibly this was a gesture of courtesy not uncommon in seafaring circles.

So I have to revise my hasty estimate of a third-hand report. The actual stages were: What Philip said to his audience, what Chaim Magressen made of it when he told Paul and what Paul passed on to Maya.

And, by the way, Maya said, Boyd-Roberts was transferred to the liner, after an arrangement by which I paid the full cost of the cruise on his behalf.

This mention of money reminded me that Maya had sponsored the whole expedition and had a good reason to welcome anything that gave it importance. (I think, like us, her interest in the cometary side was never very great.)

- Long ago, but not all that long, because I'm speaking of a time in history when civilisation had flowered and reached great heights in several parts of the world, when, in fact, mankind was settling in, becoming acclimatised to conditions here with every prospect of a long and happy possession, give or take a few pestilences, bloody squabbles, trouble-makers and the like...

However, it wasn't to be. Out in the cosmos (which mankind in general had little time for, what with his energy put into surviving and, with what was over, cultivating the extra crops that provided luxuries which included the arts) something was going on. Given there was a cosmos at all, that wasn't surprising. What were the events out there was, of course, hard to determine by those few people who gave it a thought.

It is these people, not at all numerous, nor prosperous, nor particularly cultured, tribal in fact and tending to the nomadic, whose history and its consequences for all of us that I am going to recount.

Yes, this is the start of Philip's lecture given in the ship's theatre on the cruise liner anchored for the moment within a mile of the Galapagos Islands, rendered by me into my chronicler's sober idiom.

What the audience made of it so far, or, come to that, in toto, I don't know, having no more than the memory of a member of the yacht's crew, filtered back through two or three other memories, as a guide. He took notes which Maya had even seen but neither read nor obtained a copy of them.

These people, if you haven't guessed - this is me addressing readers, not Philip to his holidaying audience - were the ancient Jews or Israelites, all twelve tribes of them, though as he pointed out, this didn't amount to all that many.

Who were they to keep clear of their neighbours, more powerful and indeed superior in most ways, and address themselves directly to a Being, a presumably creative spirit out there? That they hadn't made much of themselves didn't deter them. Jehovah, the God of Abraham, Isaac, and Jacob, according to their prophets, hadn't put them on the planet - this concept of 'putting' anyone on it is one beyond both my (Philip's) competence and time to discuss - to gain earthly renown.

They had no cities to compete with Athens, Rome, Petra, or even Alexandria, and their Ark of the Covenant was a rather small and shoddy piece of carpentry. As for their temple, it wouldn't have detained anyone long who had seen the Acropolis, not to mention the buildings at Abydos and further along the Nile.

Despite all of which, and in a sense because of it, they had a special relationship, a line of communication, and by no means one-way, with a source outside the known world, and, indeed, outside the planet - of which, apart from among the Babylonians and some Asians, no very clear image had been formed.

What basis is there for such a claim? And here we come to what I take was the climax of the talk. In history too, though seldom, as well as in private lives, the totally unexpected and almost incredible does happen.

The situation as presented by the lecturer was remarkable, but not explosively or subversively so. It was one that escaped the notice of most of the Jews' contemporaries.

It was when the prophets appeared, Isaiah, Daniel, Amos, Hosea, Jeremias, Elijah, and lifted it onto another plane, one that had not till then been dreamt of as consistent with, or even as a possible alternative to, the different planes, society, trade, politics, culture, religion, that human activity was channelled into.

They made prophecies that few among the Israelites took seriously, foretelling that the King of Israel that the Jews believed would come and lift them high above their enemies, would indeed appear in due time, but as somebody afflicted, wounded, homeless, 'acquainted with infirmity'.

If a few of the more thoughtful, with always a woman or two among them, stayed after the curious crowd had dispersed to ask the prophet to resolve the puzzle, if that's what it was and not a farce, they heard a word that they hadn't heard outside the intimate family circle and there seldom enough.

The Messiah would indeed come because he loved them. His father had arranged their composition out of particles that were plentiful enough in the cosmos - this detail didn't get into the scriptures because the scribes rejected it as senseless - and then found suitable accommodation for them on one of the planets of the so-called solar system, of which there were several billions.

The stupendous act that resulted in a universe evolving out of a photon, or quark - if there exist such entities - and filling every nook and cranny in the vast nothingness that might well, and normally should have, continued, was a lonely act. Everything was expended on it, chemicals, electronics of the most sophisticated kind, gravities, strong and weak, various forms of magnetics in negative and positive fields, yet all from the simplest formula, utilising, or activating, a few basic sub-particles, three or four, say, less than a half-dozen although the exact number hasn't yet been established, and yet it was a flop as far as the unspecified, perhaps unconscious, purpose for it remained obscure or forgotten. (I'm speaking in human terms.)

What the great chemist, physicist and mathematician had tried for was escape from his own divine isolation, not a loveless solitude, but solitude none the less. And such a going forth, such an extension of being into the consciousness of another being - not godlike, that wasn't in question, there was already, according to the later theologians, Father, Son and Holy Ghost - but lowly, lonely, unfortunate.

The one thing essential in the series of astonishing events following the initial almost undetectable ripple at the heart - if such had existed - of motionlessness, or, if, it's preferred, the Big Bang, was that no matter how much the space or time, or whatever it is that these fictitious measurements conceal, there was for various combinations of molecules to evolve, that these were sentient beings, human or animal, who could respond.

What were my feelings transcribing this as a dedicated recorder? At first, wariness. I imagined I was up to Philip and his strokes. Then bewilderment and finally admiration, for the boldness, the abandon and, I suppose above all, the sobriety. He stuck to the data as he found it.

Try as I did, I couldn't detect the sleight of hand, or mind, that I suspected must underlie the performance. The thesis was so in keeping in many ways with my own convictions - not overtaking or overlapping them but, say, running parallel - that I felt what was the solid ground, the estimation of the more central persons in this report, giving way under me.

I had thought of Philip Weisberg as a poor man's Onassis - have perhaps referred to him as such, or else discussed it with Abby. A womaniser, like the Greek magnate, a yachtsman, a promotor of successful but shady enterprises (the unseaworthiness of some of the Onassis oil tankers registered under flags of convenience for example) such as the promotion of Club Firmament.

I was confused and upset, which, of course, Abby noticed. When, after some hesitation, I told her why, she said:

- According to your sacred scriptures, wasn't Jesus most at home in the company of publicans and sinners?

- So what?

It was I who had related to her this predilection of his which I had taken a personal pride in, believing I shared it.

- If only you'd stop romanticising and read the passage in question as you would any other piece of information or news. Publicans, as I understand it, were extortionists who made use of their positions of petty authority by taking bribes and swindling. As for those described more generally as sinners, it's not meant to denote a lot of Mary Magdalens and good thieves. As I take it, from what you told me, words are used in the Gospels like the great Russians use them - to mean what they say and more than they say. Sinners, most of them, were then, as now, a nasty lot. To suppose anything else is to minimise and tone down your Jesus's actions, don't you really see that, Joel?

Yes, I was beginning to, though I had to muster all my   -

It's a matter of energy, if you ask me, Abby continued. Energy is what keeps it all going, including Paul's comets and bacteria. The centre of your religion, Joel, the Incarnation, is a supreme manifestation of explosive energy that loosens the grip inertia has on our minds and hearts. Oh, don't you see that without energy there can't be love, and yet energy has often a very ugly face.

- Another thing, she went on.

What a torrent of words she could pour out when something - mostly me - had taken the wrong turning: - I don't care for Philip any more than you do. When I compare him with Daddy and think of them as Arab and Jew I grasp something of the eternal hostility. Both have the semitic faith in their own special relationship with the cosmos and its ordering, but for the Jew that doesn't oblige him to conduct his earthly dealings on the same strict principles. His Holy Books are not inducements to tolerance, let alone compassion.

I was chastened, even aghast at what I realised had been my evading reality, which I prided myself on serving. I was cast down, but not utterly, or not for long, as I would have been if the admonition had come from anyone else but Abby.

And now, before concluding this painful but, for me, how salutary phase of the report, are two or three minor notes relating to the fortuitous meeting of the yacht and cruise liner in the Pacific Ocean.

Captain Magressen had been introduced by the Master of the liner to one of his distinguished passengers: Eileen Cabbit-Bruce. When he'd mentioned that Paul was on the yacht, that he was on what he called 'a fact-finding mission', she had known who he was. Then, recalling something that I, or Abby, must have mentioned on our visit to her, she had asked him if he had come across the writer, Joel Samson.

She had written to us and given him the letter which Paul had brought when he came to see us, a visit I have had to postpone narrating. As I also postponed reading Eileen's long letter, only glancing through it and catching what I suppose are the passages of real interest - though I could be wrong - such as the mention of the gardener who was accompanying her and her sense of being at home so close to those turbulent waters, which confirmed me in my belief in her aquatic nature. As Paul's was aerial, but very likely I am influenced in that conclusion by his space researches. And as Abby has traces of the fiery element with the impression of smouldering.

19

42

Before I relate what will probably be Paul's last visit to us in this report, I want to record that I may not have been altogether fair to him. There are others about whom I feel the same, but they are those who I ended up not caring for - it takes a time for the oscillations that people set up in me to modulate - a fact that it would be wrong to suppress. Paul, with his daring, and therefore original, imagination, the great clown, the heretical astronomer, would, had he been there at the time, have been with John the disciple whom Jesus loved. And, following the tradition of sacred scripture, I have not described him in the flesh, nor, indeed, any of the others with the exception of Abby and, sketchily, her father.

- The first time you came to see us, it struck me you set a standard that I should try to live up to.
He came out with this surprising announcement as we were showing him with secret pride - secret because it was probably only to our eyes so wonderful - our autumnal garden.
I could genuinely, not modestly, disclaim any such characteristic, the result, I suggested, of a misunderstanding. I'm aware of giving the impression, not of moral superiority - God forbid! - but of being rather unapproachable.

- I soon realised you yourself were far from living up to it. But that it was there preserved in some isolated corner of your system and not at all affecting your behaviour in the slightest way, was a consolation.

- *There's* somebody, I told Nicole, who instinctively rejects the whole set-up, lock, stock and barrel.

- That was a cause for elation because I was in the grip of the depression that results from hardly taking a step or turning a knob - outside the laboratory that is - without being assaulted, visibly, verbally, neurologically, by the forces organised for profit-making, the obscenities and lunacies of the unceasing struggle for more and more money.

- It's the boredom, Joel, old soldier! If it was a real battle, no matter that the evil power was winning, it would be supportable. But the tedium, the banality, a stickiness over everything so that you can't go to any public gathering without getting smeared with it, at home too if for some reason you have one of the bits of gadgetry for noise-dissemination.

- They are doing their best to cancel out creation. Not like de Sade with an honest raging hatred, raving and blacking out the sun, but by the supreme reductionism, the great abortion, vacuuming the living spores away and replacing them by magnetised plastic that, fed into computers, produces an endless supply of pop stars, in human guise, screaming loveless tirades about love.

We did our best to calm and console him.

- At least we're creatures, some of us, destined to perceive the truth about our origin in an instinctive way. We still come and go, weep and laugh, and all the commercial glue in the world can't stick us to the wall.

Abby could be unintentionally funny, and at the right moments.

I took Paul's visit among other things to be his way of intimating that my task as recorder and Amenuensis of several crucial years in his work was over. Perhaps his own way of life was reaching a new phase. He mentioned delegating some of the laboratory work and spending more time in the bedsitter, with Nicole presumably, where he could isolate himself from what, much as I sympathised, seemed his neurotic reaction to our society.

Much was changing, falling apart and regathering around new centres. Time was short. I am thinking of all I had still to do. I resolved to go back and start from the beginning, with a day from the diary of the terrible, if blessed, Original Chemist and Mathematician, the First Person of the Trinity. This avowal will come as a shock. It has to me and yet I can see no other way to relate the legend, or story, of love without evasion. Without in particular evading the mention, and more than a mention, of, if not a creator, an infinitely imaginative arranger of atoms into molecular structures all the way up to the human, and doubtless non-human, brain.

Yet the Void remains, and here the Second Person of the Trinity - this triune concept of ultimate reality gives me a precarious foothold on these precipitous planes, much as space and time are useful in forming models of the Cosmos.

There is a dynamic relation between father and son, as there isn't, say, between brother and sister, a stream of energy, whether unified or in opposition.

Utilising family terms for the interaction of celestial energies is, of course, also a matter of convenience.

How plant a divine seed in matter? Directly and boldly, as such leaps into the future as the original creation takes place, dropped into the womb of a terrestrial woman: In Christian terms, the Incarnation. The Son of God - to call these interventions bold is like depicting a star's centre in pastel shades - came with a mission: to ignite and bring to a furnace love on this planet. For this, as we now know, nothing is more necessary than compassion. The Messiah of the Old Testament became 'afflicted and acquainted with infirmity', a more direct reference to his wounds would have resulted in a stoning of the prophet.

It is these wounds that must be thought deeply and honestly about. They are at the heart of the event. They are bloody, as one of the disciples who doubted their reality was able to prove by thrusting part of his hand into the one in the chest.

I briefly retell this well-known story to set the scene for my comparatively modest researches into the later history of terrestrial love. It is largely a matter of documentation, if such a term may be used in connection with scraps of paper, soiled and torn farewells exchanged between men and women in desperate straits, and afterwards rolled tight and thrown onto the floor, say, of railway trucks where the guards won't find them.

And where do I suppose *I* shall find them? In my imagination for the most part.

- 43 -

In several disparate and far-flung locations, all variations - and how extreme ones! - on the central theme. About almost all of which history is ignorant.

But imagination, even the most self-supporting, must draw sustenance from facts. From, in this case, letters, a few long and explicit or obscure except for a few breathtaking passages. Several unfinished, interrupted by who knows what final catastrophe. Illegible, faded, tear-stained, blood-speckled scraps of paper. And overall the agonising sense of time running out, of the lateness of the hour, the date, the season.

What with the higher passes blocked by snow
And other routes unfinished or unmapped
It was getting clearer that I either go
Or spend another fruitless winter trapped
Here at the halfway house of the half-hearted,
Doubting your promise that if I departed
You'd come with me - that faith too was sapped -
So, wrenched from the mementos of the past,
I fled with nothing but the household pet,
Alone, I thought, fearful, at longest last
And ravaged by regret.
But then at midnight right across the track
Authority in full array was spread;
Magistrate, Counsellor, Warder and Moralist,
The horrid lot! I thought of turning back,
As 'papers', 'passport', 'visa' crossed my head.
You pulled apart your shirt and what I'd missed
Was bared, as was the bloodstain where you'd sat,
As I drove on alone but for the cat,
Over the hill to the wholehearted dead.

Coda by Abby

That Joel died before me was almost inevitable, foreseeable and a part, as he explained to me, of our relationship in time. He did not leave me with any specific hope that 'a little time would pass' and then he would be with me once more, he seemed assured that communication of some kind, silent and on another frequency, could continue. And that this was as much up to me as to him.

One other matter I should elucidate. The above poem, *Over the Hill,* as well as a reiteration of his faith in the Christian Gospels, which I never unreservedly shared, is a reminder of Noona with its celebration of the cat whose death she may never have quite got over. It is also to remind me of her and of her presence in our thoughts.